Much ado about

DUTTON

By

Claudia Dain

This book is a work of fiction. Names, characters, places, and incidents either are products of the author's imagination or are used fictitiously. Any resemblance to actual events or locales or persons, living or dead, is entirely coincidental.

All rights reserved, including the right to reproduce this book or portions thereof in any form whatsoever.

ISBN: 978-1-940940-03-8

Much Ado About Dutton

Copyright © 2014 by Claudia Dain

Website: ClaudiaDain.com

Formatting by Dead River Books

Praise for Claudia Dain's Novels

"Funny, superbly sensual, and filled with sassy wit and appealing characters . . ." ~Library Journal

"A delightful work full of bantering conversation, clever transitions from scene to scene." ~Romance Reviews Today

"Miss Dain is deucedly clever, witty, and the fabulous cast of characters she has created are a delight to revisit and learn more about each time. Don't miss this fun romp through the ton . . . " ~Sapphire Romance Realm

"Dain concocts another wonderfully witty story, complete with unforgettable characters, sparkling dialogue, a clever plot, and amusing situations." ~Booklist

"Dain is a master of the Regency romp, and this one has witty repartee and an authentic setting. The characters are engaging, unpredictable, and outrageously funny." ~Romantic Times

"Told in a delightfully dry, tongue-in-cheek voice, this romance chronicles verbal skirmishes and even a physical brawl or two as part of an ongoing battle in the war of love." ~Bookpage

"Highly amusing repartee and some wickedly attractive open ends round things out." ~Publisher's Weekly

"Wonderful . . . Great dialogue . . . Sophia the seasoned courtesan [is] so feisty and fun . . . Don't miss this fresh and extremely fun romp through romantic London. It is , as Sophia would say, "Simply too delicious to miss!" ~Night Owl Romance

Titles in the series:

THE COURTESAN CHRONICLES
The Courtesan's Daughter
The Courtesan's Secret
The Courtesan's Wager
How to Dazzle a Duke
Daring A Duke

MORE COURTESAN CHRONICLES
Much Ado About Dutton
The Most Dangerous Game (short story)
Encounters of the Ardenzy Heiresses (two novellas)
Accidentally in Love (novella)
Chasing Miss Montford (novella)
Taming Miss Grey
Chasing Miss Montford (novella)

Other Series:

ENGLISH WARRIORS
To Burn
The Holding
The Marriage Bed
The Willing Wife
The Temptation
The Fall
Tell Me Lies

WILD AMERICANS
A Kiss To Die For
Dances With Lords
Once Upon a Time in London

Dedication: For everyone who wanted Anne and Dutton's story, this is for you.

Chapter 1

London 1804

Anne, Lady Staverton, approached Dalby House on foot, ignoring the threat of rain to dwell instead on the scent of spring in the air and the feel of the cobbles beneath her feet. Anne, as the carefully proper Lady Staverton, had not walked anywhere in Town in recent memory, and certainly not to Dalby House, locked up and nearly deserted since the end of the London Season of 1802. The house on Upper Brook Street had been uncharacteristically still for the past two years.

Much had happened in the intervening two years.

Two years ago this spring, Anne had been a poor widow of a minor naval officer. She had lived in Dalby House with Sophia, Lady Dalby, and Sophia's daughter, Caroline.

In those two years, Anne had married Lord Staverton and become a viscountess. She was now a widow for the second time.

Darling, dear, sweet Staverton had died a year ago, thirteen months, to be exact. He had died without an heir, something that had not seemed to concern him, but a point upon which she could only feel was a painful dereliction of duty. That there was nothing to be done about it now did nothing to alleviate her sense of having failed at her most important duty as a woman and as a wife.

In those same two years, Caroline had married Ashdon, heir to the 7th Earl of Westlin, produced a daughter christened Elizabeth, buried the 7th Earl Westlin, and become the Countess Westlin. Caro was now pregnant again, most happily pregnant, and spending another London Season at Chaldon Hall, the Westlin family estate. That the disagreeable 7th Earl was now at his rest in the family crypt was a happy situation for Caroline and Ashdon, though not perhaps for Westlin. It was probably neither wise nor kind to think ill of the dead, but then it might be argued Lord Westlin should have lived a finer life if he wanted to be grieved in proper fashion.

That was something very like what Sophia would say and Anne tried very hard to think it, making the thought her own, without guilt. She was not successful. She did so very many things out of guilt and a sense of failed duty.

It was an utterly exhausting way to live.

She needed to see Sophia. She needed to hear Sophia's smiling counsel, always pragmatic, always shocking, and always so very, very accurate. She needed to be saved, but from what she would not say. Not even to herself.

In those same two years, Sophia had sailed to New York. Some said she had sailed precipitously, that her leaving England so suddenly was the result of the feverish activity of shocking courtships and hasty marriages and that she had inspired in the infamous London Season of 1802.

Oh, yes, it was called infamous. It was also called the Famous London Season of 1802. Many upon many girls out for their first or even their second Season wished openly, much to their mother's dismay, that Sophia Dalby, former courtesan and dowager countess, were in a position to help them achieve the perfect man for them the way she had been so readily involved in the courtships, if one could call them that, and marriages of such high rank and esteem in the 1802 Season.

Anne, though it was not widely known, had been a recipient of just such aid. How would she, a poor widow and the daughter of a failed courtesan, ever have married a viscount otherwise?

But leave England because of shocking courtships and legal marriages? That Sophia would not do. To what point? Sophia cared nothing for shock and everything for legality, particularly when the marriage contracts were written with a woman's security in mind.

And while that was true, it was also equally true that Anne had no idea why Sophia had left England for America two years ago. Neither did she have any idea why Sophia had returned, but she had. Just two hours ago, Sophia had sent round a note that she was *in* and that she would be very happy to see Anne whenever it was convenient. It was never an inconvenience to see Sophia Dalby. That much everyone could agree upon.

Dalby House, positioned quite nicely upon Upper Brook Street so that a view of Hyde Park was visible from certain windows, was as familiar to Anne as her own home. Seeing it again, its quiet and dignified façade looking quite properly British, brought tears to Anne's eyes. This place was home in a way that Staverton's home on King Street was not. Dalby House was the home of girlhood hopes and impossible dreams.

Impossible. Yes, impossible. She had married and then loved Staverton, in that not uncommon order, but he had not been her dream.

Anne brushed off the thought, sending whatever

girlish dreams remained to her to be crushed against the cobbles. She was a woman twice widowed. She had been loved well and she was secure in her place in Society, thanks to Staverton. She had an income. She was safe, finally and irrevocably safe, and she was not going to waste time in dreaming of things, or people, who might put her security in peril. She was far too mature, too worldly wise at the respectable age of twenty-two, for that brand of nonsense.

With those thoughts firmly pinned to her heart, Anne, the dowager Lady Staverton, motioned for her footman to knock on the Dalby House door.

Fredericks, Sophia's butler, answered the door before the first knock could raise an echo.

"Lady Staverton," he said, his wrinkled face creasing into a delighted smile. "Welcome home."

Of course it was entirely improper for Fredericks to make such a personal remark, and one that was so hugely inaccurate, and one could and often did hear his being an American credited for his lack of proper protocol. But, nevertheless, Anne burst into tears upon hearing the words *welcome home* upon his lips.

It was not the impression that a very mature, twice-widowed twenty-two year old wanted to convey.

"Come now," Fredericks said, putting a hand on her elbow and ushering her into the house, nodding to the footman behind her. "None of that, Miss Anne. Sophia'll set you right. She's in the white salon. In you get."

Completely and utterly improper, every utterance, but Anne grinned through her tears, nodded sloppily, and walked into the white salon as if she still lived in

Dalby House, without even Fredericks to announce her. It was unheard of. And it felt wonderful, as if she truly had come home.

Sophia rose upon her entry into the room and held out her arms, a smile lighting her captivating face. As Anne hurried into Sophia's outstretched arms, without a trace of the nobility of carriage and studied decorum she had mentally rehearsed, she fleetingly marveled that Sophia appeared not to have aged a day, then she buried all thoughts and all fears in the embrace of the woman who was more mother to her than her own mother had been.

"Darling Anne," Sophia said into her hair, "how ravishing you look. How proud Staverton would be of you."

Anne, to her horror, burst into a fresh bout of tears. Stepping back from Sophia, she fumbled in her reticule for a handkerchief.

"Now, what's this?" Sophia said, leading Anne to one of the white sofas in the room and urging her to sit beside her. Anne did not so much sit as plop. This was not the impression she had hoped to give Sophia after two years as a lady of the realm. Hardly. "You can't still be mourning darling Stavey? He would never have wanted that."

"No, truly. I'm so sorry," Anne said, wiping her nose as delicately as she could manage. "I don't know what's wrong with me."

"A pure excess of emotion and nothing of which to be ashamed," Sophia said. "If this is not for Staverton, then may I presume that this is for me? You've missed me, I daresay. Come, tell me all. What's been happening whilst I've been abroad? You simply must catch me up."

"You received my letter about Staverton? It reached you?" Anne asked, still sniffing and mortified beyond measure.

"Of course, darling. They have postal service in America, I do assure you. It's not quite as barbaric in New York as you might have been lead to believe."

"Oh!" Anne said on a hiccup of laughter. "I hardly thought that."

"Hardly?" Sophia said, her dark brows raised. "I am reassured."

"Oh, Sophia," Anne said, smiling at her, "I have missed you."

"Have you, darling?" Sophia said, looking across the room to the windows that faced Upper Brook Street. "How gratifying that is. I do adore being missed."

Anne, who had lived with Sophia for many months and who had been privy to many quiet and intimate conversations with her, and who, while not claiming to be Sophia's equal would have said with some confidence that she was Sophia's friend, heard something in Sophia's voice which gave her pause. Sophia, charming, quick Sophia, did not sound quite the same as she had two years ago. The words were the same, but the tone, the sparkling, sharp wit that was the essence of Sophia, was dulled.

What had happened in New York? And why had she left England in the first place?

"Are you well, Sophia?" she asked. "Is all well with you?"

Sophia smiled abruptly and moved to the opposing couch; they were a perfect pair of white upholstered sofas with milk blue trim, and said, "Perfectly. I only despair that I shall never get this room redone. I tired of white years ago now and I simply can't find the time to do anything about it. I've been thinking of red, a nice vibrant crimson. The color of blood, to be precise. I find myself quite drawn to that shade lately."

Anne's tears quite disappeared at that. Sophia was *not* as she had been. What had happened?

"You know about Westlin, I presume?" Anne asked.

Sophia smiled slightly and crossed her legs. "Of course. I received exactly eleven letters telling me of his demise. Naturally, I'm delighted that I was out of the country so that his death could not possibly be laid upon my doorstep. I'm sure many would have liked to do so, not the least of which, myself." Sophia laughed. "But, alas, he died without any aid from me. How very like him. He always was a most inconvenient sort of man."

The Earl of Westlin had been Sophia's oldest and most enduring enemy; the fact that Westlin's heir had married Sophia's only daughter was seen as proof by some that Sophia was the most devious enemy since the Cassius hailed Caesar. Not a single soul who knew either Westlin or Sophia believed that Caroline had accidentally stumbled into wedlock with Ashdon, and that included Ashdon himself. Of course, Ashdon was hardly complaining.

"You are not . . . "

"I am not what, darling?"

Anne shrugged and looked down at the floor. "The relationship with an adversary is sometimes the most intimate of all. Such a relationship, once ended, can create a void of sorts."

Sophia smiled and leaned toward Anne, her dark eyes alight in the old, familiar way. Anne, for the first time since she'd entered the white salon, felt completely at rest.

"Intimate adversaries? What an intriguing word pairing. How clever of you to think of it. And how is Lord Dutton? He is your intimate adversary, as we both know. I presume he is still unmarried. Is he continuing his practice of drinking himself under the furniture and flinging himself in the way of men's fists?"

Anne, who should have blushed if she had an ounce of moral fiber or proper etiquette, did not blush. She began to cry again.

"He is not. He is not married and he is perfectly sober," Anne said. "And he has been for over a year."

"Oh, my," Sophia said, ringing for tea. "Things are in an awful state. We simply must bring him round, mustn't we?"

"Oh, Sophia," Anne said, still crying like a child, a lovesick, heartsick child, which is precisely what she felt like at the moment, and in fact, had felt very much this way since Staverton had died.

She had at first thought her appalling lack of self-control was the result of losing Staverton and finding herself a widow again, but as the months passed, Anne had, with sporadic bursts of clarity, realized that it was more than Staverton being gone. It was far worse than that. It was that she'd lost Dutton just as fully as she'd lost her husband. Not that she'd had Dutton to lose, which was another tearful subject altogether. Things were a complete tangle. There was simply no unraveling it, until Sophia came home and made all right with her cleverness and her ruthlessness, for what good was being clever if one weren't ruthless enough to put cleverness to good use?

"I'm quite undone and I can't think what to do about it."

"Can't you, darling?" Sophia said, grinning, running her hands gently over her black hair. "I can."

For the first time in months, thirteen months precisely, Anne felt the tug of a true smile on her face and in her heart. She could not possibly have been more delighted.

"Can you?" Anne asked.

"But of course, darling. You cannot have doubted me."

No, she hadn't. Anne was not particularly clever and hardly ruthless enough to mention, but she was experienced enough not to waste time in doubting Sophia.

"Now, tell me everything. Do you still want him, Anne?" Sophia asked.

Put so, Anne did not know what to answer. Did she want Dutton? She ought not to. That much she knew.

Lord Dutton was a horrible man. When she had still lived at Dalby House, Lord Dutton had tried to seduce her for the sheer pleasure of it. He had likely simply been bored. He had kissed her ruthlessly (and somewhat cleverly), and had obviously expected her to fall into his bed like an overripe plum.

Needless to say, she had not fallen in any fashion whatsoever. She had not even been so tawdry a thing as tempted. But she had thought about it. Lord Dutton, as horrible men invariably were, was brutally handsome and quite certain of his effect on women. It was the only thing that made refusing him at all possible. Anne, whose mother had failed as a courtesan in that she couldn't find protectors either wealthy enough or interested enough, had starved, and Anne had starved right along with her. As a result, falling into beds was not something that Anne had trouble avoiding.

Until Dutton.

Avoiding falling into anything with Dutton had been a challenge. Dutton had, quite obviously and with great comic result, been completely unprepared to be denied. In fighting Dutton during the London Season of 1802, Anne had enjoyed the most vigorous and entertaining two months of her life. Of course, she had been engaged to be married to Staverton for half of that Season, and of course she felt as guilty as she ought for such unbecoming behavior, yet it had been quite an exhilarating time.

There was little point in denying that Dutton was distractingly handsome and that she was more than a little interested in what had ultimately become of him. Initially, for some many months, after getting into one fist fight or another, he had turned into a complete drunkard. It had been a most gratifying thing to see. Then she had married Staverton, Sophia had left England, and as Staverton and Dutton did not travel in the same circles without Sophia to guide them, she hadn't seen Dutton since.

She had heard about him, of course. He had stopped being a drunken lout some time ago, which naturally showed the very short length of a man's attention to any one woman. Then she had heard that he had gone to Redworth, his family estate, where he had proceeded to have lengthy meetings with his estate manager and made improvements to the mill on his lands. Of course no one believed that. What was whispered was that he was keeping a woman of the town in a hunting lodge on his property and that he was very busy seeing to her. No one had any trouble believing *that*.

Anne had maintained her perspective and her decorum through all of that, but what had thrown a boulder at her dignified resolve to live an exemplary life that would bring additional honor to the memory of Staverton and additional respectability to herself was that, just three days ago, she had seen Dutton riding in Hyde Park.

He should have stayed a drunken sot. That would have been a kindness to her, but when had the Marquis of Dutton ever shown her any kindness?

Lewd and suggestive remarks, yes, he was brimming with those. Or he had been, the last time she had exchanged words with him during the London Season of 1802.

Two years ago. Two long years ago, and now, when she should be a respectable widow with respectable thoughts meandering placidly through her mind, she had the ill fortune to see him riding in Hyde Park.

Two years ago, without very much effort at all, he had stolen into her thoughts and wrapped himself around her heart like a weed. She had pulled him free and married Staverton, who had esteemed her. Staverton, who had honored her with marriage. Dutton had only wanted to drag her into the nearest bed, or shove her up against the nearest wall. She was a widow twice over; nothing about men and their urges surprised her. She had made the only choice she could possibly make: she had married well and married happily.

Being shoved against a wall, her skirts a mess about her waist, was not a choice.

It had been something to remember, that long ago kiss, her back against a wall, but it had not been an actual choice. She could not have made that choice, the choice to fall into his kiss, his embrace, and his bed. She was not a woman for that.

But now, now she was a woman who was less certain of what she was and what her choices were.

How extremely embarrassing.

"Do I still want him?" Anne repeated. "How can I answer that, Sophia?"

"Honestly, darling. It is just we two. You may speak your heart to me. You know that, certainly. Do you want Dutton?"

Anne looked at Sophia, trying not to blush. Anne's hair was red and her skin fair; she blushed with unwelcome regularity. Sophia looked deeply into her eyes and waited, without censure. Anne took the first full breath she had taken in months.

"I think I must," she said.

"Oh, no, darling. You must not *must* any thing. But *do* you? It is entirely your choice. Entirely. Never forget that. A man may entice, but he has no power to impel, though they like to convince women otherwise. Whatever you do with Dutton, you must keep your wits about you, and whatever you do with Dutton, you may be assured that he will do all he can to steal your wits from you. Men, as you well know, are quite predictable in that way." Sophia, smoothed a hand down her skirt, caressing the muslin, "Do you want Dutton? I will think neither better nor worse of you, no matter your reply."

And there was that. Sophia had seen, if not everything, anything worth seeing. She had been a young girl from America, half Iroquois and half English, and she had made her way in London, alone, becoming a very successful courtesan. When she had tired of that, or conquered every man worth conquering, depending upon the source, she had married the Earl of Dalby and given him two children and much joy. Upon Dalby's death, Sophia, as the dowager countess, had lived her life as she had always lived it: upon her own terms and with a great deal of dash.

Sophia, to be blunt, had seen it all, known the best and worst of Society in the best and worst of situations and circumstances, and there was truly nothing that could shock her, least of all Anne's inconvenient desires.

"Yes. I do," Anne said. "I want Dutton."

"As what?" Sophia asked, without even the delicacy of a pause.

"As . . . what?" Anne repeated.

Sophia smiled and leaned forward. "As a lover? A diversion? A husband? Though I shouldn't recommend a husband. You have had two and that should be quite enough for any woman. You have everything a woman could possibly want, and without a man to get in the works and make a muck of it, though I did love darling

Stavey and I don't want you to think for a moment that I think ill of him, but he was a man, wasn't he? A situation entirely out of his control, yet still, a man for all that."

Yes, a man, and an entirely wonderful man, the kind of man that any sensible woman would prefer over the dissolute and disagreeable Dutton. Anne had been sensible her entire life, deliberately and determinedly sensible. Apparently being sensible was something that could run dry in a woman.

"I hadn't considered that," Anne said.

"Then consider it now," Sophia replied. "Would you prefer tea or coffee, Anne? Let's settle in and discuss this fully. We must plan your assault carefully. Lord Dutton is such an intriguing quarry, isn't he? So volatile, so elusive. He will be a delicious challenge, though nothing you can't manage."

The hair on the back of Anne's neck prickled and she felt the hot wave of a flush on her neck and chest. It was just these sorts of comments, these nearly illogically aggressive remarks concerning men that Sophia was in the habit of making that put a woman off and made her think twice and then twice more about engaging Sophia's help in anything.

However, Anne had been already been married twice, and she had seen her mother treat men with such soft passivity and a generally sloppy hope that things would somehow turn out well, meaning, to her advantage, with such dire results. Anne knew *that* never happened, not when dealing with men.

"Tea would be lovely, thank you," Anne said. "I had no intention of planting myself in your salon, Sophia, taking you away from all others who surely are eager to welcome you back to London. Please, throw me out when I become too burdensome."

To Anne's horror, her eyes filled with tears at her attempt at humor. The words were too close to the truth. She did want to bury herself in Sophia's house and Sophia's care, and she did fear it would take being tossed out bodily for she could not imagine leaving willingly, at least not any time soon.

Anne, as much as she had come to love Staverton and had loved being his wife, had never quite settled fully into her role as a viscountess. Staverton hadn't seemed to notice, and for that she was grateful, but Winthrop, Staverton's butler, had. Winthrop was far too accomplished in his position to ever say so, but she had felt his censure all the same. Winthrop, having been at the house on King Street for twenty-four years, was as much a fixture of the house as the door knocker. Anne could not even contemplate discharging him.

Anne, it was quite clear, was able to think of nothing, to contemplate nothing, to accomplish nothing that did not ultimately involve Lord Dutton. It was humiliating in the extreme, especially since she had not accomplished a single thing regarding Dutton.

"Anne, darling, what on earth is wrong?" Sophia said, leaning forward, a curl of black hair sliding forward onto her bosom. "This is simply not like you in the least." Fredericks opened the door to the white salon at that moment and Sophia said briskly, "Tea, Freddy, if you would."

Fredericks nodded and closed the door behind him.

"That's true, isn't it?" Anne said, sniffing, holding a

small handkerchief to her eyes. "I'm not myself? This is not how you remember me? I vow, I cannot recollect who I am anymore, or who I was, or what I've become."

"You've become a viscountess, darling. Never forget that. Never let anyone else forget it either," Sophia said with a smile, patting Anne on the knee. "You are a beautiful woman who has made one adequate marriage and one stellar marriage. You are in the full flush of your beauty, without encumbrances, without enemies, and without equal. You are, darling girl, in the perfect position to play with Lord Dutton. Precisely like a cat with a rat."

Anne laughed and blotted her nose. "Oh, Sophia, I've missed you."

"Yes, darling, you certainly have."

"But Dutton is not a rat. Or not much of one. And I am not a cat. I haven't the claws for it."

"Why Anne, every woman has claws. She merely may have let them grow dull and blunted from disuse. That's easily remedied. As to Dutton not being a rat, of that I am not certain. He was well on his way to becoming one. What he has become in the last two years I am eager to find out. How we manage him will depend entirely upon what sort of man he has become."

"I think he's horrid," Anne said.

"Plainly," Sophia said with a wry grin.

"In a wonderful sort of way."

"Which is the most horrid way of all," Sophia said with a grin.

It was as Anne was trying to smile at Sophia, to at

least put on the show of amiability and good cheer, that Freddy came back in with the tea cart, but he was not alone. Preceding Freddy was a woman of American Indian blood, that much was instantly obvious. She was tall and slender of form with black curling hair, dusky skin, black eyes, and a prominent, if delicate, nose. She walked into the room as if she owned the house and were alone in it, which was never the way Anne walked anywhere, not even in her own house. At her side was Mr. George Grey, Sophia's Iroquois nephew, his black hair cut a bit shorter than when last she saw him two years ago and the curls more pronounced. His eyes were as black and as full of laconic humor as they were before, his single dimple on his left cheek as readily apparent, and his nose and mouth . . . why, they were an almost perfect match to the woman at his side.

Anne rose to her feet before she knew what she was about and said, "Miss Elizabeth Grey? How perfectly delightful to meet you at long last!"

Anne was not precisely the kind of woman to bestow casual embraces upon people, particularly on those she'd never met, but she was half inclined to embrace Miss Grey in the most polite of hugs. Until she looked fully into Elizabeth Grey's eyes. Elizabeth Grey looked at her like a wolf considering a pampered pet. Anne froze, smiled, backed up a half step, smiled again, and then looked at George, Elizabeth's twin. George was smiling fully, his single dimple winking at her riotously, his expression amused.

"My niece and nephew, Mr. George and Miss Elizabeth Grey," Sophia said, eyeing them with a somewhat rigid expression. "This is Lady Staverton, a treasured friend."

Miss Grey looked at Sophia, then nodded at Anne, and sat down with economic elegance on an upholstered chair. George, winking at Anne, bowed slightly and sat in a matching chair not far from his sister's side.

Anne was quite beyond knowing what to think, or what to say. It appeared that the relationship between Sophia and Elizabeth was somewhat strained, though she could not think why. Sophia's family was quite close; they all adored each other as a matter of both habit and principle. George's response to her was also quite out of character. An Indian he may be, but George Grey had always behaved most warmly towards her, if not a bit flirtatiously on occasion, and even, particularly with Lord Dutton, positively chivalrously. It was George who had, once and quite spectacularly, knocked Dutton out cold. It had been entirely deserved.

There was a moment to make a woman blush with pleasure.

With that memory uppermost, Anne threw herself into the social breach.

"It is so good to see you again, Mr. Grey," she said. "I had not thought to even allow myself the pleasure of imagining it."

"There is much you must train yourself to do," Sophia said with a smile, "and the first is to allow yourself the pleasure of imagining things. Just think what you may accomplish."

Anne laughed lightly. "I'm sure that's true, yet will I want everything I may imagine? Is that not the stuff of nightmares?"

"Do not have nightmares. Instead, have dreams," Sophia said. "Is that not so, Elizabeth? I daresay you do not suffer from nightmares."

Anne shifted her gaze to Elizabeth, wondering how she would respond.

"Not nightmares and not dreams. Not here," Elizabeth Grey answered her aunt. A most unusual reply, quite terse and nearly unfriendly.

"Not here? Do you mean in my home? Or do you mean in England? I confess to being bewildered," Sophia replied as she poured out the tea, handing Anne a cup.

"England is your home," Elizabeth replied. "I confess to being bewildered at the distinction."

Oh, dear. That was not at all pleasant. What could possibly be amiss between Sophia and her niece? Anne hadn't expected anything of this sort when she'd sobbed her way into Sophia's white salon. On the other hand, she found this situation far more intriguing that her circular thoughts about Dutton.

George made some sort of snorting sound, something in the vein of a muffled chuckle; Anne looked at him, looking quite proper in his English coat and his simple cravat. As to that, Elizabeth, for all her lack of cordiality, was outfitted quite becomingly in a cream-colored muslin gown with fawn rosettes sewn along the neckline. A beautifully becoming gown that was fitted to perfection. Her dark hair was arranged off her face, the mass tumbling down her back to her elbows. Whatever her age, and Anne couldn't begin to guess it, she truly was of an age to have her hair up and properly dressed. Miss Grey most obviously didn't care about doing what was proper or not.

"I think, perhaps, that I see your point, Elizabeth," Sophia said, handing her niece a cup of tea with a graceful movement of her arm that had a vaguely serpentine aspect to it. "I do have homes in England, and one in France, though that property is much in dispute now, and I even, if you will recall, have a home on the northern bank of the Mohawk River. You've spent some time there, I know. When things become dull in Town, we will naturally remove to Marshfield Park and you may enjoy that home of mine as well. I am, unlike you, a woman of more than one continent."

Elizabeth Grey remained silent against this listing of properties, her gaze frozen into an expression of rigid disinterest and disapproval.

George Grey, sitting at her side, looked almost amused. Anne was not amused; she was alarmed. Contention was not an atmosphere she performed well within. Her youth had been far too tumultuous for her to have developed any sort of well-grounded stance when faced with it. She preferred, and indeed required, harmonious relations. Why she was so fascinated by Lord Dutton, a most inharmonious man who sparked nothing less than violent contention wherever he went, was beyond explanation.

"But I fear we are making Anne uncomfortable, Elizabeth," Sophia said, raising her cup to her lips for a sip. The tea service was black porcelain; it looked quite striking against the white walls and white furnishings of the white salon. It also set off Sophia's flawless ivory complexion, which was no accident. "Perhaps we should have this discussion at another time. I'm quite sure you must agree that it would be rude in the extreme to make a guest in my home feel anything less than at ease."

Elizabeth looked at Anne, a quick glance that held the shadow of honest regret within its dark depths, and then Elizabeth nodded at Sophia.

"I beg your pardon," Elizabeth said, her voice a lovely contralto. "It is not proper to discuss such things. This discussion is for family only."

"As much as I dislike disagreeing with you, Elizabeth," Sophia said, her tone of voice and the expression on her face making it quite clear she did not dislike any such thing, "Anne is like a daughter to me. Her mother was quite a good friend of mine, consequently, my affection for Anne is quite intimate. Please, look upon her as yet another English cousin. If you can."

By the look on Elizabeth's face, she did not appear to want another English cousin.

"How very kind, Sophia," Anne said. Indeed, she had felt as much, but she had not expected to hear Sophia put voice to the thought.

Elizabeth cast her dark eyes upon Sophia, a small smile flickering along the edge of her mouth. It was not a particularly pleasant smile.

"Very well," Elizabeth said. "Another cousin, then. How do you like being English, Anne? How do you like being a part of this most unusual family?"

Elizabeth's antagonism was so very plain and so very insulting to Sophia that Anne, quite unusually for her, reacted without thought and without hesitation.

"I like it very well, Elizabeth, if I may call you that,

cousins as we now find ourselves to be," Anne said, her voice a trifle sharp, but not unnecessarily so, given the provocation. "I consider it a high honor to be counted among Lady Dalby's friends. She does choose them so very carefully, and so very much regard is showered upon those who have the gift of her trust. To be as a daughter to her? I am flattered beyond measure. As her blood niece, I can but assume you feel the same."

Elizabeth smiled, a cold smile full of ill feeling. Anne had seen the same sort of smile upon Sophia's face more than once. She knew enough to be wary of such a smile, yet she was too angered to be wary at the moment.

"Lady Staverton," George said, "you have grown teeth."

As he said it with a grin, Anne answered him in kind. "And claws, I fear."

"A woman needs both tooth and claw to survive this world intact."

It was not Sophia who said it, and it was very much like Sophia to have said it. It was Elizabeth.

"She certainly does," Sophia said, setting her cup down upon the small table in front of her, smiling at Anne. "How reassuring it always is to me to see a woman's teeth so well sharpened. I know you agree, Elizabeth."

"I do," Elizabeth said, her manner easing slightly. "I had not thought, Anne, to find such sharpness in an English salon. I had, mistakenly, thought that English women would be soft. Vulnerable."

"Useless," George added with a smile. "I tried to explain to my sister that English women are as varied as the land. Sometimes hills. Sometimes valleys. Sometimes marshland."

"And what am I? I daresay, I cannot begin to guess which delineation would give me greater prestige," Anne said, holding her tea above her lap.

"You seek prestige?" Elizabeth asked.

"Of course. Is that not the way of things in an Iroquois long house?" Anne answered.

Elizabeth raised her dark brows. "You know of the Iroquois? Our traditions? Our ways?"

"As well, or as poorly, as you know English ways," Anne answered. "I claim no expertise, but I know some little bits of this and that."

"Such as?"

"Such as, a valley is more desirable than marshland in Iroquoia?"

"It is."

"In England, marshland holds higher value," Anne said. "Shall I be deemed marsh or valley in your estimation?"

"Not hill? Not mountaintop?" Elizabeth asked, a half smile hovering over her lips.

"I do not think myself so extraordinary. Mountaintops are rare things in England. I am hardly so inaccessible as a mountaintop," Anne answered.

"You, perhaps, think too little of yourself. That is not the way of women in my land."

"You, then, seek prestige as well."

Elizabeth frowned in mild confusion. "I do not think so. I think only that we, I, take prestige, value, consequence, as my right."

Anne sat back, shocked. She looked at Sophia, who

smiled and took a small sip of her tea, her dark eyes shining with delight.

"This is so?" Anne asked George.

George nodded.

"I have much to learn of Iroquois ways," Anne said.

"No, Elizabeth has much to learn of English ways," Sophia said. "She is in England now and, as a guest here, must learn the customs of this land. That is the way of travelers, is it not? One must adjust. Accommodations must be made."

Anne looked at Sophia, at the dark thread beneath her words, but Sophia smiled and tilted her head playfully, pulling Anne into her warmth, causing her to lose sight of the momentary shadow behind her black eyes.

But what accommodations had Sophia's English mother made as a prisoner of an Iroquois warrior? What accommodations had Sophia made as a child of mixed blood alone in London?

Accommodations had never before sounded so ominous a word.

"I'm certain that, whatever accommodations Elizabeth must make, she will make beautifully," Anne said, not knowing what else to say.

"Are you?" Sophia said. "How kind you are, Anne. I find I am not so certain, and have discussed my concerns with Elizabeth a time or two. I would hate to see her put a foot wrong in this new world in which she finds herself. That would be most uncomfortable for all concerned."

Oh, dear. That wasn't the most cordial of comments.

"I will not put a foot wrong," Elizabeth said. "I have never put a foot wrong."

"Not among the Iroquois, certainly. But you are not among the Iroquois now. This is a new game, darling. You must adjust yourself to a new situation."

"I have. I will."

"Have you or will you? I confess, I am confused," Sophia said, setting her cup down without a sound. Elizabeth also set her cup down, equally soundlessly.

Oh, dear. This was becoming quite heated.

"I have *and* I will," Elizabeth said. "Are you still confused?"

"I am," George said pleasantly.

"Darling George," Sophia said on a laugh, "never that. I will not believe it."

"Believe what you will, or will not," Elizabeth answered. "There is nothing I fear in this land. I understand the English, what they want, how they get it."

"What they want?" Anne asked, hoping to lighten the mood. "You cannot mean wives, for Englishmen are most averse to wife taking, unless an heir is required, then they are merely reluctant."

George grinned. Sophia chuckled, still eyeing Elizabeth. Elizabeth glowered. Good heavens, what was wrong with the woman? She seemed more inclined to snarl than smile, and in her aunt's lovely home, too. It was becoming beyond irritating. Anne felt a glower of her own rising to the surface. She tried to stamp it out, truly, but it was difficult.

"You have had two husbands," Elizabeth said. "Is that not so?" She did not wait for an answer. "They cannot be too difficult to snare."

Why, was that an insult? She, the unspectacular Anne had managed to capture two ridiculously stupid husbands, and so, what could there possibly be to it? And this talk of snaring. Really. The woman, Sophia's niece though she was, was hardly out of the backwoods shadow of a savage and uncivilized land. Oh, yes, it was Sophia's land and Anne would allow some sentiment to color her thinking, but she was not so blind that she was not aware, that the entire Town was not aware, that Sophia was as savage and uncivilized, in some ways, as the country of her birth. Oh, no. She knew that well enough. This wild and surly Elizabeth Grey could do with a large helping of polish and refinement. As to that, so could anyone. It only helped in life, after all. Hadn't she been born without it, and hadn't she worked diligently to attain some small measure of it?

She certainly had, and she was not going to be snarled out of the room by a woman who didn't know how to behave to her own aunt and host.

"Elizabeth," George said, his smile wiped clean, his tone full of warning.

"A challenge! How thrilling this shall be to witness," Sophia said in the same instant. "Will you take her on, Anne? I do believe you fully able to trounce her."

Anne supposed she had the same look of shock on her face that Elizabeth did in that moment. One did have to be so careful what one said in Sophia Dalby's white salon.

"But of course, you, Anne, shall take Lord Dutton," Sophia said, ignoring their shock entirely. "He is the logical choice for you. Or would you prefer Elizabeth throw herself at Dutton? I shall bow to your preference, Anne, though I do think Dutton should be in this somehow, no matter who is arranged for him. He is the ideal man for this sort of thing."

"Not Dutton, and not Elizabeth," George said, frowning now. How his good humor had fled at the mention of Lord Dutton. Small wonder.

"Of course, I agree with you completely, George," Sophia said. "Anne for Dutton, though that does give her an advantage since she and Dutton have something of a history, as feeble and wobbly as it is."

Her history with Dutton was not feeble! He had kissed her and pursued her for fully half of an entire Season. The only reason he had fallen off was that she had married Staverton. Certainly, Sophia understood that. Looking at Sophia's smiling face, Anne did not see any indication that Sophia understood that.

"I will not take Dutton. I will not engage in any sort of wager regarding Lord Dutton!" Anne said, a bit shrilly, to be frank.

"You'll give him to Elizabeth then? George seems to have some sort of objection to that, though I do confess to understanding why. He did not have the opportunity to see Lord Dutton in the most positive of situations. Then again, there may not be a situation in which Lord Dutton would create a favorable impression," Sophia said. "Would anyone like more tea?"

"No. Thank you," Anne said. She was more annoyed than she could ever remember being with Sophia, and she actually had no memory of ever being annoyed at Sophia. Grateful? Yes. Charmed? Yes. Delighted? Of course. This was an entirely new, and an entirely unwelcome sensation. "I am not giving Lord Dutton to anyone, as I'm certain must be absolutely plain to you, Sophia."

"Oh, good. You'll keep him for yourself then," Sophia said. "I do think that's best, don't you?"

Sophia did not give Anne any time to respond to that impossible statement. Anne had no idea what her response should have been in any event.

"Now, who shall we pair with Elizabeth?" Sophia said, looking brightly, and only slightly maliciously, at her niece. "Who's in Town this Season? Do you know, Anne?"

"I shall not be paired with anyone," Elizabeth said. "These games are not to my liking."

Elizabeth did not look at Sophia brightly as she spoke, though she did look quite unrepentantly malicious.

"Of course, this game wouldn't be," Sophia said soothingly. "It is, of course, much more fun to play at a game one fully expects to win. I can fully understand your reluctance, darling Elizabeth. You are a stranger here and, therefore, at such a severe disadvantage. I suppose it was thoughtless of me to suggest it. Forget I ever mentioned it. Anne, I do hope you're not disappointed?"

Anne was too busy looking at Elizabeth's sullenly angry face to answer Sophia directly. The look on Elizabeth's face . . . well, it was the most amusing moment Anne had experienced in months, if not years.

"Sophia, no," George said, shaking his head.

"Of course not," Sophia said in response to George.

"I don't know what I was thinking to believe that Elizabeth could compete with Anne in this simple little test. Anne has, after all, been pursued and married twice. She has a completely unfair advantage. It wouldn't be at all fair to Elizabeth."

"What sort of test?" Elizabeth said.

"No," George said, a bit more forcefully. Elizabeth ignored him completely. Anne and Sophia did the same.

"Oh, something entirely simple and straightforward, I should think," Sophia said. "A simple test of desirability, for lack of a better word."

"No!" George snapped.

"It will be entirely innocent, of course," Sophia said. "You cannot think I would risk either my niece or my darling Anne to danger of any sort, even the negligible danger of a damaged reputation."

"My reputation cannot be damaged," Elizabeth said. "It is within my own hands. I hold it."

"Precisely," Sophia said, beaming a smile at her niece. "How beautifully stated and how perfectly true."

Anne did not feel the same way about her reputation, but she kept that to herself. In her experience, reputations could be torn upon the smallest of points, or the largest ones.

"All I suggest," Sophia said, "is the smallest and most innocent, the most entertaining of diversions. Something to engage the interest and quicken the blood."

"I do not need my blood to quicken," Elizabeth said.

"Nor do I," Anne said.

"Don't you? Very well, but perhaps it will quicken my blood," Sophia said, folding her hands in her lap, looking as matronly as possible. It was not at all possible.

"Very well. I will agree to that," Elizabeth said, her dark eyes shining. "We will each engage in this test of yours, including you, Sophia. Whatever you will have of me, I will have of you."

"And what of me?" Anne said, angry at being overlooked. Hadn't Dutton done that? He certainly had, most thoroughly, until he had discovered that her mother had been a poorly maintained courtesan, *then* he had been interested. In getting her in his bed, and nothing more. She was beyond all remnants of toleration for being ignored.

"Will you, darling?" Sophia said to Elizabeth, her smile soft. "I think that can be managed. And I certainly would never forget your part in this, Anne. You are the center of it, aren't you? I think that your domination of Lord Dutton will be the measure upon which Elizabeth and I will be judged."

"Domination?" Anne said. She had no desire, and no ability, to dominate Lord Dutton.

At least, she didn't think she did.

"Subjugation?" Sophia said. "You must choose your own word for it, but I think that is in the realm of what we are proposing."

"Is it?" Elizabeth asked. "And what Englishman am I to subjugate? And how shall it be proved?"

"It shall not be," George said. "*This* will not be."

"Oh, come now, darling," Sophia said, smiling at George. "Don't you think your efforts are best served by being the judge your sister demands in this contest of ours? I trust you completely not to give her any advantage. You will be completely impartial, won't you?"

"It is not possible to be completely impartial," Elizabeth said.

"I agree," George said.

"I will not allow my brother to judge in my favor. I do not need his help in this," Elizabeth said. "This thing you propose, it is a simple thing, a luring of a man in some way, isn't it? There is nothing to that. They are lured by a smile and fall at a laugh. A man is a thing easily conquered."

"I can be impartial enough to make this a fair contest," George said, looking askance at his sister, his black brows furrowed in displeasure.

It seemed Elizabeth had the ability to nettle her twin. How very unpleasant of her.

"I knew you could," Sophia said, smiling at George. This time, George came close to smiling back at her. Anne was not encouraged. She was being thrust into a dare of some sort, a three-way duel that had Dutton at its heart, at least her heart. That was nothing to smile about. "Now, something pleasant, something simple, wouldn't you say, Anne?"

There was nothing pleasant or simple about Dutton. That was the entire problem.

"I would prefer it," Anne said. "Are you certain that Lord Dutton must be involved?"

"Aren't you?" Sophia said.

The look in Sophia's eyes was so full of mischief and delight and hope that Anne was lifted on a surge of joyous expectation not unlike the last time she had sparred with Lord Dutton. In truth, tangling with

Dutton was better than living respectably without him, especially now that she was a respectable widow of means. Really, how much did she have to lose? Neither her money nor her position. Her reputation? She would not risk that. Ever.

"I think that must depend upon what is proposed. I suppose I must draw the line at drawing and quartering him," Anne said, to which Sophia laughed outright, and to which Elizabeth smiled in what could only be termed feral anticipation.

Anne smiled in return, whether in delight or feral anticipation she refused to speculate.

"What are the boundaries to this game of ours?" Elizabeth said.

"Boundaries," Sophia said. "Yes, we must certainly have those."

"And how shall I know when I have won?" Elizabeth asked.

"Don't you mean, how shall I know when you have won?" Sophia said. "It is so lovely to see such confidence, Elizabeth. I know you have come by it honestly."

"I come by all things honestly, Sophia," Elizabeth said.

"As do we all," Anne said, her anger flaring at the insult to Sophia implied in the words, and at the continued insult to herself, the insult of being overlooked and disregarded. By heavens, but she had endured more than enough of that! Even her own butler, no, Staverton's butler . . . no, *her* butler, did not treat her with proper deference. Who was this Indian girl to ignore her so? Was she not Lady Staverton?

She most certainly was.

"Very well," Elizabeth said, in a very dismissive tone, Anne thought. "Let us decide this thing. You are to take Lord Dutton. Agreed. But what are you to do with him? And how shall it be determined if you have succeeded or not?"

Instead of looking at Sophia for instruction or guidance or encouragement, all three, to be frank, Anne looked Elizabeth Grey straight in the eye and, thinking less of Lord Dutton than of defeating Elizabeth, which was certainly not the wisest of decisions, Anne said, "We shall receive proposals. Public proposals."

Sophia smiled and said, "Proposals to do what?"

At that, Anne did not blush. She absolutely forbade herself to blush, and, shockingly, she did not blush. It was all rather remarkable.

"To marry, of course," Anne said. "All other proposals are far too effortless to achieve, aren't they?" And she looked at Elizabeth as she asked it. How many proposals of marriage had this Iroquois woman received? Even one? Doubtful. She was far too disagreeable a woman to attract a man to any lasting commitment.

Possibly. No, probably. Most assuredly probably.

"A marriage proposal," Sophia said. "That might put Elizabeth at too great a disadvantage, Anne. She knows no one in Town. Who would possibly offer for her on such a slight acquaintance?"

"Don't worry about me," Elizabeth said, crossing her legs. "Name the man I am to conquer. And name the man you are to conquer, Sophia. What man will fight for you in this place?"

"Lord Ruan," George said, staring at Sophia. He did not look particularly malicious, but there was a mischievous twinkle lurking not far below the surface. "He's always about, isn't he?"

Then Sophia did the most unusual thing: she compressed her lips, giving every indication that she was, if only for the merest moment, uncomfortable. It passed quickly enough, but it had been there, that tremor, and it caused an answering tremor in Anne.

"Yes, that would make him a convenient choice," Sophia said easily, "but whom shall we pair with darling Elizabeth? Anne, has anyone of note married while I was in America?"

"Not that I can recall," Anne said. "Certainly no one who anyone would believe would interest Miss Grey." Yes, she was calling her Miss Grey again. The cool distance seemed appropriate.

"You may call me Elizabeth," Elizabeth said, turning the entire coolly distant cordiality slap on its head. A most annoying woman, even if she were Sophia's niece. "Lord Dutton. He's young?"

"He's old enough," Anne said.

"He's old? Like your previous husband?" Elizabeth said.

Good heavens, was she implying that Anne was only attractive to *old* men?

"The Marquis of Dutton is the approximate age my first husband would have been, had he lived."

"Forty? Fifty?" Elizabeth asked. George grumbled something unintelligible; Elizabeth ignored him.

"Lord Dutton was born in 1776, I believe," Sophia said. "A date I should say that we all remember well,

Lord Dutton most especially."

"So. He is young," Elizabeth said. "I, also, would like a young man. They are more unruly, and more volatile."

True, but why did that make them more attractive as candidates in this contest?

"I think you will find, Elizabeth," Sophia said, "that Englishmen, in their youth, are less inclined to think of marriage than Iroquois men. Youth, in this contest, will likely be a disadvantage."

"Lord Ruan. He is old?"

"He is not old. I would say he is of an agreeable age," Sophia said. "Which will be so very convenient to me, won't it? I do think he is the perfect choice, and we simply must do the same for you, darling. Find you the perfect man upon which to sharpen your claws."

"George," Elizabeth said, holding Sophia's gaze, "can you give me some names?"

"George Prestwick," George Grey said. "Lord Raithby."

"What about Lord Penrith?" Anne said. It was malicious of her, true; the Marquis of Penrith was lethal to women. Lord Raithby far less so, and Mr. Prestwick least of all. Or that was what was rumored. In very many cases, rumors were entirely true.

"Is Penrith in Town?" Sophia said. "I had a letter from his mother, Julia, and as of two months ago, he was in Greece with them, examining marble piles."

"Oh. What a pity," Anne said. She meant every word. Penrith would have easily knocked Elizabeth Grey on her arse. Raithby, who cared only for riding and Prestwick, who cared only for she knew not what, but not gambling and not women and not drink, for that would have been well-documented through rumor, would likely be trampled under Elizabeth's very large, callused feet.

"Prestwick and Raithby," Sophia said. "What charming choices, George. Trust you to cut to the heart so quickly. Now, whom shall you choose, Elizabeth? They are both young and handsome and available. What more can a woman ask of a man?"

"Who is closer?" Elizabeth asked.

"Why, how very practical you are," Sophia said. "Mr. Prestwick, as it happens, leases a house on this very street."

"Then I choose Prestwick."

"Prestwick, Dutton, and Ruan," Sophia said. "We have our list, our quarry named. Our goal? A proposal of marriage."

"How shall it be made public?" Elizabeth asked.

Anne laughed. "In England, a proposal of marriage is always, and nearly instantly, public."

It was the other kind of proposal, the kind Dutton specialized in, especially with her, that was private, often for as long as a single day, if one were very, very fortunate. She had, sadly, never been fortunate with Edward Preston, 3rd Marquis of Dutton.

Chapter 2

At that moment, Lord Dutton, who did think of himself as Dutton and not as Edward, or Ned, as his old nurse used to call him when he was sick in bed, or Press, as one of his enemies at Eton had done and which still rankled whenever he thought of the man, now somewhere north of York and moldering away, God willing, at that very moment when he was being tossed into a contest upon which he had no interest and would certainly have bet against Anne if he could have done, Dutton was wondering how long it had been since he had fornicated, a word his old tutor had used quite frequently.

Dutton had learned, through tedious repetition, that bedding ginger haired women with light eyes, did not work. Meaning, his tackle, which should have worked and usually did work perfectly, upon all occasions and in any weather, did not work as it should when bedding red-haired women with blue, green, or grey eyes.

He had thought, back in the beginning, two years ago now, that he could fornicate, such an odd sounding word, his way into satisfaction and oblivion. Anne, red-haired, silvery-eyed, Anne, who had not interested him in the least until she had the gall to refuse him not only resolutely, but repeatedly, which did add to the horror of it, had with great vigor and unrelentingly force interested him. Bewitched him. Confounded him. And while he was attempting to lure her into his bed she had married another, snatched herself right out from under his hand, literally, and plopped herself into another man's bed, literally.

The obvious thing to do, besides get drunk for a month or two, was to satisfy his urge for a particular ginger-haired widow on any and every ginger-haired woman he could lay his hand to. There were quite a few around, as it happened. He was not satisfied, as it also happened. Neither were they. In a most embarrassing display of he knew not what, Dutton could not perform in that way that most mattered to a man, and if there was a woman in his bed, that most mattered to a woman.

Avoiding ginger-haired women had been one solution. Another was to avoid London. In that, he had found success. He had poured himself out of the whisky bottle and poured himself into estate affairs. Redworth, the ancestral pile, had been quietly and so very discreetly languishing. It was not now. Redworth was in better health now that it had been during his father's tenure, as it must be admitted, his father, the 2nd Marquis of Dutton, had been a man more given to the pleasures of the flesh, another favorite term oft used by his old tutor, than to the pleasures of the land. His father had also, famously, been entangled in the most lurid and lasting of Sophia Dalby's exploits. In fact, his father had been the source of what was supposed to have been a simple weekend of male amusement into a figure of fun, in the best of lights, and an object of disgust in the worst of them.

Naturally, Dutton did not enjoy thinking of that time, a time that was immortalized in a famous satire done by no less a talent than Gillray, and which showed his father, Lord Westlin, Lord Melverley having their way with a very naked and very young Sophia, looking every inch the Iroquois she was, or had been. He was never completely certain of what Sophia Dalby was, or had been, but he did know that she disliked him very much, and because he could not recall ever having done anything to offend her, he was left to conclude that it was his father, his father who had died by falling down a flight of stairs in a brothel, who was the cause of all Sophia's animus toward him.

When he was sober, he found he could not blame her. When he was drunk, he found he could blame her resolutely and enthusiastically.

It was a sign of his stellar character that he had chosen to forego drunkenness anyway. Whenever he thought of Sophia, which was seldom and yet still far too often, he hoped she realized that. Whenever he thought of Anne, which was entirely too often no matter how the matter was sliced, he hoped she fell into the Thames and drowned.

"The dark blue for the tailcoat, m'lord, and for the waistcoat?" the shopkeeper asked.

"The blue brocade. And the ivory stripe," he answered, pulling on his gloves.

"Very good, m'lord," the man said, dipping his head. "On Tuesday, then, if it pleases you."

It did not please him. It did not displease him. He did not need the coat. He was on Bond Street because he had to do something to fill the hours.

He was in London again, it was the start of the London Season of 1804, and Anne was in Town. Possibly worse, Sophia was in Town. The two of them together were an awful pair, set to destroy his sanity, not to mention his reputation, without any cause whatsoever. Whatever his father had done to Sophia was buried with the man, or ought to have been, and whatever he had done to Anne, a simple kiss, a few lurid suggestions concerning what he'd like to do with her and what he was certain she wanted done to her, and she'd reacted like no woman he'd ever known: she'd rejected him. And she'd acted like every woman he'd ever known: blown the whole thing out of proportion. She should have been flattered, or at least intrigued. What was the point of being insulted? Why inflame him at every turn and then express outrage at his logical response to being enflamed?

Women were a bother. Anne Warren Staverton was worse than most.

She was a widow again. The woman went through husbands like a turnstile.

Dutton finished with his gloves and, checking his cravat in the mirror behind the clerk, walked out of the shop and onto the bustle of Bond Street, and was jostled against the most unlikely and unfortunate man in all of London.

"Dutton," the Marquis of Ruan said. "Good to see you."

It was not good to see Ruan. Ruan was somehow inextricably linked with Sophia and the tangle that had become Anne. Ruan had understood too much; in fact, it had been Ruan who had understood and explained in patronizing terms to Dutton that Sophia had been using Anne to punish him for some perceived misdeed. He had performed no misdeed. He had simply tried to seduce Anne Warren. What the bloody hell was wrong with that?

According to Ruan, something had been bloody well wrong with it, at least from Sophia's, and yes, Anne's perspective.

Seeing Ruan again put Dutton back two years and in the completely wrong frame of mind.

"Ruan," he said. It was said a bit tersely. He was feeling profoundly terse. He was not going to apologize for it.

"I'm on my way to Dalby House," Ruan said, studying him with his sharp green eyes. Ruan's eyes saw far too much. "I trust you know that Lady Staverton will make for Sophia's side, and where Anne goes, so goes Dutton. Hasn't that been the way of it?"

Dutton stiffened. "Certainly not. Most definitely not. It was never so and is not so now. I pay no attention to where Sophia Dalby is and am even less interested in Lady Staverton, whatever her situation or condition may be."

Dutton knew the second the words were out of his mouth that he had said too much, but there was nothing to be done about it now except to keep his tongue behind his teeth.

Ruan did not smile, but his eyes did something that spoke of being amused. Dutton felt himself grow yet more agitated, a thing he had hardly thought possible.

"I beg your pardon," Ruan said. He should have cut a bow as he said it. He did not. "I was mistaken. I had thought you wanted a bit of your own back this Season. If you can forgive the assault upon your character during the 1802 Season, then I can but applaud your virtue, though I cannot believe that Lady Dalby will join me."

"No, applauding virtue would not interest her," Dutton said. Ruan gestured and the two of them continued on, side by side. Dutton could not shake the notion that Ruan had taken him under his wing. And not for the first time. Why Ruan should care what happened or did not happen to him was beyond reckoning. "Yet I was not aware that my character had been assaulted. Merely my reputation."

Ruan smiled and said, "There are not many men who would draw such a fine line between the two. I applaud you yet again, Dutton. You have matured a decade in the past two years."

Yes, he likely had. Hard work did have the habit of doing that, one of the main reasons that people likely avoided it so. That, and it took so much time every day. He'd hardly been deep in his cups for more than a year, and the last time had been at Christmas, which was surely nearly a tradition.

Dutton looked askance at Ruan. He, too, appeared to have aged beyond the normal passage of months. Ruan, older than he, harder, the rough edge of experience lying on his face and in his manner, looked harder and rougher still. Whatever he had been doing for the past two years, the affects showed upon him.

"I've been busy. Working," Dutton said. He said the word almost as a curse, almost as a challenge.

"A good use of time, working. So I've heard," Ruan said. "Your reputation, has it survived intact?"

"I have no idea. I can't say I care."

"Grown up, then. Good. She will have a tougher battle this time, won't she? She won't pink you at the first thrust."

"She?"

"Sophia. Anne."

Dutton stopped dead in his tracks. "I can't think what you mean, Ruan."

"Can't you?" Ruan said, looking back at Dutton, his head tilted to one side, his smile tilted upon his weathered face. "If you think she will stop, you don't know her. She will not stop until she has satisfaction of you."

"She?" Dutton asked again.

"Sophia, in her way," Ruan said, "and Anne in hers."

It sounded positively ominous, and ridiculous, like something out of an Italian opera. Dutton made a sound of dismissal. "You are fixated. I had not thought you the sort, Ruan."

"They are fixated," Ruan countered. "Best be prepared. And best to attack. Or do you want them to call the hour and the method?"

"Swords or pistols?"

"They are women, Dutton. They play with deadlier weapons. Seduction. Marriage."

Dutton laughed. It had a bitter sound. He didn't care. "You speak with great authority, Ruan. Tell me, are you their agent? Are you part of this vast plot against me?"

"Dutton, I have not seen Sophia Dalby in two years. I have not seen Anne Staverton since Staverton died. Yet I know what will happen to you because I know them, these women. They have made you their quarry before, to their great amusement. Do you think that they have forgotten about you? Do you think that they will not pick up this game where they last left it? Sophia Dalby does not forgive. Anne Staverton will not have forgotten."

"How can you know that?" Dutton asked. "And why should it matter to me?"

"Perhaps it doesn't," Ruan said. "Perhaps it only matters to me."

"Why should any of this matter to you?"

Ruan shook his head, giving him a rueful look. "They whipped you hard that Season. I could not stand by and do nothing. I would like to even the score, that is all. If you have moved past it all, forgotten all the slights and the barbs, then . . . " Ruan shrugged, the muscles of his shoulders rippling beneath his dark blue coat. "I should do the same, yet I do not think it is in me to do so. I'm to Dalby House now, to begin it again. Join me or not. I will not think less of you."

Which, naturally, meant that he would most definitely think less of him, but Dutton did not care what Lord Ruan thought of him. Why should he? Ruan was nothing to him. Yet, strangely, he did care. Worse, he cared what Anne thought of him, and if Anne thought that he was beaten and that *she* had beaten him, the bloody stick still in her hand, well, that wasn't acceptable, was it? No. Not at all.

"Let's stop at my house on Jermyn Street. I'd like to change my cravat," Dutton said.

"Certainly," Ruan said, his green eyes glittering.

Chapter 3

But of course, it was all a lie. Oh, perhaps not all, but most of it. The Marquis of Ruan did not particularly care about Dutton, but he did particularly care about Sophia Dalby.

He had not seen her in two years. When he had last seen her, she'd killed a man with one of the many knives she carried upon her person. She'd pulled out a knife, stuck it in the back of the man's neck, and left him for dead. It was Ruan who'd kicked the man into the water, hiding the body for the few moments it would take for Sophia to get away.

He'd not hesitated. He'd been watching her, as he always seemed to watch her, with the same fascination that a hawk watched a falcon, two predators out amongst the mice. Yes, he supposed he was a predator. How else to explain his willingness to help her kill a man? He'd not hesitated and he'd not felt anything but gladness that he could help her when she needed help.

She *had* needed help. He'd seen that in her fathomless eyes. She'd looked at him, a single, beseeching look, and he'd known he'd do anything she asked of him.

It was not easy knowledge, that.

After the deed, he'd asked her whom they'd just killed and she'd told him. The man had murdered her mother. He believed her. The look on her face, the joyous, righteous rage in her eyes, had convinced him of that, if he'd needed convincing. Strangely, he had not. She had needed him. He had met that need. It was enough for him.

Shockingly, it was enough.

A man lived a short life when tied to such service, to

such a woman. And still, he did not care. That was how far he had fallen.

No, not into love. Into fascination. Perhaps even something so juvenile as infatuation. But not love. The man who was foolish enough to love Sophia Dalby would lose his soul.

He would not relinquish his soul, what little was left of it.

Ruan paced the street in front of Dutton House, waiting for Dutton to make himself ready for the challenges of Dalby House. He had little patience, certainly not enough to tether himself to a sofa indoors; it had been two years since he'd last seen Sophia Dalby. He did not know how he had endured it.

She'd escaped him, escaped England, he'd come to find out. Slipped the leash, bolted, gone running back to America, disappearing into that vast wilderness like a shadow. He'd not expected that of her. She'd killed a man. But who had not?

He'd not expected her to run, and not so far. And not so quickly. Twenty-four hours after she'd killed her man, she was gone. Gone, where he could not track her.

She was a fire in his blood, tawdry and over-worked as the saying went, yet it was nothing but the truth. He had pursued her, stumbling in his pursuit when swift deftness was essential, blundered, righted himself, and lost her. Two years lost. He could ill afford two years.

What had she been about, this woman of many continents yet beholden to none? Oh yes, he knew that about her, though he could not have said how. Sophia trod lightly upon the earth; no country claimed her allegiance, and he supposed he could understand it.

Born a child of the Iroquois, then a young girl amongst the Americans, and eventually a young woman tossed upon the streets of London to make her way. France had played a part in her history; she had spent time in France, but what had she encountered there? He could not pierce that mystery. He had tried. He was trying still. He would seek out her secrets until his blood ran cold.

He had to have her. She was his other. Not his soul mate. He did not have enough of a soul to believe in soul mates.

Dutton came down the steps of his house, his gait hurried and eager. Ruan smiled, one corner of his mouth indulging in the practice, and then he resumed his normal expression. What that expression was he could not have said. Perhaps it was beyond description. He rather hoped so. He was not the sort of man who would tolerate having his face read.

Never mind the fact that Sophia read him like an alphabet.

Dutton, quite obviously, could not read him like an alphabet.

"You want to see Sophia, of course," Dutton said.

Ruan did not bother casting a glance in Dutton's direction. Alphabets be damned. Yes, his fascination with Sophia Dalby might have become a trifle obvious, even to a man of Dutton's powers of observation, which is to say, whisky-soaked, but he was not a fool of the Dutton variety. Dutton had, by the most singular and uninspired method, become a complete lackwit where Anne Staverton was concerned. He had cornered her, snarled at her, accosted her, and failed with her.

It was most amusing and equally ridiculous.

That he had done something of the same with Sophia was nobody's business but his. And Sophia's. No one else had been a party to his failure to arouse Sophia's amorous interest. That counted for quite a lot in Town. Dutton had lost that battle two Seasons ago. He had not quite recovered his reputation since, though he appeared to have recovered his equanimity.

Dutton was sober.

Dutton was clear-eyed.

Dutton was, perhaps and for the first time, ready to tackle Anne Staverton and bring her to heel. Or at least survive an attempt at her. He had not quite succeeded at that before, not with Sophia pulling all the strings.

Sophia did pull strings, and most efficiently, too. To be blunt, Sophia could pull any string she liked concerning Lord Dutton and Lady Staverton, as long as she pulled his string as well.

Throwing Dutton into Sophia's outstretched hands ought to serve very nicely as an entrée. He would deliver Dutton to her, and to Anne, and then he would take whatever was offered as a result. He didn't expect much, but he did expect something.

And that was all he cared about.

Chapter 4

All Elizabeth cared about was showing Sophia that she cared nothing for England, for English ways, English manners, and English protocols. She hated the English. She also hated the Americans and the French and the Spanish and the Hurons. In short, she hated everyone who was not a member of the Iroquois nation. Because of them, all of them, the Iroquois nation was more memory than actuality.

Her hate was the fire that kept her alive.

George, more traveled, told her she was wrong, repeatedly.

George, by traveling, had diluted his warrior's heart.

She would not allow the same thing to happen to her, no matter how long she was forced to dwell among the English hoard. And she was forced. Her father, at Sophia's urging, had forced her. Sophia's son, Mark, was under her father's hand in America, learning the ways of the Iroquois and the ways of the earth and sky, unlearning the ways of the city and the throng. For two years Mark had been unlearning the lessons of his English childhood. He had come to America like a babe, unknowing of the simplest of things. How to start a fire. How to kill by knife. He knew those things now, and many more. He had become a man.

It was time, Sophia had said to her father, that Elizabeth learned how to be a woman among the English. Her father had agreed. Her father too often agreed with Sophia. It was a weakness---a habit learned in childhood before he and Sophia had walked their separate paths upon the Earth. That Sophia had walked into prostitution among the French and English he held hard against his heart, blaming himself for not saving her, yet proud of the woman who had survived so well.

Elizabeth knew that survival was assured, if one was willing to pay any price for it. There was no inherent merit in survival, no matter the ferocity of the opponent. It was in saying that to her father, his brows lowered in silent disapproval, that he had made his decision that she would go to England with Sophia and that she would stay in England until summoned home.

Elizabeth blamed Sophia. There was no one else to blame.

George blamed her, for her uncensored disapproval and pride.

Sophia blamed no one. Sophia merely smiled that cold English smile of hers and set about ordering a suitable English wardrobe for her.

George had come with her to England because Sophia had suggested it, and that made having George with her, something that she would have enjoyed, turn into something she resented.

Sophia, with her English ways and her bone-deep arrogance, burned through every layer of warm goodwill Elizabeth should have felt for an aunt.

She hated Sophia for that, too.

"I was under the impression that Lady Staverton had nothing but disdain for Lord Dutton," Lord Raithby said. "Actually, I was told she hated him."

"Who told you that?" George Prestwick asked.

"Ashdon. The last time he was in Town, soon after

he assumed the Westlin title," Raithby said.

"Since his marriage, he's been out of Town more than in," Prestwick said. "He's misinformed."

"I suppose that's possible," Raithby said.

The two men were riding in Hyde Park. It was not the most fashionable hour to be riding, but then they did not care for fashion. They cared for horseflesh. Lord Raithby had been horse mad since his youth. George Prestwick had become horse mad upon becoming acquainted with Lord Raithby. It made for a most cordial friendship. Raithby instructed Prestwick on horses; Prestwick instructed Raithby on the affairs of the *ton*, of whom he was an avid observer. Prestwick, his father having become a baron fairly recently, was, as a newly hatched member of the aristocracy and as a generally genial fellow, made it his business to see everyone and, to the best of his ability, understand what he saw.

He understood more than most. He understood far more than Raithby, who did not care one way or the other what he saw or what he understood. Of course, it was equally true that Raithby did not care if he understood Society or not. For Raithby, the world was all of horseflesh.

"Sophia Dalby's back in Town," Prestwick said, keeping his gaze on the sodden path beneath his mount's hooves, "and Lady Staverton is a widow."

"So?"

"Dutton is in Town."

Raithby cast a narrow glance at Prestwick, the scar on his cheek white in the damp air. "So?"

"So," Prestwick said with a grin, "we should call on

Lady Dalby."

"Why?"

"Because that is where everything will be happening this Season. Look, Raithby, I have learned much about horses from you these past two years. It is time for you to learn much about women."

"From you?" Raithby said, his blue eyes glimmering with amusement.

"From Sophia Dalby," Prestwick said. "Who else?"

Chapter 5

Jane, the Duchess of Edenham, American by birth and English by marriage, though just barely English by marriage, and that only if her husband was within hearing, entered Lady Louisa Blakesley's salon with a flourish of very American excitement.

"Sophia's back!" Jane said, without even so much as a greeting. Jane was very, very American at times. Louisa had learned to tolerate it.

"How are you, Duchess? Feeling all the thing today?" Louisa said, her back erect and her carriage impeccable as she stood to greet her guest.

"Oh, are we doing that again?" Jane said with a grin. "One would hardly think we are related, the way you carry on."

"Related by marriage," Louisa said.

Louisa was married to Henry Blakesley, Jane's cousin, Henry's mother having been born and bred in Boston, of all places. Jane's mother, Henry's mother's sister, was from New York, but that story was rather long and involved and Louisa tried not to think of it anyway, being related to Americans to such a close and unpleasant degree. But it did prove, if proof were required, how very much attached she was to Blakes, that she would marry him, being as awash in Americans as he was.

"And I married a duke," Jane said, "so give way, Louisa. If we are to play these games, I shan't be found the loser." Jane said the last bit with her most polished English accent, her gaze most superior, and her smile most wicked.

"Oh, very well," Louisa said, throwing herself onto the tufted blue silk sofa. "It's not very much fun to pull your nose when you know I'm doing it."

"Thank heavens for that," Jane said. "Now, fetch your bonnet. We're off to Sophia's white salon and I shall finally be witness to her expert machinations. All my life I've waited for this."

"As you're married, you can witness it all quite safely," Louisa said.

"Witness what?" Eleanor said, coming into the room.

Eleanor, Louisa's younger and only sister, lived with Louisa and Blakes as no one in her right mind would choose to live with the Marquis of Melverley, their dissolute and disagreeable father.

"Sophia's back," Jane said. "How lovely to see you, Eleanor. You look so very pretty in that shade of rose."

"She looks like a blister," Louisa said, "and you must stay at home. You are far too young and vulnerable to enter into Sophia's wicked white salon."

"I look wonderful in this gown and you know it," Eleanor said, giving Jane a quick hug, "and I am not staying at home. Sophia is back in London and I'm going to see her. I am quite old enough to manage whatever occurs in her white salon."

"You are an imbecile to think it," Louisa said.

"You've been in her salon," Jane said to Louisa.

"And found myself engaged mere days later," Louisa said.

"As I am too young to marry, I shall be quite safe," Eleanor said. "I've only to fetch my bonnet and gloves and we shall be free to leave." Eleanor, looking at Louisa, who sat in a somewhat predatory posture and had a slightly suspicious look on her face, said, "I shall just wait here for Mary to fetch our things, shall I? I shouldn't want you to leave without me."

"You've always been so needlessly suspicious, Eleanor," Louisa said with a sigh.

"Needlessly? Hardly that," Jane said on a chuckle.

It was thus that the bonnets and gloves were fetched, the three women mutually guarding each other for signs of escape in the interim. Bonnets affixed and gloves drawn on, they proceeded to Dalby House. Jane was smiling, Eleanor was humming, and Louisa was scowling. All in all, it was a perfectly ordinary outing and they were each behaving entirely in character. Until they arrived at their destination.

It should not be supposed that there was a single person above the age of eleven who was not privy to the fact that Sophia Dalby was back in Town. Which is to say, when the knocker appeared upon Dalby House door, making it clear to all that Sophia was *in,* anyone who had any interest in what Society was up to, and that would be everyone, was either hurrying to drop in upon Lady Dalby or, if they did not have the social capital for entrée, loitered about on Upper Brook Street to see who was going to knock upon her door.

Lord Raithby and Mr. George Prestwick were just barely in the former category. They knew Sophia Dalby just barely. They could, and probably would, be granted admittance, but their welcome was not assured. An open door, the acceptance of a card, was not the same thing as social acceptance. Whoever it was who wrote the leading book of etiquette didn't know deuce about that. Prestwick, who had read all the books of etiquette, particularly after his sister, Penelope, had married the heir to the Duke of Hyde, knew that beyond a shadow of a doubt. There was more to social congress than any book of etiquette could ever cover.

"Why shouldn't she be *in* for us?" Raithby asked, his valet brushing invisible lint off his coat of blue superfine. "Isn't she *in* for nearly anyone?"

"It's perfectly obvious you haven't spent any time at all with Lady Dalby," Prestwick said.

He had accompanied Raithby to his father's house on Grosvenor Street for the simple reason that the horse he rode belonged to Raithby. George Prestwick's father, a man who had been made a baron because he had a knack for making money, was not adept at spending it, particularly on horseflesh, a habit he considered wasteful, indulgent, and suspect. A horse, according to the senior Prestwick, should be sound. And that was the end of his interest in the subject. On the junior Prestwick's annual stipend he could afford a sound horse, but nothing more than that. Raithby scoffed and, being a horse snob and a friend, did not encourage George Prestwick to waste his money on mere soundness.

"The purpose of this visit, I assumed," Raithby said, lifting his chin so his valet could adjust his cravat by a fraction of an inch.

"Yes, well," Prestwick said, "there is that, but doesn't the Earl have more than a passing acquaintance with Lady Dalby?"

"My father and Lady Dalby?" Raithby said, waving his valet aside and by a nod, indicating he should remove himself. The valet, whose name had not been mentioned in George Prestwick's hearing, removed himself. "What are you suggesting and where did you hear it suggested?"

"No place in particular," Prestwick said. "It is simply something known."

"It is not known by me."

"Raithby, since Sophia Dalby does not possess four legs and a tail, of course it is not known by you."

"I had heard rumors about a tail," Raithby said with a quick, sharp smile.

"Of course you did," Prestwick said with an answering smile. "I only meant to say that I think, with the Earl Quinton with us, we should have a better reception than without. Do you think he might accompany us?"

"I can but ask."

But, as it happened, the Earl of Quinton was not at home; he was out calling upon Lady Dalby, which did leave Lord Raithby stupendously speechless for all of fifteen minutes.

Chapter 6

Anne judged that she had arrived at Dalby House and been admitted into Sophia's white salon for approximately twenty minutes before the (unpleasant, it must be admitted) arrival of Elizabeth and George Grey. The details of their challenge had been set within ten minutes of that, and not quite ten minutes after that, the white salon was inundated with a steady flow of the cream of Society. Sophia had that sort of draw. Anne did not, though she was quite accustomed to that sort of bland dismissal. Well, perhaps not accustomed to it, but resigned to it.

That is, until Lord Dutton arrived in the company of Lord Ruan. Then, watching how Sophia commanded Lord Ruan's attention with the most casual and amused ease, Anne decided, if she had not decided before and she really thought she had done, that she would treat Dutton to very much the same.

He would pay attention to her.

She would be amused by it.

There truly was no other option that she was willing to consider, and it had nothing whatsoever to do with the challenge with Miss Grey, though that was a lovely fillip and it only urged her to reject fear or timidity or any of her other many failings, one could say *habits*, as an option. No, the only path open to her was the path that Sophia had laid out for herself so long ago with oh so many men. She was going to make Dutton fall ludicrously in love with her and she was going to laugh right in his face.

And wouldn't it be lovely for Miss Grey to be a witness to all of that?

It was truly so lovely to be a widow of good repute.

There was simply nothing she could not attempt, particularly with Dutton. After all, he already was a laughingstock and had more than the beginnings of a perfectly vile reputation. Who would ever take his side over hers?

So it was that, even with the arrival of the Jane, the Duchess of Edenham, whom she did quite like, as little as she knew her, and Lady Louisa, whom she positively loathed, and young Lady Eleanor, who did seem quite nice, though she bore further study as Louisa was her elder sister and there was something to be said for fruit from the same branch, that Anne, even in this crowd of witnesses, was confident that she could lure Dutton into making a complete fool of himself.

And so it was that she was able to smile quite wickedly and curtsey to Dutton with the most insouciant air that was ever seen. At least to judge by Dutton's response to her. Dutton, that fool, that wickedly handsome fool, scowled down at her, touched her hand to his lips, and when she did not blush at the contact, grumbled some nonsense about ginger-haired women who did not know their proper place.

It was a most magnificent beginning. Even Sophia chuckled. Though Miss Grey, Iroquois savage that she clearly was, did not seem to understand the point of any of it. It was going to be so difficult to win at this contest if Miss Grey did not understand the plain facts in front of her.

Ah, well, but that is what the proposal was for.

If Anne felt the slightest flutter of nerves in the pit of her stomach at contemplating wrangling a marriage proposal out of Lord Dutton she supposed that was allowed, as long as Dutton, and Miss Grey, were unaware of it. Still, she had already achieved two marriage proposals; how difficult could it be to arrange for another?

Without having had to do so much as change her shoes, which made the fact that she had chosen to wear her favorite new pair of shoes with the blue satin ribbons so fortuitous, Sophia found herself standing to admit James Hampton, 5th Marquis of Ruan, into her white salon. And how delicious of Ruan to have delivered the 3rd Marquis of Dutton into Anne's tempting web. For he had delivered him, she could see that clearly in his piercing green eyes.

How long the past two years seemed now, looking into those knowing green eyes.

Sophia promptly looked away from them and greeted Dutton with a seductive curtsey. "Lord Dutton, how wonderful you look. Lord Ruan," she said, with a dip of her head, one of her curls swinging forward to sweep across her bosom.

"Lady Dalby," Ruan said, his voice a low thrum that caressed her skin.

"Lady Dalby," Dutton said, his voice an angry buzz that promised pure entertainment.

Darling Anne would have such fun with this one, if she could but keep her wits and her heart well in control, which was always a challenge for Anne when dealing with the devastating Lord Dutton.

Ah, well, but what was life but one enticing challenge upon another?

She did not look at Ruan upon the thought. No, she did not.

"Lady Dalby," Ruan said, his eyes skimming over her face, "how long it's been, and how little it shows."

"How little?" she repeated. "Darling Ruan, it has been long enough for you to have grown clumsy in your compliments, or perhaps it is your eyesight which has grown clumsy?"

"Only my tongue, I fear, from want of practice," he said, his lips giving the hint of smile without the delivery of one.

"Now, that's better," she said. "How quickly you have found your feet in this duel."

"It's always of duels with you, I fear, Lady Dalby," Dutton said, which was so very like him as it was so ham-fistedly dreary.

"It is always of duels, of tongues and hearts, between men and women," she said. "I did think you understood that, Lord Dutton, being a man of mature years. But perhaps I am overly optimistic."

Dutton, who did look rather well after two years doing God knew what, did look quite fine. His shoulders were even broader than previously and his face more sculpted. Why, it was almost as if he'd actually been engaged in meaningful occupation, which would make the rumors true. How perfectly extraordinary. The only question now was if Dutton's being sober would make things more difficult for Anne or not. As Dutton had been amusingly obtuse while drunk, he might be more responsive to suggestion while sober. It didn't play that way very often, but he might be the exception that proved the rule. She did hope so, for Anne's sake.

"For Anne's sake, I do hope that Lord Dutton doesn't make a complete fool of himself this time," Jane said.

"Whatever do you mean? And how could you possibly know what kind of fool Lord Dutton was last time when you weren't even a witness to it?" Louisa said. Louisa sounded annoyed. Louisa nearly always sounded somewhat annoyed.

"I do have a husband, as you may recall," Jane said. "He does speak to me, as difficult as that may be for you to believe."

Louisa gave Jane a slightly scathing look, marred by Eleanor's snort of amusement, and said, "He may speak to you, but it's clear you don't understand what he's saying, Jane. Of course it's perfectly true that Dutton made a complete cake of himself two years ago—"

"Even I heard of it," Eleanor interjected, her dark blue eyes alight.

"Oh, but that counts for little as you hear everything," Jane said with a wink.

"But of course," Louisa said stiffly, reproving them for interrupting her with her eyes, "Anne can want nothing more than for Dutton to improve upon his performance as a complete imbecile this Season, and by that I naturally mean that he should and likely will appear even more foolish that he did before."

"He doesn't look foolish now, does he?" Jane said, looking as politely as she knew how at the two men.

The three of them eyed Dutton as he stood talking with Sophia, Anne, and Ruan in the center of the white salon. The three women had stood upon the entrance of the arrival of Dutton and Ruan. The three women were waiting for the men to properly greet them. The three women continued to wait.

"I'm devastated to admit it, but he does not," Louisa said.

"I know you won't admit it, but you are in over your head," George Grey said.

Elizabeth had excused herself to use the necessary ten minutes ago and George had followed her. George had not stopped talking to her about all the many things he thought she did not understand. George was a man and did not understand the way a woman engaged in warfare. Not that she could explain that to him; he was a man and he would not understand.

Elizabeth knew that more people had arrived in the house; she could hear their voices. George did not seem to care about that. George only seemed to care about telling her that she didn't know what she was doing.

It was sometimes very tedious being with George.

"I know how to swim, brother," she said, crossing her arms over her chest, staring up at him.

"Not in this river," he said.

"Swimming is swimming," she said. "Do you not think I can manage an Englishman?"

"You are the granddaughter of an English woman," George countered. "An English lady."

Elizabeth shook her head and uncrossed her arms. "Yes, and if that is what you need to remember to have confidence in me, so be it. Let me do what I must do. I shall win this contest."

"By obtaining a marriage proposal," George said. "It is a serious thing. You think Sophia does not understand this? She knows better than you what this will mean."

"A proposal, not my acceptance," Elizabeth said. "Trust me. Can you not do that?"

George smiled and sighed. "I trust you. It is the Englishman I do not trust."

"Nor do I," she answered with a grin. "I am prepared."

"But is he?" George said, but he spoke to the air for Elizabeth had reentered the white salon. George, his smile fading, followed her in.

"Miss Grey! How delighted I am to make your acquaintance," Eleanor gushed. "I have met your three brothers, did they tell you?" Eleanor rushed on, not giving Elizabeth a chance to respond. "I am so, so happy to finally meet you. I never thought to have the pleasure, and it is such a great, great pleasure. Tell me, what can I do to make your visit to England pleasurable? It is a visit? You are not here to stay with Lady Dalby for good?"

"No. I am not," Elizabeth said, cutting into the stream of Eleanor's outpouring. "A short visit. To see England. To see . . ."

"Sophia's world," George supplied when his sister seemed at a loss for words.

"Yes," Elizabeth said, her black eyes shuttered. "That."

"How very familial of you," Louisa said, her own face shuttered against this odd addition to their Society. "What a close family you are. I hardly imagine I would travel across an ocean to visit a relative."

"Oh, but you hate to travel anywhere, for any cause," Eleanor said on a laugh.

No one else laughed. Jane, most particularly, did not look even tempted to laugh. Louisa found Jane's reaction to Elizabeth Grey particularly noteworthy. Were they not both Americans of a sort? Should they not be more enthused upon meeting each other? They were not. Louisa paid attention to details of that sort. Eleanor, with her never-ending fascination for the various Indian nations, did not.

"It is a pleasure to make your acquaintance, Miss Grey, Mr. Grey," Jane said. Jane had not met George Grey and his two younger brothers in 1802; George and his brothers, and their father, Sophia's elder brother, and Sophia's son had just sailed for America. Jane and her brothers had arrived in England on the heels of their departure. But of course she had heard of them; Eleanor, if no one else, had seen to that.

Jane nodded regally, looking very much the duchess

she was, and waited for the proper response from the Grey twins.

George smiled, his one dimple wickedly charming, and how well Louisa remembered that dimple, and bowed to Jane, his dark eyes revealing nothing but pleasure and perhaps amusement. Miss Elizabeth Grey's dark eyes revealed nothing, not pleasure and most definitely not amusement. She dipped her dark head in a stiff bow of acknowledgment, and that was all.

How very vexing.

"How have you been entertaining yourself?" Louisa asked baldly.

"By making wagers with my aunt," Elizabeth said, "and with the woman she protects. Lady Staverton."

Eleanor gasped and looked quite alarmed. Jane did something quite near a grunt and looked amused. Louisa did not gasp nor grunt. Louisa spoke. "Regarding what, if I may ask?"

She shouldn't ask, it wasn't at all polite, but she didn't care about being polite in the best of circumstances, and certainly not to an American savage dressed in English clothes while standing in Sophia Dalby's home. It was a universal truth that manners and decorum went completely up the flue at Dalby House.

"We are, each of us, to obtain marriage proposals," Elizabeth replied, equally blunt.

"Each of you? You and Lady Staverton and . . .?" Louisa asked.

"Sophia," Elizabeth said.

This time both Eleanor and Jane gasped. It was Louisa who grunted.

"Mercy," Jane breathed.

"She may well require it," Elizabeth said with a most unattractive superior air.

It was not to be borne.

Louisa may well have had no love for Sophia, and indeed, she did not, nor for Anne Staverton, which she most assuredly did not, but she was not going to stand idly by while this savage woman from a savage land insulted people in her social set, even if she still couldn't quite determine how Sophia had managed to crawl her way into her social set. Nevertheless and completely to the point, the look in Miss Grey cold black eyes was not to be tolerated.

"How woefully misinformed you are," Louisa said. "One might even use the word ignorant. Yes, it's quite clear you are ignorant of so very, very much."

Eleanor and Jane didn't bother to gasp. George Grey, however, did make some sort of noise in his throat that was in the same general family as a groan. Louisa turned her gaze upon him, communicating her rage and her superiority in a single look, and he took a half step backwards. Good man.

"Sophia Dalby can induce a man to do anything. Even marry her," Louisa said. "How else could she have become the Countess of Dalby?"

"That was long ago," Miss Grey replied stiffly.

"Lady Dalby agreed to this?" Jane said. "She wants to marry again?"

"And you, are you going to marry an Englishman?" Eleanor asked.

"The wager is for a proposal only," Elizabeth said. "Obviously."

Oh, obviously. Louisa cast a glance at Jane. Jane

refused to meet her eyes. Jane had come from America for an adventure two years ago and, like Elizabeth now, had no thought to marry an Englishman. Jane was now the Duchess of Edenham. Blasted Americans were stumbling into all the best men and snatching them up. It was beyond toleration.

"Mr. Grey, did you advise your sister as to the . . . dangers involved in such an adventure?" Jane asked, a smile fighting for life around her mouth. Blasted Jane saw humor in every thing, it was one of her most irritating traits. Of course, being a duchess would induce one to having a rather sunnier outlook than was typical.

"My sister sees no danger in the wager," George Grey answered. He did not smile, but there was something shimmering in his black eyes that might have been amusement.

"And she sees no danger in Lady Dalby," Louisa said dryly. "How original."

"The wager is that the first one to receive a proposal of marriage wins?" Eleanor asked. "I should think Sophia would win that handily."

"It is a matter of whom," Elizabeth said, clearly annoyed that everyone seemed to think Sophia had got the better of her. Louisa almost felt the merest whisper of a tug of sympathy, but it passed. "I am to snare Mr. George Prestwick, Sophia, Lord Ruan, and Lady Staverton, Lord Dutton."

Upon hearing the list, they all gasped.

Chapter 7

Anne was not going to gasp, no matter what Dutton said or did, or did not say or did not do. She was Lady Staverton now, and she was more than his equal, and he was not going to toy with her.

She was going to toy with him.

"How well you look, Lord Dutton," Anne said. "Can it be possible that you are sober? How remarkable, if so."

Dutton, his blue eyes heavy-lidded with sensuality, looked at her coolly. "How remarkable, Lady Staverton, that you appear to find sobriety in a man unusual. This does not speak well of your late husband, I fear."

Sophia smiled and said, "All of duels, my dear Dutton, 'tis all of duels. I shall leave you both to it, shall I? And shall you accompany me, Lord Ruan? I must introduce you to my niece, Miss Elizabeth Grey. You will find her most fascinating, I am sure."

And with that, Sophia and Lord Ruan moved deeper into the white salon, leaving Anne alone, relatively speaking, with Lord Dutton. Lord Dutton looked annoyed. Anne was not going to be put off by it. Lord Dutton, as she well knew, was not possessed of a pleasant disposition. He was blatantly sensual and extravagantly attractive, but he was not pleasant. Everyone knew that. The surprising development was that he was sober.

Anne had not yet decided if that development was going to play in her favor or not. Probably, it would not. She did not have a history of good fortune when dealing with Lord Dutton. Why he continued to fascinate her she could not have said.

Oh, very well, she could have said; she simply

refused to.

"Miss Elizabeth Grey?" Dutton said, glancing across the room. "She is related to Mr. George Grey?"

Since Mr. George Grey had struck Lord Dutton unconscious in the not too distant past, Dutton did not seem at all pleased at the possible connection. It was thus that Anne said with not inconsiderable glee, "She and Mr. Grey are twins. Miss Grey is visiting Sophia so that she may experience London and its Society."

Dutton, his blue eyes raking across Anne for the briefest and most heated of moments, said, "Would it be very forward of me to wish to be a part of her London experience?"

"Very," Anne said, her pulse pounding.

She was not going to allow Elizabeth to walk off with Dutton under her arm, or vice versa. Where was his well-documented fascination with her? Gone into the grave with Staverton, very possibly. It might be that her entire fascination for Dutton was in her unavailability; it would be just like Dutton to be so contrary, so devoted to making her miserable and frustrated at every turn.

Yes, frustrated.

Stavey had been gone over a year, and he had been very old and not very vigorous at his best, not that a woman complained of such things, especially when the husband, old or not, made a viscountess of a woman, but she was young and she was not disinterested in the activities of the marriage bed, or the activities out of one, come to that. Not that Dutton ever need know that about her. No, he was, or had been, far too sure of himself without knowing that she had been only somewhat virginal on her first wedding night. As her first husband had never known the difference, certainly Dutton had no need to know.

But it was just this, these thoughts and these frustrations and these inconvenient longings, that made dealing with Lord Dutton so difficult. He threatened all her common sense and that was nearly unforgivable.

Nearly unforgivable.

Which was the entire problem, wasn't it?

"I don't suppose Miss Grey will mind, not when all is said and done," he said. "If you would make the introductions?"

Dutton looked at her, his look clearly full of mischief and a most unwelcome sense of awareness, and Anne felt something burst within her. It was not a blood vessel, one hoped.

"Forgive me, Lord Dutton," Anne said, lifting her chin, and her bust, it should be noted, "but I do not believe that Miss Grey, nor Mr. Grey, with whom you already have a most uncongenial relationship, cares to know you any better than she currently does. Which is to say, not at all." At Dutton's startled look, and he did look delightfully startled, and it was such a good look on him, she said, "I hope you will forgive me for being so brutally frank, but Mr. Grey and Miss Grey are terribly close, as you may imagine as they are twins, and he has told her all about you and she has stated her express desire to avoid you as much as possible without offending her aunt, which as Sophia has no great love for you should be simplicity itself. I trust you take my meaning? I only inform you of this to spare you any discomfort."

Of course it was all a lie, but how would he ever know that? As to that, it might actually be true, or at least in part. Mr. Grey must dislike Lord Dutton; he'd hit him, hadn't he? And certainly one would expect twins to be exceptionally close, no matter that Elizabeth Grey seemed to have the most unpleasant disposition, her brother likely forgave her all. No matter what was true and what was false, there could be no doubt at all that George Grey would not want his sister, his sheltered, naive sister, to be within Lord Dutton's sphere of influence.

No, there was no doubt about that at all.

"Lady Staverton," Dutton said, looking down at her, his sharp blue eyes glinting almost malevolently, which looked more fascinating than repulsive, which was such a problem, "I take your meaning precisely." Upon saying, he took her hand in his, lifted her fingers to his mouth, and kissed her knuckles.

It all looked quite proper, if one didn't know Dutton, but it did not feel proper in the slightest. For Dutton, it was quite an improvement in that two years ago he could not have even feigned looking proper. Anne wasn't quite certain if she thought it was an improvement in his character or not. Judging my her heart's pounding, it was probably a development for the worse.

How very like him.

"But we both know," Dutton said, his mouth hovering over her hand, "that you are the only woman who causes me discomfort. And I have every reason to believe that you enjoy it."

Her pulse jumped, her skin prickled with heat,

warning her of a rising blush, and her breath hitched in her throat. All completely unacceptable responses. Completely. She was a viscountess. She had to make him treat her like one. Though, knowing Dutton as she did, this was likely exactly how he treated viscountesses. He really had appalling manners. Still, even acknowledging that, her pulse continued to race. If only he weren't so devilishly handsome. If only his eyes weren't so seductive. Of course, if all that were true, her pulse would be running at its normal plodding pace.

The thought, the honesty of it, made her smile.

Dutton lifted his head and looked down at her with an expression that was not altogether pleased, and wasn't that a nice change from his usual superior mien?

"I do, as it happens," she said, which was not at all what she had intended to say, but it did have such a nice, confident ring to it. By the look on his face, he didn't seem to like that. How perfectly ideal. "Are you very uncomfortable now, Lord Dutton? Or must I do more?"

She cast a glance down his body, taking in his waistcoat and his trousers, both nicely pressed. His cravat was impeccable. It was quite an improvement from two years ago, though she had never thought to fault his valet; when one was cup-shot more than half the time, one did tend to look more dishabille than was fashionable.

"Taking stock, Lady Staverton?" Dutton drawled. "I was not aware that you were in the market."

She swallowed her gasp. She was not going to allow him to shock her into either silence or submission. She was a viscountess and she was not answerable to anyone, and most particularly not to him.

"When one has the funds, one is always in the market," she said, holding his gaze, refusing the temptation of a blush. "Are you suggesting that you are for sale?"

Dutton barked out a short laugh, the corner of his mouth lifting in a quick grin. "The lady has grown claws."

"Indeed," she said, a smile teasing her lips. "They came with the title."

"Did they?" he said. "I would not have said so, but if that is the claim you wish to make, I will not argue it."

"Because of my claws."

"Because I would do other than argue with you."

His voice was a murmur, a throaty hum that sent tingles down her spine. His blue eyes sparkled with mischief and promise, and she was a fool to fall into his seduction like a green girl. She had never been a green girl, not ever. She had lived too fully in her mother's life, shielded from nothing and no one. She knew better. She was determined to do better.

Dutton was not going to manage her. She was going to manage him, and it had nothing to do with proving herself to the disagreeable Miss Grey, though she did cast a glance across the room to see what Miss Grey was doing and was irritated to find that Miss Grey was looking quite pleased to find herself being introduced to Mr. Prestwick and Lord Raithby, who had just arrived. In fact, judging by the expression on Lady Louisa's face, a woman who rarely bothered to appear the least pleasant and who looked positively grim now, and, was . . . oh, heavens, yes, she was coming over now with a most, *most* unpleasant look about her. Even more unpleasant than usual, which was saying quite a bit.

"I fear, Lord Dutton, that we are to be interrupted," she said.

"And you are disappointed?"

"No, not at all, merely annoyed," she said, and then she smiled at him in pure Sophia fashion, meaning a look of wit and seduction and good humor. By his reaction to her smile, she succeeded quite well. "Hello, Lady Louisa," she said. "How nice it is to see you."

A complete lie. She loathed Louisa Blakesley. How her husband, Lord Henry, quite a charming man, could stand her she had not the faintest idea.

"How are you, Lord Dutton, Lady Staverley?" Louisa said, her blue eyes looking quite positively hostile. "You're looking well, Lord Dutton. Given up the bottle, have you?"

Anne could not help it. She laughed, a most unladylike laugh, too.

"One does hear such frightful rumors about Lord Dutton," Anne said. "This, I must confess, seems one of the worst. Are you as downtrodden as all that, my lord? Have you given up drink entirely?"

She gave him her most saucy look, one she had, she should but did not blush to remember, learned before she had turned twelve. When one's mother was a struggling courtesan, one did learn one's lessons early.

"Not yet," Dutton said with a lopsided grin, "but I may. Will you ladies attempt to drive me to it? With two such leaders, what can a man do but follow?"

"Lord Dutton, I am a married woman," Louisa said,

tossing her bright red head in stiff disapproval.

"That leaves you, Lady Staverton. Will you lead me?"

"I believe I'd rather drive you," Anne said, flirting as outrageously as Sophia ever had. "To ruin, I think. Yes, you are a man simply begging to be driven to ruin."

"By a woman?" he said, his eyes losing their humorous light. "I do believe it in you to try. It cannot be done, of course. No woman can ruin a man, but the effort would be most entertaining to witness."

"It is perfectly clear you know nothing of women," Louisa said. "Despite the rumors otherwise."

"It is perfectly clear," Anne said, cutting Dutton off before he could say another word, "that you know nothing of me."

"And I should remedy that?" he said, his look gone quite seductive.

"Indeed," Anne said. "You should."

Louisa seemed to catch her breath, which was quite ironic as Anne could not seem to catch hers. She was caught in a daring game of seduction, of dares and threats and challenges, a game she had never truly played and never played truly well, with the man who had haunted her thoughts and her most humiliating dreams for well over two years. She had almost become Dutton's plaything, indeed, in her weaker moments, she had yearned to become Dutton's plaything, but common sense, fed and bolstered by Sophia, had saved her.

What was going to save her now?

Not Dutton. Dutton was not a man for saving a woman. Dutton was a man for seducing a woman and using her up and tossing her aside and forgetting her very name. Dutton was a scoundrel, a rake, and a libertine.

Unfortunately, that did not lessen his allure. Indeed, quite the opposite, she was afraid. He was a devastating man and he was adept at leaving devastated women in his wake.

But not this time. Not with her. She was going to best him at his own game and get a bit of her own in the bargain. She was going to use everything she had learned about men from all her careful years of watching them and protecting herself against them; she was going to take all that, all those lessons, and she was going to fashion them into a club and she was going to beat Dutton over the head with it.

Yes, she was going to be that violent about it.

And, yes, she was going to derive great pleasure from it. Ecstatic pleasure. Unbounded pleasure. Erotic pleasure. Yes, that too. Because, now, no matter what else happened, she was going to take Dutton as her lover. She was going to use him as she had dreamed of using him from her first look, and she was not going to pay any price at all.

She was a viscountess.

She was a childless widow.

She was independent.

She was going to play.

She was not going to pay any price for that, not even with Lord Dutton.

What could he do to her? Nothing. She was free to do as she wished and she wished to do whatever she wished with him.

How perfectly extraordinary.

Chapter 8

"How perfectly extraordinary," Jane said, staring at the grouping comprised of Dutton, Anne Staverley, and Louisa. "Didn't someone tell me that Louisa disliked Lady Staverton?"

"Yes. Louisa told you that," Eleanor said, taking a sip from her cup. "It's just that she hates Dutton more."

"I wouldn't have thought that was possible," Jane said, not taking her eyes from the clearly animated conversation taking place across the room, and also taking Lord Dutton's full measure, or as full a measure as could be taken without actually speaking to the man. She had heard about the Marquis of Dutton for two years now, and all that she had heard was . . . well, it was all really quite extraordinary. Dutton was, if the tales were even half true, dangerously debauched and recklessly rakish . . . and if only she could think of another pairing that described him half so well. Heinously handsome? Very possibly. Brutally beautiful, also true. Oh, not as beautiful as Edenham, but quite, quite dashing in an entirely different manner. An entirely more dangerous manner. Yes, that was it exactly. The Marquis of Dutton looked very much like a wolf among the sheepfold. It was Lady Staverton's good fortune that she was behaving nothing at all like a lamb. "Isn't it true that Louisa once thought herself in love with Lord Dutton?"

"Which is why she hates him," Eleanor said. "Not that she did love him, not really, but she hates him on principle, she said. Because, even if she did not actually love him, he should have loved her. Unforgivable, really, according to Louisa."

"And why does she hate Lady Staverton?" Jane

asked.

"Because Lady Staverton, though she was just plain Mrs. Warren then, got him. Or got his attention, anyway. Also unforgivable."

"I see. Yes, that does sound like Louisa's logic," Jane said.

"It's why she hates so many people, that logic of hers," Eleanor said, grinning at Jane.

Jane smiled back at Eleanor and then they both cast a glance at Miss Grey, who had moved off to the edge of the room, her brother at her side, surveying them all like a hawk surveys field mice. A most unappealing simile yet completely apt, for all that. Miss Grey was not a very pleasant person, and it was equally clear that she did not bear much fondness for her aunt, the glorious Lady Dalby. Oh, yes, certainly glorious as well as infamous and glamorous and outrageous. All of that and more.

Jane, still quite the American even if she were married to an English duke, could guess why. Lady Dalby was more English than American, and more aristocrat than Indian, and that would not sit well with an Iroquois. The Iroquois, organized and worldly wise, a nation of astute warriors and diplomats, had been torn apart by the wars between the French and the English and then by the English and the Americans; they had, for the most part, sided with England, and England had lost. Iroquoia had fallen, piece by piece, throughout it all.

No, Miss Grey, Iroquois, would have no instinctive love for an English aristocrat and that is precisely what Sophia was now. Not that the English saw her in precisely that light. Jane, because she was an American, saw that more clearly than anyone she knew here in England. Sophia was Iroquois and American and British . . . and she was none of them.

She loved Sophia and she was annoyed with Elizabeth Grey for not accepting her aunt, yet she understood why Miss Grey would resent Sophia.

The Earl of Quinton entered Dalby House far later than he had intended and was immediately surprised by the crush within her white salon. He was also surprised to find his son, Raithby there, as well as Raithby's more constant companion, George Prestwick. To be truthful, he was not happy to see his only child. To be equally truthful, he was not happy to see that Sophia was so fully occupied. He had hoped to see her alone. He should have made an appointment.

"Darling, it is delightful to see you again," Sophia said, leaning forward to brush a kiss against his cheek. Lord Ruan looked on carefully. As did the Duchess of Edenham, Lady Eleanor Melverley, Lady Louisa, Lord Dutton, George Prestwick, Raithby, and two Indians standing in the corner.

Two Indians? They must be relatives of Sophia's.

"Welcome home, Lady Dalby," he said. "You've brought family, I see. Lord Ruan," he said with a nod of greeting.

"Lord Quinton," Ruan answered with a slightly more curt nod. He and Ruan were not on unfriendly terms, but as their paths had crossed only briefly and only in relation to Sophia, they were not exactly on friendly terms either.

"My niece and nephew," Sophia said, signaling her butler to have more refreshments brought in. It was usual when one was At Home to have visitors stay for a few minutes, minutes devoted to the most inane conversation, usually involving mutual acquaintances and also involving remarks of the damning with faint praise sort, which was why he hated this sort of thing, but at Dalby House, no one left at the proscribed time and so Sophia's At Homes almost always turned into assemblies. "My brother insisted they come, and so, of course, I was most happy to have them. You've met George, have you not?"

"No, I have not," Quinton said.

"Oh, he's adorable," Sophia said, her eyes shining mischievously. "He and Elizabeth are twins, but they are not as alike as one would suppose."

"One being male and the other female," Ruan said with a quirk of his lips.

"Adorable, is he?" Quinton said. "I've never heard anyone refer to an Iroquois warrior as adorable before now. Trust you to do it, Sophia."

"Well, I am his aunt," she said. "I do think he has many adorable qualities."

"For instance, the way he fights," Ruan said. "I happen to have seen him lay Dutton a blow that knocked him out for more than a few minutes."

"Dutton was drunk at the time, so I'm not sure that is quite fair," Sophia said.

"It was most certainly unfair to Dutton," Ruan said.

"Does his sister, Elizabeth, fight adorably as well?" Quinton asked.

"You must judge that for yourself," Sophia said, her dark eyes shining now with more mischief than before. "And I do so hope you will."

"Ah," Quinton said. "There is something you want to teach her. Hence her arrival here."

"How to take a punch?" Ruan said. "Or does she know that already?" Ruan was looking at Sophia with all the hunger of a lover thwarted. Sophia was not looking at Ruan unless she had to. That explained it all quite clearly.

"She has been carefully reared," Sophia said by way of answer.

"Which is not quite an answer," Quinton said.

"The best sort of answer, that," Ruan said.

Quinton eyed Ruan. He was a brutal looking man, a man who wore his life on his face, and not an easy life by the look of it. Ruan was dark-haired, green-eyed, his skin weathered by sun and wind. He had the look of a man who had been in a tussle or two, the look of a man who had borne himself well, with honor, in situations and circumstances where honor was not common.

Of course, no man's face could reveal all that; Quinton, once he had learned that Ruan was caught in Sophia's net, had found out a thing or two about the man. What he had found out had reassured him. What he had not been able to find out, such as how the man had come to his weathering and just what sort of situation he had occasion to display his honor, was troubling. Tales of that sort, of honor in harsh climes and harsher circumstances, were usually broadcast with a liberal hand. That tales of Ruan were thin on the ground . . . troubling.

He would not see Sophia dallied with by a troubling man.

She would laugh in his face if she knew he was concerned about her, particularly in anything concerning a man. She thought herself, well and truly and with good cause, well prepared to deal with a mere man. But he still thought of her as a girl, a stalwart, brilliant, resilient girl, but a girl, nonetheless. So she had been when he first met her and so she would remain. In his heart, always a girl on the verge of catastrophe. And always a girl who would fight for, and achieve, her victory.

Her niece, Miss Grey, had something of the same look about her. Something, not much. That was, perhaps, the point of this trip to foreign shores?

"She is to be educated abroad," Quinton said, looking across the room at Miss Grey. "Something in the nature of a tutorial?"

"How clever you are, my lord," Sophia said sweetly. Sophia never spoke sweetly. "Yet how wrong you are. What could I, a dowager countess, possibly teach such a lovely, and, to be perfectly honest, such an innocent young woman?"

"How not to be quite so innocent?" Ruan asked, his expression grown somber.

"But how could I, a woman, teach her that?" Sophia said lightly, looking only briefly at Lord Ruan. "That is a man's province, is it not?"

"Is that a question?" Ruan asked. "Or is it an offer?"

Sophia looked hard at Ruan then, her black eyes

flashing. "Not a question and not an offer. Merely an observation upon which we shall surely have no dissent."

"Then there shall be no dissent," Ruan said. "Not between us, Lady Dalby. Not if I can help it."

"But can you help it?" Quinton said.

To which Sophia did not so much as smile. Which is when Quinton knew that Ruan and Sophia already had a history, but a history of what?

"Which one is mine?" Elizabeth Grey asked her brother.

"Dark hair, dark eyes, smiling," George answered her.

They were standing on the edge of the room, near the door to the dining room, having finally gotten rid of the annoying English women. Elizabeth studied her quarry. He was acceptable, if a bit ordinary. He should prove easily conquered. "Why does he smile?"

"He is that sort. A smiling man, very congenial, very pleasant."

Elizabeth snorted under her breath. "This is not the way a man should describe another man. Where is his heat? His fierceness? His power? No. He smiles."

"He is that sort," George repeated. "He reminds me of myself. I like him."

Elizabeth laughed and looked at her brother. "You? Smile? Since when?"

George smiled at her, his dark eyes dancing with

amusement. "The English women like my dimple."

"A dimple as your weapon," Elizabeth said, shaking her head slightly. "Where is your knife?"

"Why use a knife when a smile will do? Learn from me, Elizabeth," he said. "A man may be disarmed by a smile."

"If he is armed to begin with."

"Different nations, different weapons."

She snorted, not quietly. Several heads turned in her direction, one of them the man standing at Prestwick's side. "That one," she said. "Who is that one?"

"His friend, Lord Raithby. Raithby's father is there, talking to Sophia."

"The look of a warrior about that one," she said, meaning the father, looking at the son. The son, Raithby, looked at her for a moment longer before shifting his gaze to his father and Sophia and the green-eyed man. "And him?"

"Lord Ruan. He pursues Sophia. The other is Lord Quinton. He served the British in America twenty years ago. He and Sophia have a history. I do not know what. Father knows, but he will not speak of it."

"She probably opened her legs to him," Elizabeth said scornfully.

"You do not understand her."

"I understand all I need to."

"Father disagrees."

"Father feels guilt and that blinds him."

George smiled, releasing the power of his single dimple. "You do not understand him either."

"He is my father as much as yours."

"And Sophia is his sister. Would you have a brother

abandon his sister? Would you have a brother forget his duty?"

Elizabeth looked down at her brother's feet, his shoes of the English type and his clothes fashioned by an English tailor, his true nature and calling buried in English wool and English leather. It was not hard to imagine losing oneself in such a place, surrounded by such a people. Look at Sophia. If she had ever been Mohawk, where was that woman now? Why could the men of her family not see that Sophia had died decades ago? This woman was no part of them.

"A man must behave honorably," she said, still staring at the floor. "And so must a woman."

"That is so."

"And so I must seduce this man, this Prestwick, into an offer of marriage. Introduce me. Let it begin," she said, but her eyes strayed again to Raithby.

"She's coming this way," Prestwick said, his lips unmoving.

"I can see that," Raithby said, his lips moving quite obviously and without any attempt at subtlety.

Prestwick sighed, then smiled, then sighed again. "You're staring."

"My first Indian sighting," Raithby said. "Allowances must be made."

"If you ask for allowances from her I suspect you shall be disappointed. Immediately and severely."

"So be it," Raithby murmured, and in the next

instant Mr. and Miss Grey stood before them. Raithby and Prestwick bowed quickly and economically, a brief movement of the head for each of them, awaiting Mr. Grey's introduction of his sister.

Mr. Grey did not have the chance.

"You are Mr. Prestwick?" Miss Grey asked, eyeing Prestwick in a quite animated manner. Raithby, who was not very attentive to females in general, found himself a trifle astounded that she was ignoring him so fully. He may have lifted his chin just a bit, but that was only because his valet had tied his cravat a trifle vigorously.

"And you are Miss Grey," Prestwick answered, smooth as always. Prestwick did have such an easy time of it, his manner so warm and convivial, so effortless.

Raithby was not of the same temperament, though that had never caused him any concern before. He did not think of women often. He would marry when it was time to marry, and he would marry a woman who would provide him with the necessary social connections and financial benefits that were common in marriages within his set. He did hope she was pleasing to look upon, and of course, she must be fertile or the marriage would have been a complete waste of time, but as those things could not be precisely arranged, he did not bother about any of it too much. Social connection and financial benefit, those were the issues, the issues that could be controlled. He had known that since leaving the nursery.

Why he was thinking of all that now was slightly disconcerting. It could only be because Miss Grey did not, by her very existence, fit within any classification of female he had yet encountered.

That she was ignoring him was beside the point.

"My sister, Miss Elizabeth Grey," Mr. Grey said, making the introduction a bit late. "May I present Lord Raithby and Mr. Prestwick?"

"You have," she said.

Naturally, he had noticed her upon first entering. She did not have an English look about her, that was the bald truth. It had not so much to do with her coloring, dark and exotic, but with her demeanor, which was also, strangely, equally dark. She fairly rippled with anger and frustration and derision. It was most unbecoming. Most.

"It is good to see you again, Mr. Grey. London has been dull without you," Prestwick said.

Grey grunted and grinned, whereupon both Mr. Grey and Prestwick cast quick glances across the room to where Dutton stood talking to Lady Staverton and Lady Louisa. And now that he looked, *that* conversation looked to be growing quite animated. Raithby looked to where Sophia stood, wondering if she would take any action to bring the conversation in her salon back to something more sedate and decorous, and boring, which was the way these At Homes usually went, which was why Raithby hadn't been to one in three years. Or it might have been four. But Sophia, in smiling conversation with his father and Lord Ruan, looked entirely unaware of the mood of the room, which was just a shade too raucous to be considered proper.

No wonder Prestwick liked Lady Dalby so well, if this was her manner of entertaining.

"How are you finding London, Miss Grey? Not dull,

I hope," Prestwick asked.

"Not dull," she echoed, staring boldly into Prestwick's eyes. Entirely inappropriate. "Yet not exciting. Perhaps you would like to show me something of London's attractions?"

Mr. Grey shook his head and touched his sister on the elbow. Miss Grey ignored her brother. Prestwick smiled. Raithby did not smile.

"As your brother is familiar with London, he is the suitable companion for your excursions, Miss Grey, not a man unknown to you," Raithby said. It was quite a pompous little declaration, he was quite certain he had never before uttered anything like it, and yet he could not find it in himself to regret a single word.

Miss Grey turned her dark eyes upon him, piercing him with her gaze, or at least the attempt was made; he could see her intent to do so quite clearly, and said, "I know my brother. It is this man I would know better."

Whereupon Prestwick came perilously close to dropping his jaw. Mr. Grey cast a grim look to Lady Dalby. And Raithby nearly growled from some dark, primitive place deep in his throat that he hitherto had never suspected existed within his very proper English soul. It was all completely beyond the pale.

He felt not a moment's shame.

He didn't have time to consider any of it further because in the next instant, Lady Dalby, Ruan and his father in her wake, was making her way into their little grouping. That his father was with her . . . well, that was beyond his control. As was, apparently, Miss Grey.

Chapter 9

Unfortunately, and entirely predictably, wherever Sophia went, there went everyone's attention. Anne was not in any frame of mind to relinquish Dutton's attention, bold as it was of her to admit it, and, ignoring every decorous lesson she had learned in the past few years, she said, "I do believe there is going to be something of a contretemps between Sophia and her backwards niece. I do think we should be involved, don't you?"

That she directed this question to Dutton and that Louisa answered was entirely predictable.

"I agree with you completely," Louisa said. "Do come along, Lord Dutton."

To which Anne rolled her eyes. And to which Dutton chuckled. In that moment, that brief, twinkling moment, Anne and Dutton shared a moment that was entirely at Louisa Blakesley's expense.

It may have been the most perfect moment of her life.

Anne, to Louisa's clear annoyance, led the way to the other side of the white salon where Sophia was facing off against the irritating Miss Grey. That the arrival of three more to the company was ignored by the combatants only fed Anne's determination not to be ignored. Not by Dutton. Not by anyone. She assumed Sophia would understand entirely.

"I do hope you have not played your hand too boldly, Miss Grey," Anne said before anyone else could say a word. That the party was now neatly huddled into one very unattractive mob at one end of the white salon was not going to be mentioned by Anne, though it was clear that Sophia found the situation as repulsive as Anne herself did; whatever one chose to say about

Sophia Dalby, no one had ever accused her of anything but flawless deportment and impeccable manners. "It appears that you, by an appalling lack of discretion, have betrayed our wager here today."

At which all the men in the room, with the exception of Mr. Grey, looked equally alarmed and intrigued. As well they should.

"What sort of wager?" Dutton asked. Of course Dutton would be the one most intrigued by a wager. He was that sort entirely.

"I have betrayed nothing," Miss Grey answered, her black eyes as hard and cold as flint. "'Tis you, now, who lays all bare."

"Whom is being laid bare?" Mr. Prestwick asked, his grin contagious.

"I am," Anne said with a boldness that she was determined would become habitual. "My dear sirs, a wager was struck just before you arrived. You, Mr. Prestwick, and you, Lord Ruan, and you, Lord Dutton, are, part and parcel, the very meat of the wager."

"I have no objections to being the meat of anyone's wager," Ruan said, to which Anne smiled, Sophia snorted, and Elizabeth Grey scowled, which was so very like her.

"Nor do I," Mr. Prestwick said with a most cordial smile, which was so very like him.

"I should think that would depend entirely on the wager," Dutton said. So true to form. Really, it was nearly monotonous.

"The wager was marriage, Lord Dutton," Anne said, hoping to shock him. He did, in truth, look a trifle shocked. It was so gratifying. "Is there any inducement, do you suppose, that would entice you to offer for me? That was the challenge and, upon reflection, indeed, upon further conversation with you, our first in two years, if you will recall, I find that there is nothing I would do or could do that would possibly convince you that I would willingly suffer a proposal of marriage from you."

Upon which Sophia chuckled and Elizabeth appeared to grind her teeth. She did hope so. Dutton merely looked annoyed, a condition that she sincerely hoped would become habitual for him.

"I concede the game," Anne said, her smile brittle and bright. On purpose. "I confess that I do not possess the talent for deception that it would require to convince Lord Dutton that I entertain the slightest interest in a legally binding relationship in which he is the binding partner."

"Oh, my," Jane said, blinking. "That is quite a statement, isn't it?"

"Some relationships bind more than others," Louisa said.

"How very, very true," Sophia said, looking askance at Ruan. Ruan smiled in response and Sophia shifted her gaze to Dutton. "It is quite remarkable how effortlessly you bring out Lady Staverton's most ardent, one could say, violent emotions, Lord Dutton. I have seldom seen a simple wager go so wrong, so quickly. Well, there it is, then. Our wager has been exposed."

"Ah," Prestwick said impishly, "only the wager has been exposed. One can't help but feel the most profound disappointment."

"Dutton was to have proposed to Lady Staverton?"

Raithby asked, ignoring Prestwick entirely.

"And Mr. Prestwick to Miss Grey," Sophia said. "I am so sorry that my niece could not have the fun of a---"

"An engagement to a British lord?" Ruan asked.

"It was only in fun. A simple wager. Of course, it was never to be taken seriously," Sophia said.

"I take it that you were to lure . . . ?" Ruan prompted. Sophia stared at him, her gaze flat and markedly steady. "Me?" When she did not answer, Ruan said, "I can assure you, Lady Dalby, that such a wager would not have resulted in anything other than seriousness."

"At least she stood a chance with you," Louisa said. "Miss Grey, who has no knowledge of anything, least of all Mr. Prestwick, would have fared most poorly." Louisa said it without the least trace of pity or warmth, for which Anne could have kissed her. Miss Grey, true to form, looked ready to spit live coals from her mouth.

"Is that true, Mr. Prestwick?" Elizabeth asked, her dark eyes scouring his face.

Mr. Prestwick, ever amiable, bowed lightly and said, "I would have stood defenseless against you, Miss Grey, as I am now."

"How very polite you are, Mr. Prestwick," Louisa said. "One might even call it excessive."

Eleanor giggled. Jane smiled. Anne, it must be admitted, smirked sarcastically. She could not help herself. She did not even mean to try.

"What will happen now? Without a wager to occupy everyone?" Eleanor asked, her question seemingly addressed to the room at large.

"I imagine that things shall proceed normally and after sipping tea and nibbling cakes, we shall wander to the next At Home," Jane answered. "I do believe that is precisely what we should do. Jane? Louisa? We must go."

"Must we?" Eleanor said, looking at Sophia with piteous, eager eyes.

"Not that you must, but perhaps you should. Is not the delightful Penelope hosting an At Home today?" Sophia said.

"I would hardly call Penelope delightful," Louisa said with a sniff.

Anne did not know for certain, but having seen the Blakesley family at a few social events during the past year she did suspect that Louisa liked Penelope more than she cared to admit publicly.

"Yes, I'm afraid we must be off. It's been wonderful seeing you again, Lady Dalby. I, for one, am delighted that you are back in Town," Mr. Prestwick said, pausing to glance at Lord Raithby, clearly expecting him to make his departure in concert with his as they had arrived together. Strangely, Lord Raithby was studying his father, the Earl of Quinton. The earl was plainly making no move to depart. As to that, Lord Ruan looked ready to stay for days.

As to that, Anne, for reasons she did not care to explore, was going to stay or go entirely dependent upon what Dutton did. As of yet, she could not discern what Dutton planned to do; most likely, he had no idea himself. Dutton did seem to be the most changeable sort of man. Where was the man who had pursued her with all the hunger of a starving dog, and yes, the analogy was entirely intentional.

With very little fuss, the room was cleared of all but what Anne believed to be the key players in what she was not going to term a farce: Dutton, Ruan, Quinton, Raithby, the Greys, Sophia, and herself. That Elizabeth Grey was very likely not welcomed in the lovely home of Penelope Blakesley was most inconvenient; she knew it was more than likely that George Grey, whom had made such a fine impression upon one and all, with the notable exception of Lord Dutton, during his last visit to England, would have been most heartily welcomed into Lord Iveston's salon. Penelope would have found George fascinating. If George Grey were determined to only go where his sister was welcomed, he would find his days spent in Sophia's salon and no where else.

Hard thoughts for a fresh acquaintance, but Elizabeth Grey was justly deserving of it. Anne had no doubts about that.

"Please, be seated," Sophia said, sweeping one hand toward the white upholstered furniture that dotted the dark wood floors of the white salon. On one wall stood a tall cabinet of Chinese influence and upon its shelves were examples of ancient Chinese pottery in various shades of remarkable celadon. Anne took a seat upon the small sofa across the room from the cabinet, her gaze on the celadon and not on Dutton, who sat stiffly upon a small chair next to the cabinet. The porcelain was lovely; why shouldn't she study it? "Now, what shall we discuss since our wager has been rendered useless?" Sophia said, nodding briskly at Fredericks, presumably to bring in fresh refreshments.

"Useless?" Elizabeth asked. "Are not all wagers useless?"

"No, not all," Sophia said with a serene smile.

"This one would have been most interesting," Ruan said. "How did you plan to induce a proposal of marriage of me? I am, as you must be aware, an accomplished bachelor."

"It is what you are accomplished at that is intriguing, Lord Ruan," Sophia said. "It is quite certainly not for being a bachelor. Bachelors are thick upon the ground and they are most often quite unworthy of notice."

"Thank you. I think," Ruan said, his smile all in his eyes.

"The wager is truly over?" Quinton asked, crossing his legs.

"But naturally," Sophia said. "As all has been revealed, it would not be at all sporting."

"How can a woman ensnare a man if he knows she is hunting for him?" Dutton said. Of course Dutton would say something like that.

"You suppose there are women who do not hunt men?" Sophia asked. "How charming. Lord Dutton, you do surprise me. I would never have taken you for a romantic."

"Perhaps Lord Dutton is not a romantic, but merely disillusioned," Anne said. "It is quite likely that no woman has hunted him. Would you say so, Lord Dutton?"

Unfortunately, Lord Dutton did not reply. Miss Grey did. Miss Grey was a most inopportune sort of woman.

"If the hunter is good, the quarry is unaware of being pursued," Elizabeth said, a slight smile hovering around her mouth. Even her brother smiled. It was a somewhat amusing observation. Perhaps Miss Grey could be civil, when pressed.

"And are you good at the hunt, Miss Grey?" Raithby asked, his dark brows raised.

"I am better than most," Elizabeth answered.

"And could you have caught Mr. Prestwick in your snare?" Raithby persisted.

"Very likely."

"We shall never know, shall we?" Sophia said on a sigh. "Such a pity. It was such a thrilling wager."

"One may assume you expected to win," Quinton said.

Sophia's glance bounced off Ruan for the merest of moments before she said, "Completely. I expected to win handily as I had Lord Ruan's good nature and willing spirit to rely upon. I have, in the past, come to understand that Lord Ruan makes a most pleasant compatriot in endeavors of this sort."

"Marriage proposals? Wagers?" Elizabeth asked.

"Unusual and delicate situations," Sophia said, gracing Ruan with a longer, warmer glance.

Anne was at a complete loss. She had known that Ruan was interested in pursuing an alliance with Sophia, that was hardly much of a secret, but she was unaware that the two of them had anything beyond a casual conversation or two to mark their acquaintance.

Once again, and more forcefully, Anne was convinced that everyone was proceeding at a wildly successful pace, achieving all sorts of connections with interesting and dangerous men while she sat dreaming and dozing by the grate. It was simply not to be borne.

She was going to do something with Dutton and she was not going to hesitate a moment longer.

"Sophia, you have the remarkable ability to align yourself with the most agreeable sort of men," Anne said. "I do wish I could say the same." She glanced at Lord Dutton as she said it. Quite, quite intentionally.

"Not all men are equally agreeable, that is unfortunately true," Sophia said, her glance sliding across Dutton in the most artful of insults.

"I daresay that being agreeable is in the eye of the beholder," Dutton said.

"But of course it is," Anne said. "That is the entire point, Lord Dutton. Such things are, however, a matter of consensus."

"Public opinion," he said.

"Precisely," she said.

"I fear you are referring to me, Lady Staverton, and if you are, I would say that private opinion differs."

"Private opinion? How private? One person? One female person? That would require that we trust you to interpret that opinion. I'm afraid that is entirely too much to ask, Lord Dutton," she said, staring into his eyes. Staring him down, truth be told.

"I'm afraid that such things are beyond a vote in the House of Lords," Dutton said.

"You are afraid, aren't you? I find I can well believe it," Anne said. She was going to have him. She was going to do whatever she wanted with him. She was not leaving this salon without having marked Dutton by whatever means, or words, necessary.

"A man should not fear a woman," the annoying Miss Grey said. Though, to judge by Dutton's expression, the comment might have done something in her favor.

"Precisely," Anne said. "Do you fear me, Lord Dutton?"

"No. I do not, Lady Staverton," he said.

"I think I may," Lord Ruan said, smiling at her.

"A woman is a thing to be feared," George Grey said, "in situations such as this."

"And this situation is?" Anne prompted.

"The hunt," George said.

"The hunt without artifice or stealth," Sophia said. "The wildest hunt of all. You know something of that, do you not, Lord Dutton? At least by hearsay, I should think."

Dutton's blue eyes glittered in the late afternoon light, his expression hardening, closing, which did not suit Anne's purposes in the slightest. Of course. Sophia was referring to the wild and debauched hunt that Dutton's father had instigated against Sophia when she was but a girl. It was a hunt immortalized in a satire by Gillray, a print which had all but ruined the men involved. The 7th Earl of Westlin had suffered the most obvious malice from it. Louisa's father, the Marquis of Melverley, gave every appearance of having suffered the least. What Dutton suffered was by Sophia's hands entirely. Lord Dutton had been but a boy when it had occurred; he bore no part in it, yet Sophia seemed to have a special interest in Dutton, an interest that went beyond Anne's inconvenient interest in him. This talk of hunts was not to her purpose. She wanted Dutton. She did not want Sophia to toy with him. Not now. Not when she had the freedom to do as she wished. Not when she could toy with him as he had once toyed with her.

She had waited two years for this. She was not going to let a faint heart, which she was determined not to have, stop her now.

"By hearsay," Dutton said amiably. "At least."

"Are such discussions common among the Iroquois, Miss Grey? They are not common among the English," Lord Raithby said, studying her in his quiet way. Anne did not know Lord Raithby well at all, but he did exude a rather quiet intensity that she found restful. The same could not be said of what Lord Dutton exuded, not at all.

"No. Not among my people. Only Sophia, I think," Miss Grey said.

"How very sad for you," Anne said immediately. "How lovely it is for you to finally be with your aunt. You will learn so much from her. If you have the wit."

Elizabeth Grey turned her black and glittering eyes upon Anne. Anne met the look without flinching, even though a part of her wondered if flinching might be entirely appropriate.

"I am here at my father's will," Miss Grey said. "I am to learn all I can from Sophia."

She said it very unenthusiastically. She was clearly an imbecile of the highest order.

"I am beginning to feel like the most tawdry sort of school mistress," Sophia said. "Can an ill-fitting costume of somber brown be far behind?"

"Lady Dalby, I would take instruction from you in anything," Ruan said. "In a brown costume or out of it."

"How very gallant, Lord Ruan," Sophia said, a smile toying with the corners of her mouth. "You do have the habit of saying the most delightful things. One can't but wonder if you were tutored in it? Perhaps in your youth?"

"It is a natural skill, dependent entirely upon the company," Ruan said with a modest nod of his dark head.

"Social niceties," George Grey said to his sister in a voice loud enough to be heard by one and all. "The

English excel at it."

"Thank you, Mr. Grey, but you are being too modest," Anne said. "You are one of the most charming men of my acquaintance, though as you are as English as your aunt, perhaps the compliment is redundant?" Of course, what that said about Miss Grey she had no idea. The woman had no social niceties whatsoever.

"Thank you, Lady Staverton," Mr. Grey answered, his dimple twinkling at her.

"A compliment can never be redundant," Sophia said. "I think that must be the first lesson of today."

"And any day," Lord Quinton said, his face expressionless.

Lord Quinton had quite a nice looking face for a man of his mature years. He must have been quite remarkable in his youth, much as his son Lord Raithby was remarkable now. Raithby had the look of something between a woodland elf and a satyr; he was singularly attractive and the small scar he sported on the top of one cheek did nothing to diminish his appeal. In fact, the scar may well have enhanced it. It wouldn't do Lord Dutton a bit of harm to have a small scar of his own and, in fact, she would be more than willing to give him one.

Dutton, quite typically, was looking at Miss Grey as if she were the most fascinating female he had ever seen. It was most annoying, particularly as Elizabeth Grey was so completely repellent in both her bearing and her manner.

"It is quite disheartening that our wager was cut short before it was properly begun," Sophia said.

"It was hardly a proper sort of wager," Raithby said, looking first at Sophia and then at Mr. Grey. "I can't think that a brother would countenance that sort of thing, even if an aunt should."

"An aunt such as I," Sophia said.

"A brother such as I?" Mr. Grey asked upon Sophia's heels.

"Raithby," Quinton said, "do leave off. These are deep waters."

"I agree with you, Lord Raithby," Miss Grey said, looking positively regal. It was particularly loathsome.

"Of course you do," Anne said. "But what you cannot have comprehended, being as new to Town as you are, and as unfamiliar with your aunt as you clearly are, is that anything which Lady Dalby attempts, as irregular as it may first appear, has only beneficial results."

"Beneficial to whom?" Miss Grey rejoined.

"Beneficial to all who are allied with her," Anne said promptly.

"And detrimental to all who are not allied with her," Dutton said, his blue eyes glittering like ice.

"But who would be foolish enough to not be allied with Lady Dalby?" Ruan said.

"Those who are foolish enough, or confident enough, to be arrayed against her," George Grey said, very determinedly not looking at his foolish sister, it seemed to Anne.

"My, my," Sophia said with a beaming smile, "I am formidable. How perfectly lovely. I do confess, I have always striven to be found formidable. It is so gratifying to have achieved such a worthy goal, and at my age, too."

"Do women want to be considered formidable?" Raithby asked, upon which his father shook his head in mild disapproval, perhaps even dismay.

"Yes," Miss Grey answered instantly.

"Most definitely," Anne said, looking at Dutton as she said it. Dutton, remarkably, was looking directly at her, his face, for once, wiped of all arrogance.

"An accord," Ruan said. "How remarkable."

"Formidable," Dutton said, staring at Anne, at Miss Grey, his gaze swiftly scouring Sophia before moving relentlessly back to Anne. "A formidable women does not often marry, I shouldn't think. It's not at all what a man looks for in a wife, is it?"

"Isn't it?" Miss Grey said, staring at Dutton as if she would like to cut his heart out just to see what it looked like. Anne understood the inclination entirely.

"Not every woman wants to marry," Anne said.

"And certainly not every woman wants to marry every man," Sophia said, freshening Lord Ruan's cup.

"The wager was a marriage proposal," Dutton said, lounging back as far as the petite chair upon which he was sprawled allowed him.

"Precisely," Anne said. "A wager for a proposal. It was nothing at all to do with an actual marriage. You, of all people, Lord Dutton, should understand the nuances of a wager." She was not sprawled upon her chair. No, she was very much afraid she was lunging toward him in overt aggression. She did not change her posture in the slightest degree. Let him feel her aggression, if he was capable of feeling anything at all. Which she very much doubted.

"A proposal of marriage without a marriage to follow. That's quite scandalous, isn't it?" Dutton said, staring at her with his blue, blue eyes, trying to intimidate her, no doubt.

"Is it? For some, perhaps. I do not find it so," she answered.

"I was under the very firm impression that you were very devotedly determined to avoid any hint of scandal, Lady Staverton," he said, pinning her with his gaze.

In his eyes she read the past as they had shared it, bits and pieces, fragments of moments, a kiss in this very room two years ago, a heated glance that had lasted mere seconds, a hand brushed against her shoulder, a lingering, wondering gaze . . . a scattering of moments, like wet leaves on cobblestones, they had pressed themselves on her heart and mind. She had been, and was still, too aware of him, of his casual interest, his purely carnal interest in her that came and went like an erratic wind.

She would have no more of it. No more. Not one instant more. She would have him as and where she wanted him. Somehow.

"It must, I suppose," Sophia said languidly, "be explained to you, darling Elizabeth, that in English Society, what a woman may do without scandal changes very much once she has made a spectacular marriage. It is one of the many, many reasons why it is so important for a woman to make a stellar marriage. Done well, it solves all sorts of future difficulties."

"I know very well, darling Aunt, that a widow may take lovers without scandal. At least in this Society," Elizabeth answered waspishly.

She was quite a waspish, buzzing woman, so ready to sting for no cause at all.

"As I am of this Society," Anne said, "I do think that makes the point. Lover or husband, I am free to do either."

"Or neither," Sophia said.

"And will you do either?" Dutton asked, his shoulders revealing a certain tension beneath the wool of his coat.

"Oh," she said, leaning forward to put her cup on the table in front of her, "one more than the other, most certainly."

"Hardly a definitive answer," Dutton said with a definite snarl of aggression.

"As I don't answer to you," Anne said, "I don't see how it pertains."

"But as you don't answer to anyone, darling Anne," Sophia said, "perhaps an answer would be illuminating for poor Elizabeth, who must learn some lessons while in England, after all. We can't have her trip here be a complete waste."

Anne looked at Sophia, studying the dark lights in her black eyes, saw the glimmer of humor as well as the glint of blazing intent, and over all was the shine of Sophia's never ceasing good will. All that in a glance. All because Anne knew Sophia very well and understood her motives and her methods. And because she trusted Sophia, about all. Because of all that, Anne said what Sophia clearly wanted her to say.

"I shall take a lover, of course," Anne said. "When I find a man who intrigues me."

She would never know why she did it, but Anne did

not look at Dutton as she spoke. She looked directly at George Grey, Iroquois warrior.

Chapter 10

Dutton was not going to sit quietly while Anne chose another man over him; not again, and certainly not when all she wanted was a lover. He was the farthest thing from interested in Anne Staverton as a wife; he was, and always had been, very interested in her as a bed mate. She knew that very well.

Which was likely the problem. Women were very contrary creatures. It would be just like a woman to refuse a man simply because he wanted her, no matter that she wanted him just as much. Perhaps more. Dutton studied Anne, her rich red hair and her pewter green eyes, and her smirk of disdain and dismissal aimed precisely at his head. It was perhaps possible, just perhaps, that she didn't want him as she had once done.

Possible, but not probable.

Still, a man did like to be certain of a woman's interest before he began even the most tepid of pursuits. Or at least he did, given his experience at not knowing any women who were not interested in him, at the very least, in the most tepid of ways, which did not describe his experience at all. Or not as a rule. Still, Ruan's counsel regarding Sophia still ringing in his ears, he had never in his life experienced any sort of trouble with women at all until he had run up against women who had stirred Sophia's interest in some way. There was something to that. It was not possible that such a thing should be merely a chance of fate. No. That was not at all possible.

Which, meant, obviously, that in order for his star to rise to the heights it had once occupied, he must make peace with Sophia Dalby, or that is what Ruan advised. Since he had done nothing to cross Lady Dalby and much to flatter her, he could not make himself sue for peace with a woman known for the looseness of both her morals and her bodice ties.

No. He had done nothing. Nothing beyond what any man of his years, means, and position had done. He would treat Sophia as he had always done: with cordiality and amiability. Nothing more was required.

As to Anne, she was, as they said, fair game. She was unencumbered. She was desirable. She was interested.

Or she had been. He couldn't quite shake that doubt, a wormlike thing, wriggling in his thoughts. Most annoying. He would simply make certain of her interest and then proceed, likely right into the nearest bed.

It would all be so very simple, so supremely uncomplicated.

It was most aggravating that he was certain it would be nothing of the kind.

It was completely obvious by the very conceited look on Lord Dutton's face that he expected nothing less than Anne should fall effortlessly and eagerly into his bed.

Nothing of the sort would happen. Anne was entirely certain of that. The fun would be in taunting Lord Dutton with that inescapable fact. She was equally entirely certain of that. She would not fall into George Grey's bed either, and she did hope George understood that, and she was quite certain, or nearly certain, that he did; he was a most congenial man, after all, and he had quite a bit of experience at the deviousness required of a Season in Town so it was likely no surprise to Mr. Grey that he was being called upon to offer the most elegant and subtle of inducements to drive Lord Dutton quite mad with jealousy, rage, and any other elegant and subtle emotion Anne chose to foist upon him.

Yes, Mr. George Grey had always been so amenable to plans of this sort. Certainly he would give every appearance of lurid interest without actually requiring or even expecting any sort of . . . oh dear, what to call it?

Anne swallowed a bit heavily and looked at Mr. Grey most earnestly. It was all a game, a game to thwart Dutton and to bait Dutton and to bedevil Dutton. George could see that, she was certain of it.

Nearly.

It was a contest, Elizabeth saw that clearly enough, but a contest to what end? George was being called upon, and he would play his part. He loved any kind of contest and he played to win. Who did not?

If George would play, then so would she. They played at many things, the two of them, twins in mind and in purpose, they each played to win. Most often against each other.

This game, it was a game of seduction, plainly. How far? To what end? How was the winner to be named victorious?

She would find all that out later.

If Anne Staverton played with George then she would play with . . .

Her gaze scoured the men in the room. Lord Ruan was too lethal. Lord Quinton was too knowledgable. Lord Dutton was very possibly too perfect. Lord Raithby . . . her gaze skimmed over Raithby. He was too young, too intense, too unpredictable. Lord Raithby was not the sort of man to play games with.

Lord Dutton.

She would play this out with Dutton. To a point.

Elizabeth looked askance at her brother, marked the glint of amusement in his black eyes, the shadow of his dimple twitching, and decided that the point would be as far as George took it. As for how far Dutton took it, she had no interest at all.

Ruan watched with scant interest the currents swamping the younger inhabitants within the white salon. They would play their seduction games, for what else interested men and women, and Sophia would sort it all out. That was without question.

What he wanted, indeed, what he would have, was Sophia. He wanted her attention, her regard, and her trust. He believed he was well on the path toward achieving all of that. Once he was in firm possession of her attention, regard and trust, he wanted what he suspected no one else had ever achieved. He wanted her heart.

He'd wanted her for years now, and that was not like him at all. He did not want. He did not care. Yet he wanted her. He cared for her.

He had not cared for anything, or anyone, for a long time. He probably should not want to enter into that fraught landscape again, the world of caring and need and pain, but he wanted her and so he did. He did not give it any more thought, or any more hesitation, than that.

He only needed to get her alone. She was always surrounded, the young puppies squabbling at her feet, making their messes, trusting her to clean it all up and make them proper puppies, properly trained.

Ruan smiled, a faint thing that barely touched his mouth. A courtesan training others in propriety. Only Sophia Dalby could manage such a thing. Yet it was not quite propriety, was it? It was more subtle and more essential than mere propriety. It was that she took aim and fired where all others thrashed in the mud. Sophia was a woman who had a warrior's heart and a soldier's self-discipline. He had no doubt she came by both quite honestly.

But he had waited too long. Too many years had passed since he had seen her and wanted her, since the fire for her had been lit within him. He had danced to her tune, by her rules, and at her pleasure. He was not where he wanted to be. He was not where he would be with her.

There she sat, her dark hair still as black, her smooth skin still as white, her black eyes still as shuttered and as alluring; the mystery of her hovered in the air, and she smiled at the deception even as she spun her magic. She was thinner than she had been two years ago, the bones of her face more sharply drawn, her neck more slender, her eyes more prominent, and more shadowed. Her travels had changed her, perhaps wearied her, if he could be bold enough to claim to know any part of her.

Oh, yes, he knew her, some small splinter of the secret part of her. They shared a murder between them.

He wanted more. He had always wanted more. He knew that she would never willingly give him more.

Enough. Enough of this game that they ever played between them. He would not play by her rules any longer, the rules of sit and wait, the rules of obedience and supplication.

The Marquis of Ruan smiled. It was not a particularly pleasant smile. He rose to his feet, staring at Lady Dalby, ignoring everyone else in the room.

Lady Dalby, his enigmatic Sophia, looked at him pleasantly, her own smile not quite formed upon her aristocratic mouth.

Ruan bowed, a crisp bow of duty and chivalry and dismissal. To hell with all the rules, her rules. To bloody hell with this game they played to no purpose and no end. But not to hell with her. No, never that. But a new game, played by his rules.

Would she play it? Would Sophia have the courage to play a game not of her own making?

"Lady Dalby," he said, his eyes for her and only her, as it ever was, "it has been most pleasant, but I fear I must depart."

"How very cordial of you to drop round for a visit, Lord Ruan," she said. "I do hope to see you again soon." She turned to Anne Staverton before the words were quite out of her mouth, dismissing him, certain of his compliance.

"I cannot, in good conscience, encourage you in that hope," he said, dragging his eyes from her, looking to Lord Dutton, who did not rise and would not be accompanying him from Dalby House. Fool. He would never win Anne under Sophia's very roof. "I wish you well, Lady Dalby, in all your many endeavors."

Sophia looked sharply at him, everyone else in the room forgotten. He could see that in her eyes, sinking into the sensation of it. As it ever was.

"You are leaving," she said. It was not a question.

"A matter of conscience," he said.

The room was still. His heart was still.

"A matter of pride," she said, her voice soft, her gaze brittle.

"Perhaps both," he said. "We each must answer to both, must we not?"

"We must," she said. Did he imagine it? Was there a throaty weight to her words?

"Good-bye, Lady Dalby," he said, turning toward the door, turning away from her in what would not, surely not, be the last time.

"It has been a sincere pleasure, Lord Ruan," she said. "Until we meet again."

"Will we meet again?" he asked, turning to face her one more time. As it ever was.

"Most assuredly," she said, her eyes devoid of all emotion but raw intent. "It is a matter of pride, you see."

As it ever would be.

Chapter 11

Anne understood that something very profound had just occurred between Ruan and Sophia, something not entirely pleasant yet entirely powerful, something to do with pride, of which she had little, and conscience, of which she had an abundance. It struck her, sneaking a look at Dutton, who looked as entirely captivated by the exchange as the rest of the occupants of Sophia's white salon, that she could do with considerably more pride and less conscience.

Upon Ruan's departure, the party within the salon shifted. George Grey moved to stand behind Sophia's chair, Elizabeth Grey stood and walked toward the windows facing Upper Brook Street, George's eyes following her with dark warning. Warning? Dutton, naturally, looked at Elizabeth, but not before looking at her, to make sure she noted it.

Blasted man. He was as contrary and arrogant as a stallion.

She wanted him. She had wanted him for quite a long time, Lord Staverton not withstanding, and she meant to have him.

Oh, dear. Had she just admitted that?

Why, yes, she had.

The earth did not open up and swallow her whole.

Her hair did not turn white.

The ceiling did not fall in on her.

More pride and less conscience. Precisely.

Anne stood up, smoothed her skirts with one careless hand, her palm lingering upon her right hip for a moment or two longer than was quite necessary, but it was necessary in an entirely different sense, and she did not look to see if Dutton had noted her hand, her hip, or her linger, because she had pride and because she did, after all, think that he had looked because she was Anne Staverton and he was Dutton and that was the way things were between them.

So, yes, her hand lingered. And yes, she knew, she simply knew, that his eyes were upon her. Perhaps even lingering upon her. Yes, that. Precisely that.

"Sophia, I must take my leave as well. As much as I would love to linger in the comfort of your white salon, I find I simply cannot." Oh, yes. She said *linger*. It was all quite amusing. "I must hurry if I am to leave with Lord Ruan. Please excuse me."

And with that, she dropped her head in a cursory curtsey and left. The silence in the room was complete and utter. She did hope that Sophia knew that she did not have any other purpose in dropping Lord Ruan's name other than to annoy Dutton.

Surely that was obvious to Sophia. She did so hope that it was not at all obvious to either Dutton or Miss Elizabeth Grey. As long as she was honing pride she did not see why Miss Grey should not benefit from it.

Anne took her wrap from Fredericks, smiled at him cheekily in response to his raised brows, and hurried out the door and down the stairs of Dalby House, her footman at her heels. She simply could not allow Lord Ruan to escape without her at his side. She was quite, quite certain that would annoy Lord Dutton dreadfully. It simply must be brought to pass. Simply must. She could not allow a moment to annoy and bedevil Dutton to pass her by without grabbing hold with both hands. And if that meant grabbing hold of the Marquis of Ruan, so much the better. She was nearly certain that

Lord Ruan would understand.

Nearly.

Lord Ruan, quite conveniently, was standing only one house down, his right heel banging against the curbing stone, looking quite like a man waiting impatiently and determinedly.

"Lord Ruan?" she called out. "May we walk together?"

"Lady Staverton," he answered, turning to face her, "I should be delighted."

She did have the strange thought that he may have been waiting for her, but that was absurd. She hadn't known she would fly out of the white salon until moments before she actually did so. Lord Ruan was a most confident man of the world, but no man was that prescient. Indeed, most were the farthest thing from prescient being rather more dim and indeed, obtuse, than was entirely complimentary. Naturally, she was referring to Dutton.

"I did begin to wonder if you were coming at all," Ruan said, casting her a sideways glance as he offered her his arm.

She took his arm, her hand positioned politely and entirely properly upon his sleeve. She did not return his glance. She kept her gaze before her, watching where she walked. Entirely the right course when dealing with Lord Ruan, that much was immediately clear. This was the man who was dancing a strange and possibly dangerous dance with Sophia; such a man was perhaps not the best choice to dangle in front of Lord Dutton. Or perhaps he was the perfect choice.

Yes, it could be that he was entirely perfect.

"You expected me," she said, keeping her voice level and her face free of blushes. She had become quite accomplished at both at her mother's knee. "Or was it that you expected anyone? Perhaps Lady Dalby?"

Ruan exhaled sharply, an almost laugh of something that was not quite amusement. "You have grown, Lady Staverton. It suits you."

"I have grown older, Lord Ruan, and I hope wiser." Prouder, is what she really meant.

"What game are we playing, Lady Staverton, and how may I assist you in winning it?"

The Marquis of Ruan kept his eyes forward, his manner congenial, his gait measured, yet for all that there was a sizzling intensity that she could feel upon her very skin. Ruan was a man who kept much buried, most obviously his motives for doing anything. Why on earth should this man want to help her?

She was wise enough in the ways of men to understand fully that men were always and ever interested in serving their own needs in their own fashion. She did not fault them for it, but that was only because she was entirely aware of it and able to defend herself appropriately. And it had not taken any sort of 'older and wiser' nonsense for that to be so. No, hardly that. Once again, she had her mother, her hopelessly naive and drearily hapless mother, to thank for that.

Some lessons were learned early in life, some late. Most of her most important lessons, the lessons governing survival, had come to her early. The later lessons, the lessons regarding pride and a certain degree of aristocratic arrogance and indulgence, those lessons would come to her now. She was quite determined about it.

"Lord Ruan, I do believe it would help my cause and possibly my reputation if I were to dissemble and flirt, to bewilder and bedevil you, leading you to my aid without you being quite aware of what was happening until all was safely settled."

"In short, behaving like Sophia Dalby," Ruan said.

If there was a trace of bitterness in his tone, she missed it. On the other hand, if there was any praise in his words, she missed that as well. It appeared she could not read Lord Ruan even the slightest bit. Plain speaking must then rule the day. Besides, she could be plain with Lord Ruan; it was the Marquis of Dutton who deserved and indeed, required, all her subtlety.

"It is far beyond me to mimic Lady Dalby successfully."

"You are in a crowded field with that observation," Ruan said.

Ruan seemed in a bit of a temper. As to that, so was she.

They reached the corner and stood for a moment in front of the house that the Hydes had on let to the Prestwicks, the glass of the conservatory glinting in the gray afternoon light. The rain had stopped, but the skies had not cleared. It seemed a metaphor for the moment, this moment when she would change everything, even if nothing appeared to change. She would know the difference, and Dutton would feel the difference.

"Shall we continue on?" Ruan said, looking down at her, his green eyes as murky as the light. "I would happily walk you to your door."

"Happily?" she said, smiling. "If it's to be done happily then how may I refuse?"

"You may not. I will escort you. I shall display happiness. You shall bear witness to it, if asked."

Anne stopped cold. Ruan stopped and looked at her solemnly, his face expressionless.

"I will not be a party to anything, any conversation, any plot, that is designed to torment Sophia," she said.

Ruan smiled, a small tilting up of one corner of his mouth. "I applaud your honor and your loyalty. I also find I am intrigued and, indeed, charmed by the idea that I have the ability to torment Lady Dalby. Quite intrigued. Quite fully charmed. Please, do explain, Lady Staverton."

Oh, bother. She really didn't have any sort of facility for intrigue. How was she to manage Dutton when she couldn't manage intrigue?

"Lord Ruan," she said, casting a glance back at her footman, who took her meaning readily enough and slowed his gait, putting more distance between them, "I will not put you in the position of either agreeing or disagreeing with me; I shall simply state as fact that in matters of subtlety, you and Lady Dalby far outpace me. There is no shame in this as Lady Dalby, most certainly, and you, most likely, rank far above me in both experience and sophistication."

"But not intelligence, Lady Staverton," Ruan said, his mouth quirking in amusement.

"Thank you for that, Lord Ruan," she said, lifting one corner of her mouth in an answering smile. "Now, since we are agreed that while I may be intelligent, and I would so love to think so, I do not excel at subtle manipulation, I ask you most boldly and most inappropriately, would you help me in my endeavors against Lord Dutton?"

"Not *with* or *for* Lord Dutton?" Ruan asked without the courtesy of hesitation or confusion.

Ah well, she was not subtle and there was no point in being dismayed that Ruan had abandoned subtlety in dealing with her. What was to be gained by being subtle at this point anyway? She was widowed and she was safely free of all but the most egregious departures from propriety. Surely Dutton, who had wandered often in such feminine fields of acceptable licentiousness, was equally free of moral hesitation and societal censure. He had certainly proven so in the past. With her, no less.

"Phrase it as you wish, Lord Ruan. I am not so particular as to the wording, only the outcome."

"And the outcome you desire?"

"Lord Dutton," she said, being far too blunt, she knew, but for some reason, she trusted Ruan's integrity and honor.

Of course, the very fact that she was asking for his aid in such a thing as this, and fairly confident of achieving it, proved that both his integrity and honor were not quite what they should have been. But she was in no position, and indeed no mood, to dither over particulars. She'd done quite enough of that her entire life, by necessity, surely, but she was past such necessity. How perfectly glorious.

"Lord Dutton? As simple as that, is it?" Ruan did her the courtesy of not grinning in ribald humor, but his eyes were definitely twinkling. "What is it you want of Lord Dutton, or is it simply a matter of wanting Lord Dutton and being assured of having him?" Before she could answer that, and she was not entirely certain she could form a coherent response, Ruan continued, taking her elbow lightly as they turned down Davies Street. "I do think you must know, Lady Staverton, that the Marquis of Dutton has been yours for the asking from the first moment he laid eyes upon you. Women are very adept at that sort of knowledge, no matter their sophistication."

"But their sophistication, or lack thereof, does impact their responses to such knowledge," she said. Small wonder that Sophia was so intrigued by Ruan; he was so exceedingly clever. "I find I have become just sophisticated enough to be able to respond as I would like."

"Then what part is called upon for me to play? You are sophisticated enough and Dutton is eager enough. I fail to see where my aid is needed."

"You must not flatter me, Lord Ruan. I do not require it."

"If I must not, then I shall not," he said pleasantly enough, but he did not sound quite completely pleasant. He was Lord Ruan; he was not known for being pleasant. If he had been, Sophia would have tired of him after the first five minutes. And she knew without doubt that Sophia had not tired of him. She was not certain what Sophia did feel about Lord Ruan, but it was definitely not ennui. "I will aid you, in any way you desire."

That sounded suspiciously seductive. She did not require seduction from Lord Ruan.

"You are not in some sort agreement, some form of arrangement with Lord Dutton? I was under the mild impression that you two had a pact of sorts between you, something concerning Sophia?"

"Does not all concern Sophia eventually?" Ruan asked, his eyes upon the cobbles, his hand upon her elbow.

"Is that an answer?"

She would not be cowed by him. Would not, no matter that he nearly compelled it. He was a daunting, dangerous sort of man, quite the type for Sophia. Dutton was quite daunting enough for her.

"Lady Staverton, I will accommodate you in any way you wish. There is no need to bandy words and meanings with me. I am entirely at your disposal."

"Why, Lord Ruan? Why are you so entirely at my disposal?"

"Because, Lady Staverton," he said, his green eyes gleaming quite wickedly beneath his black lashes, "I suspect it would please Lady Dalby."

"You want to please her."

"I want," he said, his voice soft, so soft that the sound of the wheels on the carriages and the footfalls of the horses nearly swallowed his response, "I want . . ." His gaze stayed on the cobbles, his head held at a low angle, his voice pitched equally low.

"Yes, Lord Ruan?" she prompted.

He lifted his head slowly and the suggestion of a smile touched the corners of his mouth. "I want what all men want. To be of service to a worthy lady, and to be found worthy because of that service. Now, how may I assist you? What bedevilment is planned for the not-so-innocent Marquis of Dutton?"

She should not have prompted him. Ruan had been close, very close to a moment of pure revelation but she had pushed and, like all men, he had immediately withdrawn. The trick, she hoped, was to push so hard and so quickly that a man had no time to withdraw. And the man she had in mind for that was, naturally, Dutton. She wanted to push him quite hard, quite soon.

"I do not know, Lord Ruan, and hence I ask your help."

"You do not know or you do not dare to speak it?"

They were nearly at Staverton House, the monumental size of it rising up like a tombstone, covering her in its shade. It was ridiculous, she knew; it was her home and she was the master of it, yet she was not quite the master of it and therein lay the problem. But if she could not master her house, her staff, how could she hope to master Dutton? And master him she would. Into what, and how, and for how long she had no idea. Her plans, truthfully, had no flesh or muscle, only the skeletal wish to dominate, to succeed, to . . . bedevil.

"I confess to having no plans, Lord Ruan, merely wishes." And desires, but she was not going to confess to that.

"Shall we take tea together, Lady Staverton?" Lord Ruan said, looking down at her, looking at Staverton House, looking at her again with a slight smile on his face. His very handsomely rugged face. Dutton's face was nothing like it. Dutton's face was devilishly handsome and wickedly sensual, his eyes promising physical delights. His mouth also promised physical delights but she was not going to believe anything his mouth said. She was not such a fool as that. "Shall we not firm up whatever it is you wish to do to Lord Dutton? Is the time not now?"

"Yes, Lord Ruan, I do believe that the time is most assuredly now." And upon those words she led Ruan up the steps and into the opening maw of Staverton House.

Chapter 12

Upon the departure of Lady Staverton and Lord Ruan from the white salon of Dalby House, the mood of the gathering abruptly shifted. The shift was not entirely pleasant, but it was interesting.

Sophia had yet to come upon the time in life when she did not enjoy a change, any sort of change, that resulted in things becoming interesting.

Of course Sophia knew without question that neither Ruan nor Anne were in any way interested in each other. Anne was all for Dutton and Ruan was all for her, and Anne would not do anything to interrupt Ruan's pursuit of the infamous Lady Dalby, and yet would do nearly anything to fire Dutton's pursuit of her.

And so it was explained. And so she would make certain it would come to pass. Sophia loved Anne like a daughter and if Anne wanted to play with Dutton, and, truly, what woman would not, then she would aid her in every way possible.

There were so many ways possible. Men made such delicious playthings. She rather doubted that they realized it, poor things.

George and Elizabeth were looking quite mysterious and dangerous, which was so clever of them. The English did expect Indians to exhibit certain characteristics and were so very put out when their expectations went unmet. They were behaving quite up to expectation.

Lord Raithby looked quite completely taken with Elizabeth, which was a bit of a surprise as she had it on good authority that Lord Raithby cared for women only peripherally and for horses quite devotedly. Of course, all men did grow up eventually and leave the playthings of boyhood behind. How Elizabeth would manage Raithby she did not dare to conjecture, but it would be interesting, of that she was certain.

What more was there to life?

"Sophia, I must speak with you. It is, I believe, quite urgent," Lord Quinton said, pulling his chair closer to hers, his knees almost brushing against her skirts. How very unusual of him.

"If you believe it to be so, then I am convinced," Sophia said, leaning forward. "What is it, my lord? What urgency requires our combined efforts?"

"Do not flirt with me, Sophia. You know I am deaf to it." But he smiled as he said it, and she was quite comforted by that smile.

Lord Quinton was a fixture, however brief the moment, of her distant past, a past rooted in the soil of New York and long before she had achieved the rank and fame of Lady Dalby. In any other man, such knowledge of her past would have made him her avowed enemy, but Quinton was not such a man. He was a true friend, and she had few enough of those in this misty, dark land. This England.

"And blind to it, I suppose," she said on a breathy sigh. "I suppose I must be content."

His light eyes grew serious, his expression relaxing into a near-scowl. Quinton was a man to the core. There was nothing of the dandy in him, and nearly nothing of worldly sophistication about him, at least sophistication as measured by London standards, of which there were many and which were generally useless as a true measure of anything.

Quinton, strangely enough, was more perfectly fitted to the Iroquois model of a man, and that perhaps was why she trusted him so throughly. She liked him, and they both knew it. She really should see more of him. Why had she let him escape to a dim corner of her life? He was man to keep in the bright sunlight of each day's thoughts.

Lord Ruan, in all her musings and determinations, was not far from her thoughts, indeed comparisons. If he dwelt in shadow, that was his preferred place. Clearly.

"There has been some . . . speculation," Quinton began, his eyes glancing briefly around the room, noting the placement of people, lowering his voice, quieting his demeanor to a less intimate mien. "In fact, gossip, about you, in the years you have been gone from Town."

"I would expect nothing less, my lord," she said lightly, signaling for more tea. Freddy spoke to the lone footman, who promptly left the room. Freddy positioned himself nearer to Sophia.

"Not of that sort, Sophia," Quinton said, staring hard into her eyes. "Not the usual sort of talk."

"How very disappointing," she said, smiling.

Freddy slid a half step closer to her, his hard gaze upon the other occupants of the white salon. Elizabeth had left her brother, who was now sprawled upon a small chair and looking pointedly out a window onto Upper Brook Street, and she was talking coolly with Lord Raithby, who did not look cool in the slightest.

"There was a man murdered, knifed, and your carriage was reported to be in the area," Quinton said.

Sophia did not feel the shiver of apprehension, nor

did she feel the heavy weight of disaster. What she felt was the warmth of appreciation. What a dear friend Quinton was, how heavily he carried the weight of worry for her, and for so little cause.

"My carriage," she said, grinning. "My carriage? I'm afraid that my carriage and I are in many places, Lord Quinton. I cannot be held responsible for all misdeeds while my carriage and I are out upon the streets, can I? Who is spreading these wild tales about my poor, innocent carriage? I may just respond in kind and tell interesting tales about his phaeton."

"'Tis Aysgarth, Sophia," Quinton said, his voice a rumble of worry and discontent.

Robert Godwinson, the Earl of Aysgarth. Of course it would be he. Lord Aysgarth.

Always and ever had he loathed her, loathed her because he feared her. Oh, yes, feared, even though she had been hardly more than a child when she'd first crossed his path in France.

"I'm certain Lord Aysgarth must have a phaeton I can disparage," Sophia said. "Or is he too old for the dash of a sleek phaeton? I would imagine him more attuned to the rough spring of a mail coach at his age."

"He is a formidable enemy, Sophia. He is making much of your carriage and the dead man. He has sworn that the man was a Son of Liberty once, and thereby connected, however distantly, to you."

"However distantly, indeed," Sophia said. A Son of Liberty had murdered her mother. A Son of Liberty had ripped her virginity from her when she was barely more than a child, but an Indian child, and that had been the deciding factor, apparently.

Quinton took her hand in his, her soft palm laying upon his roughened hand. It was not a caress, merely the touch of human kindness. Quinton had always had a very highly developed sense of kindness. One could only wonder how he managed life at all, kindness not being conducive to long life. Of course, he kept it well-buried. Only those who knew him well, of which there were few, were aware of his deep well of humanity.

"Sophia, he is not making your connection to this particular Son of Liberty a secret in certain quarters. The talk is growing, suspicion against you rising above a murmur."

"I care neither for talk nor murmurs, darling, but I know you do. You have played Galahad to my Guinevere, have you not? Or is that Lancelot to my Guinevere? I cannot keep the point of that particular legend straight in my mind. Was Lancelot not Guinevere's crucible? She would have been far better off without such an inconvenient fellow, I am quite sure."

"Sophia," Quinton said, looking deeply into her eyes. "You must take care."

"Darling, you know full well that I always take care. Very special care," she said, turning her hand in his to squeeze it soothingly. *Particularly of my enemies*, she added, but only to herself. Poor Quinton was quite overwrought enough as it was.

※

"You are overwrought," Raithby said to Elizabeth

Grey. "I have misspoken."

"I am not overwrought. You *have* misspoken. Again," Elizabeth answered.

Elizabeth was well aware that George could hear every word spoken and that he was likely laughing himself sick. In silence.

"I am unaccustomed to the social courtesies common in America," Raithby said.

"Yes," she said, staring him full in the face. He seemed most discomfited by the experience. She widened her eyes and stared at him as a wolf tracking a house cat. He was like a cat, this Lord Raithby. His blue eyes were narrow and quiet, observant and wary, the hint of a predator in their depths. But she was a wolf, child of the wolf clan; he was no match for her.

"As you are unaware of the way of things in England," he said. "It is to be expected, though as your aunt has spent most of her life here, it might have been otherwise."

The cat eyes glinted in the light. Amusement? Hostility? She did not know. She hardly cared.

"I have nothing in common with Sophia."

"Nothing? Not your blood?"

"Blood thins as it runs dry."

"Sophia's blood is dry? No one will agree with you on that point, I'm afraid."

He did not look afraid. He looked both amused and hostile, very much like a cat.

"She left her people. She lives with the English, and has become English," she said. It was more than an indictment; it was a curse.

"Her people are also English. Her mother was

English, was she not? As your father's mother was English. Same mother, same father, same blood."

Hostility, yes, much of that. Not so much amusement now. He knew Sophia's story, or that part of it. From his father, most likely. Quinton had been part of Sophia's life in New York, after Sophia had stayed with her English mother. John, her father and Sophia's brother, had stayed in the deep woods of the Mohawk and Ohio valleys, looking for . . . but Raithby could not know that, as Quinton would not know that. Sophia would not have said that much. Sophia, for all her Englishness, was not so English that she would say so much to those such as these. These English.

"Much time and much distance between then and now," Elizabeth said. "Even blood ties run thin after so much of both."

"She has taken you in. You and your brother."

"For my father she has done so. Her bond is to him."

"And yet that bond still holds, fast and strong."

"Why is it so important that you think so?"

"Why is it so important to you that it not be so?"

And so, again, too much said, too many words misspoken. There was no talking to this man. He was all bristle and claw. Mild scratches, true, but she did not like being scratched.

"If you cannot see that I am nothing like her then I have nothing more to say to you," she said, turning to go, turning back to catch one more look at his blue cat's eyes, the scar just below one eye glinting white in the fading light.

That scar spoke to her, of wars waged and honor accrued. It was a man's face, showing the marks of battle. If he would only close his English mouth and let his scar speak for him. But he was English. He did not know how to stop his mouth.

"You are nothing like her," he said softly, "and everything like her. You are the call of the wolf in the night. You are the mare running across the hills. You are the narrow track into the deep and shadowed wood. You whisper danger and caution and seduction. You whisper, and I lean forward to listen."

She stood still, his words falling against her, finding their way into one small corner of her heart. He had so many words, too many words. A woman did not need so many words from a man. Yet they leapt, alive, and she could not find the will to kill them.

"You have too many words, English," she said.

"I do," he said, his voice low, his eyes gleaming, his hands in fists at his sides. "With you, I do. You must excuse me," he said. And upon the words, he bowed his departure to her, to Sophia, to his father, to the room.

He was gone without another word spoken between them. She ought to have been thankful. She worked very hard to be.

Chapter 13

Anne was determined to be thankful for Lord Ruan's help. It was not difficult. Lord Ruan seemed to push all obstacles from his path. It was most refreshing. Upon entering Staverton House, a moment which always caused her to hold her breath slightly and stiffen her shoulders, facing Winthrop, the butler, the entire cause of all her anxiety, Ruan, without any breath holding or stiffening whatsoever, handed Winthrop his hat and gloves and paid him no more attention than that.

It was all quite completely breath-taking, in an entirely non-Winthrop way.

Lord Ruan really was quite wonderful. Winthrop, as was perfectly common for butlers in fine established houses of impeccable name and location, did not so much as blink an eye at Ruan's behavior. It was something to behold, and something to consider, that was obvious. If she had attempted such an act with Winthrop it would surely have been perceived as being high-handed and ill-considered and she was quite certain she would have been paid back in full by a month's worth of soggy biscuits and unwaxed floors. Lord Ruan did not give any indication that he would tolerate any sort of pay back from a butler.

It was completely awe-inspiring.

Anne led Ruan to the most intimate and cozy of the rooms at Staverton House, the room in which she had spent the most time as the bride of Staverton and which she spent the most time as the widow of Staverton. In fact, it was the only room in the house in which she felt any degree of comfort and domesticity at all. The room, a small drawing room, was on the first floor at the front of the house, the noises of the street quite clear when the windows were open. It was the noise of London, even this distinguished part of London, that made her feel so at home.

The room was done up in silvered green damask on walls and upholstery, a fine walnut writing table with tapered legs in most delicate proportions, and a white marble fireplace surround designed in the simple lines that gave the room its charm. It was a soft, feminine room bathed in pearled light for most of the day. The fire drew well and the furniture was well-stuffed. It was not as intimate a space as Sophia's white salon but it served the same purpose. It was a room designed for intimacy, for quiet conversation, for reflection, for the writing of correspondence. If only she had someone with whom to correspond.

"Please, be seated, Lord Ruan," Anne said, indicating the sofa opposite her own. Like Sophia's white salon, her salon had matching sofas flanked in front of the fireplace. She often suspected that Staverton had modeled this room on Sophia's; it would have been quite like him to compliment Sophia in such a subtle yet public manner.

"What a charming room, Lady Staverton. I feel quite at my ease in it," Ruan said, sitting gracefully upon the sofa, his long legs stretched out in front of him.

"As do I. It is my favorite room in the house."

Winthrop stood between the window and the corner, looking quite bored and yet equally disapproving. In other words, his normal expression.

"Will you take tea, my lord?" she asked, looking at Winthrop.

"Thank you, yes," Ruan said, ignoring Winthrop

entirely to ponder the landscape painting hanging above the mantle.

"If you would, Winthrop?" Anne said.

Winthrop, in response, waited a full two seconds and then with an almost audible sigh, departed to see to the tea.

The moment he was out of the room, and in a voice most alarmingly audible, Ruan said, "Sack him."

"I beg your pardon?"

"Your butler. Sack him."

Ruan looked pleasant enough; he did not look enraged or outraged or particularly engaged in any way, yet he was certainly *something*, wasn't he?

"Winthrop," Anne said. "He and I have a difficult relationship at times." All the time, but she didn't feel the need to share every mortifying detail.

"Lady Staverton, there is no need to have a difficult relationship with one's servant. In fact, it defies the very concept of having a servant in the first place."

"He was very devoted to Lord Staverton."

"Lord Staverton is dead. Winthrop's devotion belongs to you. Or it should."

What an alarming thought. She could admit to having similar thoughts in her room at night, the blankets pulled to her chin, the fire in the grate gone feeble and she too nervous to ring for a servant to see to it.

"Yes, I can see that should be so," she said. It had nothing to do with Dutton, of course, and she had invited Lord Ruan in so that she could talk to him about Dutton, but it was not enjoyable to shiver in one's bed at night. "I do think giving him his papers is a rather severe solution."

"Then he should have thought of that when he chose to treat you without the respect due you, Lady Staverton. The necessary result of his misbehavior rests entirely upon him, not upon you. As mistress of this house, you must discharge your duties faithfully. The future of Staverton House rests upon it."

"Yes," she said, her voice small and tight. He was correct, of course. Was she to allow Staverton House to fall down into rubble because Winthrop was free to mismanage the affairs of the house? The heir to Staverton House, a man she had not met yet as he was traveling in the Holy Land, deserved better. "Yes, put that way, I can see that you are correct."

"What other way is there to put it?" Ruan asked, his eyes glinting in the candlelight, his legs crossed at the knee, looking quite at ease in her salon. She did not know why but having Lord Ruan at ease made her feel a bit uneasy. She could not think why. Those glinting eyes, so green, so sharp and knowing. He was a man to give a woman shivers of awareness. He clearly knew it, too.

"Lord Ruan, are you attempting to seduce me?" she said, crossing her legs at the ankle, tightening her body against his gaze.

"By sacking your butler? That would be original. And daring," he said. "I do believe you put too much upon my abilities, Lady Staverton. I am not such a man as Lord Dutton. He, I am quite confident, could and would seduce a lovely widow upon the back of a shoddy butler."

Anne laughed. Oh, it was too ridiculous. She could

not help herself. Upon the back of Winthrop, indeed. There was an image to savor. Ruan smiled at her laughter, his face lightening, his mood visibly lifting. That was an odd realization; Ruan's mood was normally somewhat dark. He was not a light-hearted man, and she could not think why that should be so. He was a man in full health, title, and wealth. Why not be light-hearted?

"You are quite as I expected, Lord Ruan," she said.

"I am delighted to have fulfilled your expectations, Lady Staverton."

"But you did not allow me to finish," she said, leaning back to gaze at him with what she hoped was a sophisticated gleam. "You are what I expected; you are a man who allows other men to stand in the light while you prefer the mystery of shadow."

It was true. She had not known quite what she was to say until she'd said it, but having voiced it, she knew it was true. Ruan stayed in the shadows. He was unlike any man she had known. She suspected that she would be very glad that she did know him, even more glad that she could name him friend. She did hope that she would be able to call him friend.

"You, perhaps, think me more mysterious than I am," he said. The very words were a withdrawal.

"I would love to be found mysterious," she said, redirecting the conversation. "Do you think it possible? Or even desirable?"

Winthrop returned with the tea tray as the words left her mouth. It was most unfortunate. Winthrop scowled. Ruan smiled his cat's smile. Anne stiffened her spine and said, "Thank you, Winthrop. You may withdraw. I wish to discuss something with you later. At half five, shall we say?"

Winthrop looked almost stunned. "At half five?"

"In this room. Until then," Anne said, dismissing him.

When Winthrop closed the door behind him, Ruan winked at her. "Nicely done, Lady Staverton."

"You are either a very bad influence or a very good one, Lord Ruan. I have not yet decided which."

"Probably not something that should be decided. Let the tide roll as it may. Let it take you where it will."

"Oh, that was definitely bad, not at all the thing a handsome man should say to a lonely widow. I am quite on my guard now, my lord, weak as my guard may be."

And, against all her experience and all her training, she winked at him. Lord Ruan, magically and wonderfully, laughed out loud. It was perfectly delightful.

"Now that is the sort of thing you should say to Lord Dutton," Ruan said. "And with just that sort of sauciness. He'll be a pudding in no time at all."

"Do I want him to be a pudding?"

"Don't you?"

"Lord Ruan, all I am certain of is that *I* don't want to be a pudding."

"Quite rightly," he said. "Now, first you will sack Winthrop and then you shall dangle the lure for Dutton. I shall instruct you, if you need it, and I don't think you do, not truly."

"Not truly? But somewhat?"

"Lady Staverton," Ruan said, smiling at her. She quite liked it. "You are a beautiful woman with experience of the world. You have had two worthy men marry you, devoting themselves to your welfare. You have made a fast friend of Sophia Dalby, a woman who is highly selective in her associations and who will not suffer fools. Is that not a correct estimation of your accomplishments?"

She sat back upon her chair, quite breathless. It was true, wasn't it? There was not a false element in his list. She was beautiful; she had known that for a fact since she was a small child. Being beautiful in a world where beauty was a commodity, and her sole commodity, was not something a poor girl ignored. Her two husbands had loved her, provided for her, cared for her. She counted Sophia as her closest confidant, a relationship she cherished perhaps above all others, including her husbands. And she was not stupid. She might be nervous and unsure and out of her depth more than she wished to be, but she was not stupid. Her very life proved that point neatly.

"You are most astute," she said.

"It is merely that I am not blind."

They smiled at each other. Really, Lord Ruan was such an agreeable man. What was keeping him from Sophia's side? They would get on so well together. Somehow, things had become bungled for them. She couldn't think how.

"Why must I sack Winthrop first? He can't have any part in my mission to turn Dutton into a pudding," she said. Oh, how she liked the sound of that.

"Because, Lady Staverton, you must catch hold of your power and position. Mastering your butler is the first step. Dutton will follow, night as to day."

"You are certain?"

"I am more than certain. I am confident."

Confident? When had she last felt confident of anything? She was almost entirely certain she never had. How distressing.

Before the thought had quite settled, Winthrop, that annoying excuse for a butler, announced and then admitted, without a by-your-leave from her, Lord Dutton. Of all things, she had not expected that Lord Dutton would seek entrance. She was not entirely certain she would have admitted him, her plans not quite in place, her strategy for snaring him far from secure, but Winthrop thrust him into the room and if she needed any further prompting to give him his papers, and she did not, then this would have done it.

Dutton looked, as was his habit, seductive, dissolute, and wayward while at the same time looking entirely respectable. Well, perhaps not *entirely*. He bowed, making a sarcastic mockery of it, she dipped into a very cursory curtesy, and then she and Lord Ruan resumed their seats facing one another. Dutton could find his own seat, across the room, preferably.

Dutton, that scoundrel, shoved right in next to Ruan, their knees bumping. Ruan's eyes glimmered. Her eyes, she did hope, glowered and flamed. Dutton's eyes did what they always did, which was to smolder speculatively in her general direction. Speculatively, indeed.

"Whatever has brought you round to my salon, Lord Dutton?" she asked, pouring a tepid stream of tea into a fresh cup. "I did think you quite enchanted by the charm of Lady Dalby's salon."

To Dutton's left, Ruan gave the tiniest shake of his head. One degree to the right, another to the left, and then he was done. She took a very shallow breath and continued before Dutton could draw breath to answer. "I have modeled my salon after hers, you know. I do hope you will make a flattering comparison."

"And if I do not?" Dutton said, because, of course, he was endlessly and tiresomely contrary.

"Then I shall have Winthrop throw you out, my lord. I do not endure anything but the highest praise."

"Again, modeling upon Sophia Dalby," Dutton said, not at all pleasantly.

"I could not hope to find a more excellent model of all that a woman should be," Anne said, her eyes drilling into his.

"Well said," Ruan murmured, shifting his legs so that Dutton was crushed against the arm of the sofa.

"And well done," Dutton said, a gleam of appreciation in his blue, blue eyes. She did hope it was appreciation. One never quite knew with the Marquis of Dutton.

"I must make my departure," Ruan said, standing quite abruptly, it seemed to Anne. "I have other calls to make."

"Do you?" Dutton said.

"You do?" Anne said in the same instant. She swallowed hastily and added, "Of course. How kind of you to have walked me home, Lord Ruan. I did enjoy it." Whereupon Dutton looked annoyed. Anne felt a rush of satisfaction, one could even, if generous, call it a flood of joy. She decided she would do just that.

As did I," Ruan said, making his bow. Winthrop

opened the salon door for him, gave Anne an odd glance, and walked Ruan out. Leaving her quite alone with Lord Dutton. Something really must be done about Winthrop. She had been far too lax with him. And with Dutton, come to that.

The moment they were alone, truly alone, alone as they have never yet been in their entire acquaintance, was a moment of great weight. For Anne, at least. What Dutton felt she had no idea. She ought not to care. And she didn't. Not really. But they were alone, in her house, nothing but servants, negligent ones, a room and a closed door away, the fire in the grate, the light fading and the shadows lengthening, her breath catching in her chest.

No. Not that. Not with this man. His breath must catch. His heart must race. His blood must pulse. It was Dutton's turn to be off step and off balance, to wonder what she wanted and if she wanted him. She was not the woman she had been. She had power now, some position in the world, and she meant to use it.

They had both stood upon Ruan's departure, as was only proper, and now they still stood. Dutton waited for her to seat herself. She decided that sitting was too passive; she walked to the window that fronted the street and looked out. Dutton did not accompany her. She did not know if she had wanted him to or not.

"If you have your heart set on Ruan, you are destined to disappointment. He is all for Sophia Dalby."

Anne kept her back to Dutton. The back of her gown had quite nice pleating and she did not think it would hurt her efforts to show it off. "I do not have my heart set on Lord Ruan."

"Your loins, then," he said. He had not moved. His voice had not moved.

"My loins, Lord Dutton, do not have a mind of their own."

She kept her back to him. She was embarrassed she had said such a common thing. She was also, almost equally, delighted.

"Are you certain of that?" He moved toward her; his voice was closer.

She had spent many nights pondering that voice. She had pushed thoughts of his voice from her mind when Staverton performed his marital duty upon her. She had ignored memories of his voice when she had stood at Staverton's side on their wedding day, and every day thereafter. She had listened fractionally to that voice in her head when Staverton was laid to his eternal rest. As the months had passed since that day, Dutton's voice, the memory of it, the seductive lure of it, had grown louder and less easily dismissed and discounted.

Now there was no reason to dismiss it. Or him. Now, she could and would do precisely as she liked.

Who was there to stop her? Who to disapprove? What price to pay for this dalliance with Lord Dutton? There had been much ado made of Dutton, deserved or not. Now, she was determined to do something about all that.

"Not as certain as I should be, perhaps," she said, turning to face him, quite well aware that the last light of the dim sun would do wonderful things for her hair. "Let's put it to the test, shall we?"

She had the supreme satisfaction of seeing Lord Dutton's jaw unhinge a fraction of an inch.

She was going to have the time of her life. Dutton simply must do his part.

This was not the Anne he remembered. Nevertheless, this Anne, any Anne, was the one he wanted. Had he always wanted her? He neither knew nor cared. He did not live a contemplative life. What motivated him hardly mattered. What he achieved, that was all that mattered. And he would achieve Anne now; now she was playing in his arena. Now, she would succumb, finally succumb. He had her precisely where he wanted her, where he had always wanted her.

"Yes. Let's," he said, moving across the room toward her. She was lit from behind, her hair glowing red, her legs outlined, their shape plain to see. She had lovely legs. He wanted them wrapped around him. He wanted that now, instantly. He had wanted it forever, eternally.

He reached her in quick, long strides, aware only of her. A swift catch of her breath. A flush of pink in her cheeks and on her neck. A widening of her eyes. Beautiful eyes, pewter green and hazel gray, neither and both, changeable, mercurial, quicksilver eyes.

"Lord Dutton," she said, holding a hand up, her other hand gripping the window sill behind her, "is this to be an assault?"

"Yes," he growled, and in the next instant his mouth descended upon hers.

She was warm and soft, open and responsive. She put a hand on his shoulder, tilted her head just so, made pleasant sounds in her throat.

A widow twice over. She knew how to kiss, knew how to welcome a man. He knew that. He knew that and he wanted more than practiced submission and acquiescence. He wanted her raw and out of control. He wanted her naked longing and clumsy, hungry passion. Not this. Not this casual acceptance of his kiss, this polite response.

"I'll strip you naked, Anne," he said against her mouth, one hand on her jaw, tilting her face up, the other hand on her hip.

"Being naked is the entire point, is it not?" she said, smiling softly, nearly humming her pleasure. God, she could smile and hum? No. By God, no. He wanted her screaming, clawing, thrashing. Not this. Not what she had shown her husbands. He was no husband to be managed.

"Why now? Why this, now?" he said, moving his hand forward to cup her.

"Because now I can afford you, Lord Dutton. Afford this," she said.

He pulled back and studied her face. She was flushed, with pleasure, not with passion. She was content, but not satisfied. She was managing him.

"Afford me?" he said. "You cannot afford me, Lady Staverton. I will ruin you."

"You can try," she said. "Please. Do try." And she leaned up to wrap her arms around his neck and kissed his jaw, a trail of kisses that ended at his mouth.

He pillaged her, ravaging her mouth with his, hot and demanding. She met him thrust for thrust, moaning. He wanted more than that, far more.

It was at that moment that her butler opened the door. Dutton released her instantly and stepped back. The man's face was a mask of contempt and satisfaction. Dutton took a step toward him, his fists clenching. Anne laid a hand upon his arm, halting him, and said with cool civility, "Yes, Winthrop?"

"You have a caller," he said. He did not address her properly, or at all.

"An urgent caller, one must assume," she said. "Lord Dutton, you must forgive me. This matter must be addressed immediately." Dutton assumed she meant the caller. She did not mean the caller. "Lord Staverton thought much of you, Winthrop. I have been under the assumption that you held him in high regard, as did I. I am Lady Staverton. Lord Staverton is gone from us both. You will likely be more content in another situation. I give you until tomorrow morning to remove yourself from Staverton House. Thank you for your years of service."

Anne had delivered the entire speech in the cool tones of the landed gentry. Winthrop appeared quite as shocked by the speech, and his dismissal, as Dutton was. When had Anne become so . . . so aristocratic?

"Who is the caller?" she asked.

"Mr. James Caversham," Winthrop answered.

The Duke of Aldreth's by-blow? How had Anne come to be acquainted with Caversham?

"I see," she said. "If you will excuse me, Lord Dutton? I am certain you must be eager to be on your way."

"Certain, are you?" Dutton said.

"Thank you, Winthrop," Anne said, dismissing him.

"Show Mr. Caversham into the library and provide him with whatever refreshments he desires. I will join him presently."

Winthrop, obviously unaccustomed to being dismissed, backed out of the room. He came close to slamming the door.

"If you will excuse me, Lord Dutton. I should not have dismissed Winthrop in such a way, in your presence, but I felt I could wait not a moment longer."

"I completely agree. The man is quite beyond the pale. Has it always been thus?"

"Forgive me, Lord Dutton," she said, running a hand up the back of her hair. "I did not mean to give you the impression that the operation of Staverton House was open to discussion. The matter, I trust, is closed. May I also trust that you will keep your own counsel as to my breech of form?"

What was this? Her breech of form in sacking her butler, but not in kissing him in what, he was certain, given just a few moments more, would have become flagrant abandon?

"When have I ever given you the impression that I could be trusted, Anne?" he said softly.

She chuckled. Chuckled! "Oh, Lord Dutton. You are not quite so fierce as you pretend. Are you?" Her pewter gaze eyed him appraisingly. It was most galling, especially as she was quite right; he would not divulge to anyone anything that had occurred in this room.

"I leave it for you to judge," he said.

"But of course," she said blithely. "Now, if you will excuse me? I have an appointment with Mr. Caversham that quite slipped my mind."

"An appointment? I was not aware that you and he knew one another."

"Oh, yes, for quite some time. You know him?"

"Not well," he said.

Caversham was hardly alone in being the by-blow of a man of title; they were thick upon the ground. Caversham was slightly unique in that his father, the duke, and his mother, the French actress, were still together after more than two decades. That was hardly usual. Caversham had been tutored and been educated at a respectable school. Caversham did not trade on the duke's name or on the connection. Again, unusual. Certainly it was not uncommon for men such as Caversham to be awarded an honorary title of some sort, but the word was that Caversham was not interested in any such thing. What James Caversham was interested in, Dutton had no idea, nor interest.

"He is quite a delightful man," Anne said. "Quite delightful."

Dutton came perilously close to snapping. He managed to ask in moderate tones, "You are well-acquainted, then?"

"And hope to be more so," she said. "I really must go into him, Lord Dutton. Thank you for calling. I hope you shall call again?"

He was being dismissed. Thoughts of how Winthrop had been managed came to mind. It was entirely unpleasant.

"Trust upon it," he said, making for the door. "Shall I make an appointment, following Caversham's lead, or will you accept me whenever I knock?"

He opened the door and Anne proceeded him out

of it. The scent of her hair, something vaguely floral, wafted past him. He resisted the urge to inhale deeply.

"I do think an appointment would be best, Lord Dutton, if you wish to follow in Mr. Caversham's lead, though I confess to being surprised you do. I am interviewing for a lover, Lord Dutton. To receive my full attention, and avoid the risk of interruption, I do think appointments are best. Thank you again for stopping in."

The hell she was.

Chapter 14

James Caversham was waiting patiently in the library, studying a landscape painting above the writing table to the left of the hearth. It was quite a nice table and quite a nice landscape. Most of the contents of the room had been acquired by the 3rd Lord Staverton. She had added nothing and did not intend to. Winthrop would likely have been most reassured to know that.

Anne was quite astounded with herself. She was managing things with brutal and open efficiency. It was completely unlike her. She was entirely thrilled. Winthrop was gone, or soon would be. She must begin the search for a new butler, someone devoted to both Staverton House and to her, much as Fredericks was to Sophia.

But that was secondary. Dutton held, as he ever had, the primary position in her thoughts. And now her plans. That was a change. Never before had she allowed Dutton to play any part at all in her plans. Now she could afford to. Oh, she had meant that. She had meant little else in what she'd said to him, but she did mean that. Unless he were horridly indiscreet, which she sensed he was not, she could play with Dutton to her heart's content.

She was not interviewing for lovers. How completely absurd. That Dutton had believed her, if only for a moment, was both insulting and gratifying. Oh, she'd make him dance a dance for her. That she would. She was Lady Staverton. She was not a woman to be trifled with. Even Winthrop knew that now.

Anne opened the massive door to the library and James Caversham turned at her entrance. The library was massive, one of the larger rooms in the house, and had been Lord Staverton's sanctuary. She had rarely entered it whilst he was alive and she was less prone to use it now. It had seemed the perfect choice given her revolution against Winthrop and Dutton and the whole of her life. She was not going to hide in corners any longer.

"Mr. Caversham," she said, "what a lovely surprise."

James made her a bow, she dipped a curtesy to him, and then she waved him into a seat upon a deeply upholstered sofa across from the hearth. She took the chair next to the grate, facing him at an angle. The room was on the south side of the house and the light was good until an hour before dusk, when it was sent into quick shadow. It was less than an hour from that now. The room was softly lit, the smell of leather bindings strong, the rug warm beneath her feet. The 2nd Lord Staverton had purchased the rug.

"Lady Staverton," he said. "I do hope you are sincere. I have burst in upon you and if you send a bad report to my mother, I shall be in for it."

He said it with a devilish smile. Fear his mother, indeed.

Zoe Auvray was the most cordial and amiable of women. French, she had come to England well over twenty years ago, had been, in the way of things, a struggling actress and then a struggling courtesan until the Duke of Aldreth had become her protector and the father of her only child. They were still together, still quite devoted, and any gossip about them had died years ago. Or should have. The Duke's wife had died while still quite young, two children to her credit, and Aldreth had not sought out a companion until she was in her grave.

It was all as proper as these thing could be. That Zoe and Sophia were friends then and friends now, that Sophia was rumored to have had a hand in arranging affairs between Zoe and Aldreth, and that both Zoe and Sophia had been friends with Anne's own mother made Anne's feelings regarding James Caversham, bastard son of Aldreth and Zoe, quite, quite warm. She felt almost a sister to him, albeit distantly related and having no childhood memories shared between them. Still, their mothers and Sophia went back decades, they were both the bastard children of courtesans, and they had both made their way in Society quite nicely.

Or she had. She wasn't quite sure what it was that Jamie Caversham was about of late. How perfectly dreadful. She felt immediately guilty.

"Mr. Caversham, you are the most charming liar of my acquaintance," *Lord Dutton notwithstanding*. "Now, how may I assist you? I am entirely at your disposal."

"May I first tender my condolences upon the death of Lord Staverton? He was beloved of all who knew him."

"How very kind you are, and how very true the sentiment."

James Caversham was in his early twenties, lean of frame, and sharp of feature. He did not strongly resemble either parent, though he had something of Aldreth's coloring, though of a more intense contrast. His eyes were light blue and his hair pure black and worn quite short and brushed forward toward those remarkable eyes. He was an intense looking man and gave the appearance of high drama and yet his manner was entirely pleasant and warmly jovial. He confounded expectation.

Anne wished people would say that of her. She feared she was entirely predictable. Or she had been.

Jamie leaned forward, his brows drawn low against his eyes. He really had the most remarkable eyes, the purest, lightest blue, quite unlike Dutton's blazing blue gaze. Anne shifted in her seat, feeling uncomfortably tingly. "I do have something to ask of you, Lady Staverton. I need information, the sort of information that only women truly know."

"You want to know about another woman?" Anne said, grinning.

"Precisely," Jamie said, smiling briefly.

"Please, you must address me as Anne. We share too much history for such formality." He nodded, his eyes closing briefly at the movement. He lifted his head and opened his eyes and it was quite the most sensuous instant of the last five minutes. Life was definitely on the uptick when a woman could measure sensual moments by the minute. "But why not ask your mother? Surely she knows everyone and everything."

"There are certain topics one does not open with one's mother," he said, a chuckle buried beneath the words.

"Women?"

"Women."

"Who is the woman?" Anne asked.

"Before I reveal her name, I must ask for your confidence, Anne. If my mother knows, then Sophia will soon know, and if I asked Sophia for this information, she would surely reveal all to my mother. I trust them both, but I want to . . . that is, there are certain times . . . "

"When a man does not want his mother involved," Anne finished for him.

"Yes. Simply that. The situation, as all dealings between men and women ever are, is complicated."

"Of course. The woman?"

"Her name is Elizabeth. She is blond, beautiful, blue-eyed. A simple miss, so she informs me. She lives west of Charing Cross."

"No last name? No address?"

Jamie shook his head, and not a bit shamefacedly. "I met her in the Reading Room of the British Museum. I followed her home, or nearly so."

"Oh, my."

"Yes. My thoughts precisely."

"Your intentions?"

"Honorable."

"How honorable?"

"Highly."

"You mean to provide for her?"

"For the rest of my life," he said, his voice intense, all joviality burned from him.

So here was the truth of his looks. Beneath the easy boy stood the hardened man. Well, so it ever was, at least in the best of men. No woman worth her salt wanted an easy boy as a partner in any endeavor whatsoever, however fleeting.

"Yet you know not her name," Anne said.

"I know all I need to know. Once I know her name, I will change it to make it mine. She will be mine."

Oh, my.

"You will marry her," Anne said. "Upon such a brief and casual acquaintance?"

"Brief, not casual. But, yes," he said, getting up to walk the width of the room, his lean legs moving quickly, his scowl deepening. "I would not ask openly for her name lest I do her reputation some harm."

Anne's heart melted a bit around the edges. This is how love and passion, commingled, appeared. Dutton would, simply *would* be driven to this! She would show him not one whit of mercy.

"Do you know her?" he asked, staring down at her.

Anne shook off her thoughts and plans for Dutton. "I do. She is Miss Elizabeth Ardenzy. She has a twin sister, I believe, named Elena. Their father, Mr. Sebastian Ardenzy, is the son of a minor French aristocrat, very minor according to the rumors, and perhaps not even that according to other rumors, who came to England in the 1780s. In fact, I am not certain if some rumors repute Austria as his place origin. In any case, he made his fortune and is determined to see his daughters well wed."

"Meaning, into the peerage."

"Meaning that, yes."

Which was poor luck for Jamie. As a bastard son, he was not ideal marriage material. His father was a duke, and it was not entirely uncommon for such sons to be granted titles of their own. Jamie had never wanted it, according to Sophia, who had it from Zoe, who could not comprehend his reasoning. Sophia, by a certain light in her eyes and a tilt of her head, indicated that she could.

Nevertheless, Aldreth had his legitimate heir in the

Marquis of Hawksworth and as far as Society was concerned, that was that. No one gave much thought to Jamie Caversham, which Jamie seemed to find both comfortable and reasonable.

"I am sorry, Jamie," she said.

Jamie sat down upon the sofa and crossed both his arms and his legs, his eyes gleaming in the cool northern light. "It is nothing more than I expected, and it changes nothing. I mean to have her. I will have her. She is mine already, Anne, though I do not expect you to comprehend that."

"Are all men as confident?"

He smiled. "When they find the woman, I suspect so."

Damn Dutton. She would make him suffer so.

"I don't know what more I can do to assist you," Anne said. Her thoughts were all of Dutton; she did care about Jamie and what happened to him, but not as much as she cared what happened to the dreadful, mesmerizing Lord Dutton. She was a selfish shrew, when she considered it. She had always been a lovely, caring person. She blamed Dutton for the change in her. He was entirely responsible. Vile, irresistible man.

"What do you know of her father?" Jamie asked, his long frame coiled rigidly into stillness. He put her in mind of one of those black panthers of America, all smooth, silky, dark danger.

"I met him once, perhaps twice. He is quite aware of both his current place in the world and where he wants to be in it," Anne said. "But I am quoting Sophia, of course. For myself, he seemed a pleasant man, if not a bit intense in his goals. I believe he has high hopes for his daughters to marry well. He has the funds to make them quite attractive."

"She is attractive enough without funds to sweeten the deal," Jamie said, a bit tersely, she thought. It was quite lovely of him. James Caversham was really quite an attractive man, so virile, so dynamic.

A thought. A lovely, delicious thought began to spring to life. Delicious. Oh, yes, completely delicious.

"As I have been introduced to Mr. Ardenzy and his daughters, it is entirely acceptable for me to call upon them," she said. "Would you care to accompany me, Jamie?"

His blue eyes lit up like flares, hot and bright. "I would. Now?"

"If we hurry, we can. Shall we hurry?"

"I'd love to hurry. In fact, hurry seems to be the word of the day," he said, rising to his feet.

She did not know quite what to expect in respect to Winthrop. He had been sacked but he was not in receipt of his reference; was he still on the premises? She preceded Jamie out of the library, her heart only slightly in her throat, only to come face to face with Winthrop, her hat in his hands, a very respectable look on his aged face.

"My lady will want the carriage brought round?" he said. Her lady's maid, Mary, stood ready to help her with her matching spencer.

"Yes, thank you, Winthrop," she said calmly.

He did not act like a man sacked. He also did not act like a butler who thought himself better than his lady. A definite improvement. Well, it would all be sorted out when she returned and had time for Winthrop. She most certainly did not have time for him now. How nice that Winthrop realized that.

"It is not far. I believe we could make better time if we walked," Jamie said.

"Yes, for we must hurry, mustn't we?" she said, thinking that walking suited her purposes far better. "No carriage, Winthrop. Have William accompany us."

William, a particularly nice looking and easy mannered footman, appeared.

It was with minimal fuss that they departed Staverton House for the home of Mr. Sebastian Ardenzy and his twin daughters, Elizabeth and Elena. That Mr. Ardenzy lived only a street away from the Marquis of Dutton was nothing if not a happy coincidence.

Jamie offered her his arm, she took it, and he matched his stride to hers with admirable control. She could feel the urgency coursing through him.

"I do not know what you expect to happen at the Ardenzy's," she said.

"An introduction?"

"And after that?"

"A marriage."

He was so intense in his drive to possess Miss Ardenzy. It was such a pleasant, even inspiring thing to see. It was certainly inspiring her.

"Mr. Caversham, might I propose something?" she asked.

"Lady Staverton, you may," he said, casting her a sideways glance as he guided her across Duke Street.

"I believe that it may raise Mr. Ardenzy's estimation of you if he believes that you are visiting him at my insistence and not your own. In that I do think he is the sort of man who will hold you in higher esteem if he perceives that you hold him in small esteem."

"Why do you think that?"

"Because of something Sophia said about him," Anne confessed. "Has she ever been wrong?"

"Not according to my mother," Jamie said with a quirk of his lips.

"Nor according to mine, who did not heed her counsel." *To a grim end*, she could have added, but didn't. Jamie was as likely aware of the fate of her mother as anyone was. "I believe that if you hold yourself a bit apart, show a bit of superiority, Mr. Ardenzy will look upon you with favor."

"And his daughter? How will she look upon me if I do so?"

"I trust you to manage his daughter."

Jamie grunted in reply. He did not sound overjoyed at the prospect. She could hardly blame him.

"And do you not want something from me, Lady Staverton?" he asked. William walked a few steps behind them and they were keeping their voices low. They would not be overheard. "I have learned that women are very generous in doing a man a favor or in giving him a prize, but only when they receive a favor or a prize in return."

"That is quite a harsh view of women."

"I don't think so. I think it shows a practical turn of mind and a very businesslike quid pro quo. It is hardly a fault. Now, by taking me in hand and ushering me into the Ardenzy's drawing room, what favor am I doing for you, Lady Staverton? I am willing to be used in nearly any manner you wish."

She laughed. She could not help herself.

"I do admit to having an idea," she said, casting him a sideways glance. The afternoon was drawing to a swift close, the sun dipping down behind the buildings, the air freshening. The day had begun in drizzle with skies of pearl. It was ending with pink flags of cloud and a soft breeze; she liked to think it was propitious.

"It involves a man, I trust," he said. "All the best ideas involve a man."

Anne laughed again, modestly. They were upon public street, after all. Still, she had not felt so lighthearted in an age. "Since you are Zoe's son and not some ill-informed country cousin, I assume you might guess the man?"

"If the man is the Marquis of Dutton, then, yes."

Strangely, and wonderfully, she did not feel the slightest embarrassment in his knowing of her connection to Lord Dutton. It was quite liberating.

"I have been advised," no need to say by whom, "that, well, I don't know quite how to put it, or as to that," she said, considering the footman not three paces behind them, "if it needs to be explained. I have decided to . . . acquire Lord Dutton."

"Acquire?"

She did not blush. She would not permit herself a blush.

"In all the word may imply."

"And all that it may not imply," Jamie said under his breath.

"I beg your pardon?"

"Forgive me. It is your plan. Proceed with it as you

will. How may I assist you?"

Anne cleared her throat and said, holding her chin up and her resolve firmly in hand, "I gave Lord Dutton the impression that I was interviewing for lovers. I told him that was the reason for your visit." Jamie's eyes twinkled and his eyebrows rose fractionally. "I would like him to continue to believe that. I would like Lord Dutton to . . . to . . ."

"To feel himself in competition for a post and to find himself . . . the loser?" Jamie finished.

"Yes. At least at the start."

"Yet you mean for him to win."

"No," she said, looking at him. They were at the gate to Ardenzy's house, the slanting light striking the windows and turning them golden. "I mean for me to win."

Jamie's eyes widened at that, in shock, most likely, but she was past caring about shocking people. Unless that person were Dutton. Dutton she most assuredly wanted to shock. She didn't think she'd have much trouble doing that.

Before Jamie could utter a reply, she led the way up the steps to the Ardenzy's; the butler opened the door moments after her knock. The Ardenzy butler was entirely forgettable; he was prompt, discreet, and clean. She might try to hire him away from the Ardenzy's. She was in that sort of mood.

The door to the drawing room was opened, the Ardenzy family rising to greet them. Mr. Ardenzy was lean, slightly stooped across the shoulders, with light brown hair and watery blue eyes. He looked a despot. His sister, Miss Edwina Ardenzy, was thick, slightly stooped across the top of her back, with light brown hair and watery brown eyes. She looked a tyrant. It was something about the set of their jaws and the narrowness of their eyes. That, and every rumor of them.

The girls, Elizabeth and Elena, were a perfectly matched pair. She could not tell one from another. They were each possessed of blond curling hair, porcelain complexions, and sky blue eyes. They smiled sweetly. They curtseyed prettily. They sat upon a settee done up in glowing damask and smiled their identical smiles at the identical moment.

She did feel very sorry for Jamie. How was he to tell one from another? Perhaps it did not matter to him. She, whichever one she was, was a pretty girl and surely either one would make him a pretty wife. If he could persuade Mr. Ardenzy to accept his suit.

She did have grave doubts as to that. In fact, she thought Jamie was on a hopeless quest, but as she had engaged in many a hopeless quest herself, with success, she did wish him all the best and was determined to help in any way she could.

"Mr. Ardenzy," she said as she rose from her curtsey, "how nice of you to receive us. Mr. James Caversham and I share quite a long history. I think the two of you have quite a lot in common." The men nodded their heads at one another.

"You are a man of business, Mr. Caversham?" Mr. Ardenzy asked as they all took seats about the room. Elena and Elizabeth sat side by side on the settee near the hearth, pressed against one another like two pearls in the same shell.

"I am not, Mr. Ardenzy," Jamie answered. Jamie had chosen to sit in the chair next to Edwina Ardenzy, the girls' aunt. "I have a keen interest in business and in trade, but then I have a keen interest in many things to which I have not yet laid my hand."

Jamie's gaze swept over everyone in the room. Anne distinctly noticed that he let his gaze rest a second or two longer on one girl's face as he said those words, whereupon the twin reached out and clasped her hand.

So that was Elizabeth, and that was Elena. How had he known which was which?

Men really were marvelous creatures on occasion. She fully expected Dutton to prove that to her at the earliest opportunity.

Edwina Ardenzy scowled. Elizabeth eased her hand out of Elena's and presented a bland expression in Jamie's direction. Jamie slid his gaze back to Mr. Ardenzy, his own expression politely blank.

"I urge you to lay your hand to the plow, as it were, and not look back," Mr. Ardenzy said. "It does a man no good to spend his days considering and contemplating. Choose your field, sir, and take action."

"I take your meaning, Mr. Ardenzy," Jamie said, his blue eyes sharply twinkling, his smile contained. "I have decided upon my course. I will act upon it."

"What field do you intend to plow, Mr. Caversham?" Anne asked, feeling very much like Sophia as she said it. But, really, with such an opening, how could she resist walking through that door?

"Canadian fields," Jamie said. "I plan to make my life in Canada."

"In timber, sir?" Mr. Ardenzy asked, his eyes lighting

up. The man was a complete businessman, that was clear. "They are rich in timber and the supply is reputed to be endless."

"And the navy always in need of ships and ships always in need of timber," Jamie said. "Yes, sir, I do think it shall be timber."

"You have capital?" her father asked. Oh, yes, business and nothing but business. The man had seen to the education of his daughters, that was obvious, but he left himself open to ridicule with such blunt talk in mixed company.

"That is hardly our concern, Sebastian," Edwina said stiffly, still giving her nieces a narrow look. The elder Ardenzy female had quite a stock of ill looks, it seemed to Anne. What a trial to be subject to her tutelage.

"When do you leave our shores, Mr. Caversham?" Elena asked.

"As soon as I have finished my business in England, Miss Ardenzy," he said.

"Do you not think you shall miss England?" Elizabeth asked.

Jamie looked at her. Did no one else notice the intensity of that stare? She did hope not. Jamie was not being nearly as discreet as he should have been. "I will take with me all that I cherish from England, Miss Elizabeth, rest assured. I am eager to begin anew, on a new continent, the old world behind me, the new world under my feet. I shall make my life there, a new life for a new century."

"It sounds wonderful," she said, her voice coming out hardly more than a whisper. "A new life. A new world."

He stared at her and she returned his stare. The room and all its occupants clearly faded from the pair's awareness. The ripple of longing and desire was almost palpable. And Anne knew, if she had not known before, that when she and Dutton were in the same room, dancing their dance, that it was the same. They shimmered with desire. They glowed with longing thwarted.

She had been ashamed of that before, before Staverton, but now she was not ashamed. She gloried in it. This was the meat of life, this passion, this radiant joy. She wanted it. She would deny herself no longer.

"I take it you are not married," Edwina said, breaking the moment, bringing Anne back to the present situation. "A good English wife might find such a move difficult."

"I am not married. Not yet," Jamie said. "But I soon will be."

It was as clear a proposal as Anne had ever witnessed, albeit a discreet one. Elizabeth Ardenzy fairly quivered in her seat. Elena reached out and laid a hand upon her knee, pressing down.

"I would think that a good English wife would follow her husband anywhere, quite happily," Anne said. She had to help them, this pair who loved so suddenly and so resolutely. Or was it a resolute love? Was Elizabeth playing at romance? She knew Jamie was not; Jamie Caversham did not play at love, not with the example of his parents ever before his eyes. "Or perhaps I am romanticizing it. What do you believe, Miss Elizabeth?"

"I believe," she said, laying a hand over Elena's,

ignoring her father and aunt, "that a good wife of any continent or nation walks wherever her husband wills, and that what he loves, she loves."

Anne smiled.

"And what she loves, he loves," Jamie said, his eyes blazing.

"So their love is made perfect, in harmony and in unity," she said.

"As their bodies are made one, so are their lives," he said.

It was a vow. It had the tone and weight of a wedding vow. Now, all that was left was to get them legally married before the next boat for Canada. Oh, and the father must be got round somehow, and the aunt. The aunt was a wolf among lambs.

Anne was no lamb and never had been.

"Elizabeth was reading *Romeo and Juliet* earlier today," Elena said, breaking into the moment.

"A heart-rending tale of love gained and lost," Anne said.

"If only they had moved, the loss could have been easily avoided," Jamie said, his eyes touching Elizabeth's face before looking fully at Anne.

"And lived on what?" Edwina said. "Children marry as they must, not as they will."

"A parent may smooth the way or hinder it," Elena said. "Do you not agree, Father?"

"I am not familiar with the play," he said, neatly closing the subject.

Anne looked at the clock upon the mantel. The time for their visit was spent, the time for Jamie to walk out of her house upon them both. Something must be done to help the pair, but she could not think what. She had read *Romeo and Juliet* a few years ago; the only thing that came to mind was poison and a false death. She did not think that was the answer in this situation. Besides, the results had been disastrous.

There was nothing for it. They must make their exit.

Anne was just rising to her feet, Jamie slowly following her lead, when another caller was announced.

"The Marquis of Dutton is calling, Mr. Ardenzy," the butler said.

Anne barked a laugh. Elena leaned toward Elizabeth and whispered in a voice that carried to the entire room, "Was he in the Reading Room, too?"

Before anyone could say anything, and what was there to say?, Lord Dutton was admitted to the drawing room.

Dutton, dismissed from Staverton House, had not left the vicinity. Of course not. He did not for a moment believe that Anne was interviewing for lovers; that sounded entirely like something Sophia Dalby would arrange simply to annoy him. He could understand why Anne had gone along with the plan. It was very difficult for any woman to stand against any plan Sophia put into play. One had only to consider the horrifying rash of marriages of the 1802 Season to see that.

He did not believe Anne wanted to marry again. He did believe that she might want a lover. He most certainly believed that she could be persuaded to take a lover, namely, himself.

He would have her. He would have her the way he had always wanted her---in his bed. There was nothing more to it than that, and there never had been. Now that Anne was free it would surely happen just as he planned.

It was, therefore, something of a puzzle when he watched Anne and James Caversham leave Staverton House, thick as thieves in their manner, and proceed directly and quite hurriedly to a house on Duke Street where they were admitted without delay. He did not know the house. He was not aware of who lived there. Neither of those facts stopped him from knocking and asking for admittance. It was the hour for callers. Very well. He was making a call upon . . . ah, Sebastian Ardenzy.

He did happen to know Mr. Ardenzy.

During the past two years, whilst making improvements to Redworth, he'd had reason to make the acquaintance of Mr. Ardenzy. Ardenzy had made a fortune in tin futures; Dutton's estate manager suspected Redworth might have a pocket of tin, therefore Dutton had contacted Ardenzy for information. The exchange had been entirely pleasant, though conducted fully by the post. It was time to thank the man in person, wasn't it?

Of course it was.

The drawing room into which he was admitted was gracious in size, generous in light, and tastefully turned out. It all spoke most loudly of respectability, which was the norm when newly acquainted with fat pots of ready money.

"Lord Dutton," Ardenzy said, "what a pleasure. It is delightful to meet you at last."

Ardenzy was a narrow man, narrow of frame and of face. He looked eternally hungry, which was likely a very apt description of his state of mind. Ardenzy introduced his twin daughters, identical beauties of blond hair and blue eyes, just the type that could be expected to make stellar marriages, and it was no secret that he expected them to do just that. When a man had a fortune and had beautiful daughters, certain truths were entirely self-evident.

An aunt to the girls was introduced, Ardenzy's unmarried sister. He nodded and dismissed her instantly. All his attention was for Anne. Even Caversham received little more than a glance. Anne's beauty outshone the blond virgins by yards. She sparkled with knowledge, experience, and humor. The Ardenzy girls glimmered with virginity and innocence. He had never been attracted by either.

The occupants of the room shuffled somewhat and Dutton found himself seated next to Anne, the aunt seated next to one virgin, Ardenzy seated on the other side of Dutton, and Caversham seated next to the other virgin. Dutton was where he wanted to be; he did not care where the others cast themselves.

"I was not aware you knew Mr. Ardenzy, Lord Dutton," Anne said. "Your field of acquaintance is impressive."

"I am delighted that I have impressed you, Lady Staverton," he said to her. He could feel Ardenzy staring at him; he could even feel the man's hunger that he pay attention to his blond daughters. "I know how difficult that is to do."

"You make me sound quite daunting, Lord Dutton," she said. "How refreshing. I have rarely been thought daunting in my life. It is quite invigorating to have grown into such a condition."

The air sparked between them. It fairly shimmered. He wondered if the others could see it. They were blind if they did not.

"I was not aware that women sought to be daunting in this new age," Miss Edwina Ardenzy said in clipped tones. The woman clearly thought herself a dragon. She was, at best, a biting fly. "It does not sound at all desirable." She cast a glance at the virgins, in warning, most certainly.

"It must depend upon the man," Dutton said.

"Not the woman?" Anne responded. "How disappointing."

"I do not believe you could disappoint anyone, Lady Staverton," Caversham said, his legs thrust out before him, crossed at the ankles. He looked both at ease and on edge, exactly where he wanted to be and desperate to fly away. Dutton knew the feeling precisely.

"You and Lady Staverton are well-acquainted?" Ardenzy said.

"Old and good friends," Caversham said, looking at Dutton with a lazy smile. "Going back years, is that not so, Lady Staverton?"

"Quite so," Anne said, handing her cup over to the fly to be freshened.

But not intimate friends. Not yet. He knew it simply by looking at them together. No man could be so easily cordial to Anne once he'd bedded her. He knew that with complete certainty.

He also knew, could feel in the shimmer between them, that she only wanted him in that way, in the way of beds and heaving sighs and tangled sheets. Anne might think she could taunt him with James Caversham, but it was a wasted effort. She was for him. He could feel awareness, a shivering energy, coming off of her skin.

He wanted to bury himself in her, to twine his hands in her hair, to nip her throat, growl against her bosom, to possess her. He stared at her, his desires plain on his face, and had the satisfaction of seeing her squirm in her seat, a faint blush rising on her throat.

"And how did you become acquainted with Mr. Ardenzy, Lord Dutton?" Caversham asked, casting a knowing glance at Anne.

"Mr. Ardenzy was kind enough to help me with a developing project at Redworth," he said. "I have been busy bringing Redworth into this century. My father left much neglected." He would have, as he was cup shot more often than not.

"It was little enough. A bit of information," Ardenzy said, lifting his chin proudly.

"Sometimes little bits of information can be decisive," Caversham said, looking briefly at one of the virgins. Elena? Elizabeth? He could not remember which was which. He did not suppose it mattered as one was the same as the other.

"True enough," Dutton said, watching Anne. She looked flushed and aroused, likely remembering that searing kiss they'd shared. He wanted more of that, much more. He intended to have it, too. All that longing and intention he put in his eyes, willing her to see it and not caring who else saw it. In this room, the only person who mattered to him was Anne. Perhaps that was true of any room. He did not care to examine himself that minutely.

Anne, in response, said, "I'm afraid we must leave. We have other calls to make, is that not so, Mr. Caversham?" Anne stood. Caversham stood. Dutton, very slowly, stood. Everyone stood. "Thank you for entertaining us so beautifully, Mr. Ardenzy, Miss Ardenzy. Your daughters are quite the loveliest women of the Season. I'm certain they'll do brilliantly."

"Indeed. Thank you for saying so, Lady Staverton," Ardenzy said, puffing his chest out a bit. He looked ridiculous.

"Lord Dutton," Anne said, "a pleasure, as always."

"Until we meet again, Lady Staverton," Dutton said. One of the virgins sighed in either sentiment or arousal. He was inclined to think the former.

Anne and Caversham left, leaving him trapped in the tepid waters of the Ardenzy drawing room. With Anne gone, he had little interest in staying and, given that he didn't care a fig for any of them, he would have left abruptly. However, Ardenzy truly had done him a service and the man did know his business. He was not as brutal as all that, no matter what Anne whispered about him to Sophia.

And he was quite certain that she did whisper about him and he was delighted by that fact. He did not care what she whispered. He assumed she made all sorts of pronouncements and protestations, just the sort of thing women devoted themselves to doing, but he knew that a woman not complaining about a man was the worst thing of all. When a woman was at the point of not talking about a man, that meant she was not thinking about that man, and that was death.

Anne, he was quite certain, talked about him in her sleep.

He planned to be there to witness it, quite soon, too.

Dutton paid his courtesies upon the Ardenzy household, though what was discussed he could not have said. Polite chatter, nothing more. The virgins paid him polite attention only and he was barely enough aware of them to realize it. His thoughts were all of Anne.

He made his departure after the appropriate interval, dipped his head to Viscount Redding as they passed on the steps, and was out on the street less quickly than he would have liked. He saw no sign of Anne, nor of Caversham, as to that.

It was the time of day when life slowed. The sun was behind the buildings, the whole world turned to shades of gray, candles lighting the windows, warm welcome in a night going chill. He had a home, true, and the candles would be lit, his servants were quite good, and he had an evening appointment to dress for, people to talk to, conversations to partake of.

Shades of gray. 'Twas all shades of gray.

He wanted Anne. He had wanted her for all his life, hadn't he? It felt like all his life.

Endless games, ceaseless plotting, years of maneuvering and did he have Anne in his bed?

He did not.

The time for games was done. He did not care what Ruan advised. He did not care that Sophia plotted against him and for Anne. He did not care if he won or lost the duel with Anne in the eyes of Town, as long as he had her.

King Street was not far. She lived almost around the corner from him. What was he waiting for? Hadn't he waited enough?

By God, he had.

Without hesitation, pushing all negative thoughts to be ground beneath his feet, Dutton strode to Staverton House. The house was dark, the candles not lit, damned butler, and still he knocked, waited an unreasonable length of time, knocked again, more forcibly, swore not very discreetly, and the door finally opened. The damnable butler stood before him.

"Yes?" the man said, chin lifted arrogantly.

"The Marquis of Dutton to see Lady Staverton," Dutton said, stepping forward.

The door closed slightly in his face. "She's not in."

"Who's not in?" Dutton said, clenching his fists. Damned sot, not calling Anne by her title. She was the lady of the house. She had damned well earned her title. "Your mistress? I trust you know her name?"

"My mistress?" the butler asked, his mouth looking quite smirkish for a butler facing a marquis. "Perhaps yours, my lord."

He was not drunk. No one could say that he was drunk.

No, it was in complete sobriety that Lord Dutton hit the butler of Staverton House dead in the middle of his smug face. It was the thud heard on St. James, or so it would be named.

Chapter 15

"You said her name is Elizabeth?" Penelope asked.

"Elizabeth Grey, but I do think you're missing the point," Louisa said.

"Details are always to the point," Penelope said stiffly.

Eleanor sighed and leaned back against the sofa cushions in the Hyde House music room.

Jane closed her eyes and smiled. Louisa and Penelope, married to brothers, each woman strong-willed and often sharp of tongue, loved each other fiercely in their peculiar way, which nearly always gave every appearance of a fight to the death.

"The point, Penelope," Louisa said, "is that Anne Staverton is free, Lord Dutton is sober, and they mean to have at each other. If they have not already done so."

"Eleanor," Jane said, "it might be time for your . . . "

"Nap?" Eleanor said, laughing. "I assure you, Jane, I am mature enough for such a conversation. I watched Louisa throw herself at Dutton since, well, since forever."

"You are an innocent girl," Jane said. "Aren't you." It was not a question. "Some topics are not for innocent ears."

"Oh, Jane, stop being such an American for once, will you?" Louisa said.

Yes, Jane was a duchess, but she was also an American by birth and inclination, a state of affairs she made certain the duke, her duke, never forgot.

"I can't understand why Lady Staverton and Lord Dutton are of more interest than an Indian girl residing in Mayfair," Penelope said, pouring out more tea for Jane.

"She is beautiful," Eleanor said. "Black hair, black eyes, regal bearing."

"And very ill-tempered," Louisa snapped. "Arrogant in the extreme, and for what possible cause? A most disagreeable woman. She makes her brother look almost gallant."

"Oh, you just don't like George Grey because he hit Dutton," Eleanor said.

"Dutton deserved it," Penelope said.

"And how would you know? You weren't even there," Louisa said.

"Iveston told me. Blakes told him," Penelope said, offering to pour more tea for Louisa, Louisa shaking her head. "You can't argue with what your own husband said."

"Can't I?" Louisa said, to which they all laughed. Louisa could and did argue with anyone she had a mind to. When Jane wasn't exhausted by it, she found it admirable. Being an American, she would.

"Did Dutton deserve it?" Jane asked, not really caring.

Lord Dutton occupied the women of Hyde House to such an intense degree that Jane found it nearly laughable. Who cared what one marquis did? True, Louisa had once pined for him, but Blakes had taken care of that once he'd kissed her. Or Louisa had kissed him. Louisa insisted that she had kissed Blakes, bringing him to ruin. Blakes only smiled when she said that so Jane was quite at a loss as to determine what had actually happened.

"Oh, most definitely," Louisa said, getting up to look out the front windows, the last light of the day turning her fiery red hair even hotter. Louisa was a beautiful woman, quite delicately formed with fragile features; there was nothing remotely fragile about her. "The more Anne Staverton refused him, the worse he became."

"He was cup shot half the time," Eleanor said. When Jane looked at her disapprovingly, mercy, was there nothing these English protected their children from?, Eleanor said, "Well, he was, Jane. Everyone knew it. And discussed it. *Everyone*."

"He did make a rather spectacular spectacle of himself, Jane," Penelope said, taking a sip of her tea. "If one does not wish to become a spectacle, one must not behave as he did. Public drunkenness is difficult to hide."

"He wasn't drunk today," Jane said.

She sounded prim. She knew she sounded prim, and that sounding prim was very close to sounding unsophisticated and that being unsophisticated was nearly equal to being American. She did not care. Oh, she'd used to care, but she no longer cared. Her duke did not care, so why should she?

"No, he wasn't," Louisa said. "Do you think he might be drunk by now?"

"Louisa, you are singularly single-minded," Penelope said.

"Dutton is singularly predictable," Louisa countered.

"Is he?" Jane said. "It's been two years since Anne married Staverton and two years since Anne and Dutton have been in the same room."

"Are we certain of that?" Eleanor said, her dark blues eyes alight with speculation. "They could be having a very discreet affair."

Jane sighed and looked at Louisa. Eleanor was not her younger sister, she was Louisa's. If Louisa didn't care enough . . . and by Louisa's contemplative look at Eleanor's remark, Louisa didn't care in the least that Eleanor was not at all behaving as a sheltered miss about to make her come-out.

"Did they look like there were having an affair?" Penelope asked.

Penelope put far more weight upon accuracy than diplomacy or decorum. Jane found it both confusing and refreshing, very confusing when one first met her, quite refreshing when one realized that Penelope was blunt to the point of hilarity more often than not. It would not be quite true to say that Penelope did not have a mean bone in her body, for truly, who could make that claim?, but she was doggedly devoted to her family and friends. There was hardly anything better to be said of anyone.

"I shouldn't think so," Eleanor said.

Now, really, that was just too much.

"They looked the way they always do," Louisa said. "They looked exactly like they were about to draw blood and tangle themselves in the sheets, equal parts violence and passion, loathing and lust."

Eleanor stared at her sister, her eyes wide.

"Oh, my," Penelope said, setting her cup down with a clatter.

"Yes," Jane said, blinking. "Yes, that's just what it was."

"The point is, what are they going to do about it?" Louisa said.

"Strangle or tangle, one or the other," Penelope said, her voice a bit strained.

"Or both," Jane said.

Whereupon they all looked at her in something like shock, and Louisa laughed abruptly.

"And you act so innocent, Jane," Louisa said, her blue eyes glittering like ice.

"It's not an act," Jane said. And then she smiled. "Except when it is."

Anne and Jamie walked out of the Ardenzy's with no new plan of action, or at least she had none. She had done what she could, provided the man with an introduction, and that was the extent of her manipulative powers.

"It did not go as I expected," she said.

She had expected something to happen, to happen as it inevitably did when Sophia arranged these things. She had not expected to see Dutton in the Ardenzy sitting room. That had been a little bit of wonderful. She was not so dim that she did not understand that Dutton must, surely must, have followed her. He had no real acquaintance with the Ardenzy's and would certainly have no interest in the Ardenzy twins. Virgins were not at all to Dutton's taste, she knew that well enough. All of Town knew that well enough.

"Nor I," Jamie said, his voice tight.

"I have nothing further to offer you. I am not adept at these sorts of manipulations." But she would so like to be. It was a worthy goal, to be sure.

"Nor I," Jamie said.

They continued on for a few steps, each step slower than the one before it, each more hesitantly taken.

"Shall we admit defeat?" she asked, knowing the answer.

"No." He spoke it firmly, desperately, yet firmly. She felt exactly the same way about it.

"Shall we go where we will find solutions?" she asked. Sophia must be consulted. How had they thought to make a success of it without her?

"Where we shall find the way to our heart's desire?" Jamie added, looking at her askance. He knew quite well her dilemma with Dutton. Zoe's son was no fool.

"*My* heart's desire? Is he?" she asked.

Jamie smiled. "Isn't he?"

No, she would not be that effortlessly transparent. It was too humiliating.

"Is she?" she countered.

"Yes. All my heart. All my desire," he answered instantly. He did not appear humiliated in the slightest.

Anne increased her pace, her steps sounding brisk and purposeful on the stones. What a lie her steps made of her. She was neither brisk nor purposeful. She was all at sea, caught between timidity and exasperation, longing and confusion.

And she knew, she truly knew, that she had nothing to fear any longer, and no need to drown in confusion. Or in longing, for that matter. It was a habit of thinking from her old life, before she had become Lady Staverton, before her place in the world was high enough to protect her from nearly everything.

For a girl born in a brothel, that was quite an accomplishment.

Now, if only she could make herself remember it.

Sophia never had any trouble remembering her exalted station, and certainly she relished reminding others of it if they were reckless enough to treat her badly.

"Then we must ask the woman who knows all about love and desire, mustn't we, Jamie?" she said. Her voice matched her steps, brisk and purposeful.

She vowed to turn the illusion into the truth.

***

They were admitted by Fredericks and led to the yellow salon, the larger and more formal of Dalby House's public rooms. Jamie paced the floor. Anne sat in only slight agitation upon a chair near the hearth. The fire was lit, the orange glow of it shining out into the sunny yellow room with flagrant cheer. She was somewhat blind to cheer, flagrant or otherwise.

That they had been admitted to the yellow salon as opposed to the more intimate white salon was something to ponder. That they were then made to wait longer than Anne expected was even more to ponder. Was Sophia entertaining someone in her white salon? And if so, whom? Not Ruan. Ruan had left with her. Of course, he may have returned. She had returned, after all. But he had not behaved as a man who planned to return. Still, a man very seldom had his plans reach fruition when dealing with Sophia; it was Sophia and her plans that were ascendant.

That is precisely how it should be. Dutton had his plans for her. She had her plans for him. Her plans would surmount.

It was only the merest detail that she was not completely certain what her plans were to be. She only knew she wanted him. She knew equally that she wanted him to want her. In a sexual manner. Entirely in a sexual manner. She wanted for nothing else. She had money, means, position. She did need a butler, but she did not see how Dutton pertained to her staffing concerns. No, she was in the perfect position to take a lover. Why not Dutton? He was so well suited to the role.

Jamie still paced. Anne shifted her weight and let the idea of taking Dutton into her bed settle into her mind. The idea also settled into her loins. She shifted again.

Sophia finally joined them, bringing with her life, energy and conversation. It was fortunate that Jamie hadn't noticed the want of conversation as Anne could not have managed a syllable whilst imagining her body pressed into the sheets by Dutton's hot and gleaming body.

With a shiver to shake away the image, Anne turned her attention to Sophia and Jamie.

"Darling! What a splendid looking man you've become. Of course, your darling mother told me as much but one does have to edit what a mother says, love being blind and all that, but she did not do you justice, Jamie. You are quite, quite perfectly delicious."

Sophia concluded this welcome by kissing Jamie upon each cheek. Jamie took it all in apparent good humor. As Sophia and Zoe were the oldest of friends, this was not Jamie's first tilt in the arena of flirtation with Sophia Dalby. For both Sophia and Zoe, flirtation was a high art. Sadly, Anne's mother had never mastered the skill. Anne, Dutton as her target, intended to.

"And you, Sophia, have not aged a day. You are still the reigning the beauty of London," Jamie responded, playing his part to perfection.

Had Dutton ever said anything half so cordial to her?

He most assuredly had not.

Sophia turned to give Anne a brief hug, Anne hugging her fiercely in response. She needed help. Again and again, she needed help. It was disgraceful and demoralizing. It did not change the fact that she felt all at sea whenever Lord Dutton was concerned.

"Yet not your beauty, isn't that so?" Sophia said to Jamie, very nearly ignoring Anne and her raging need for counsel and guidance. "You are in love, Jamie. It shines from you like a beacon fire on a cliff. It is quite charming, I assure you. Who is she?"

"Miss Elizabeth Ardenzy," Jamie said.

"We just left the Ardenzy's," Anne said. "I thought to introduce him to Mr. Ardenzy. Lord Dutton arrived just as we were leaving."

There. She'd said it. What to make of it but that Dutton had followed her? And what to do about it?

Sophia turned her attention to Anne for the briefest of moments, her gaze intense. "Lord Dutton? But how unusual."

Yes! It was. Now, help me to plan my next step in this dance that never ends.

"Yes, much that Dutton does is unusual," Jamie said, redirecting the moment entirely, "but about Elizabeth. I intend to marry her."

"And the length of your acquaintance?" Sophia said, directing every bit of her attention to Jamie and leaving nothing for Anne.

"I met her today. In the Reading Room," Jamie said.

"How romantic," Sophia said, sounding as if she actually meant it. She sipped her claret. Anne downed her claret. Freddy refilled her glass immediately. "And how inconvenient. You are leaving for Canada shortly, are you not? Hardly the best time to put for a successful suit of . . . ?"

"Matrimony," Jamie said.

How intense he was. How determined. There was some of the same in Dutton in relation to her. Of course, matrimony was not the goal in her situation. Not any longer.

"But of course," Sophia said. "I would have expected nothing less, darling."

If there was an insult to Dutton in that reply, Anne was deaf to it.

"My leaving for Canada is the least of it. Her father will never accept me," Jamie said.

"And, if the rumors are true," and Freddy confirmed this by a nod, "Miss Elizabeth Ardenzy is nearly engaged to Viscount Redding."

Jamie whirled away from the women and strode the length of the room in his frustration. Did Dutton stride rooms for her? Did Dutton grind his teeth in despair?

It was something to aspire to, certainly.

Jamie strode back and dropped to his knees in front

of Sophia upon her chair, the very image of the gallant knight in supplication to his lady.

It would be so very nice to get Dutton on his knees to her.

"I will do whatever you tell me, Sophia," he said, his light blue eyes lit with holy fire. "I will follow your every command. I, who have known you longest, know you can work your magic on any man, even a man as old and practical as Sebastian Ardenzy. He will follow where you lead, Sophia. As will I."

It was the most beautiful declaration she had ever heard a man utter.

Sophia reached out to him, her hand under his chin, her eyes searching his face with a fondness that was tender in the extreme. "Why, darling, how charmingly put. Of course I shall assist you. All shall be managed. I will arrange everything. But you must tell me, is the girl willing?"

"Yes. Most definitely, yes," he said.

Jamie was a knight set to slay the dragon, any dragon, and claim the girl. He was fire and smoke, blazing and unquenchable. He was all a man should be when he wanted a woman.

And in the barest shadow of it, in the remembered blaze of scattered memory, Dutton had this. Some of this. A great deal of this. Dutton burned. Dutton claimed. Dutton demanded.

Anne shivered and squirmed.

Sophia looked at Anne, for confirmation of Jamie's declaration, certainly. Not because she shivered and squirmed. Anne nodded, smiling.

Dutton had this intensity. Even in part, he had this.

And that was nearly everything, wasn't it?

"Then let us each dress for the evening. It shall all turn out as it should, and as you like it, darling. Have no fear."

She was speaking directly to Jamie. She was also speaking to Anne. Anne was certain of it.

The process of arranging for an invitation to the Countess of Helston's dinner that night, Jamie to escort her, did not take long. It had taken only moments to discover that the Ardenzy family would be attending the Helston's that night and that if Jamie wanted to carry Elizabeth off, this was his best chance. Anne had nothing left to contribute to the cause.

Whilst Jamie paced Sophia's yellow salon, and Sophia made her inquiries and arrangements, Anne blurted out her own frustrations with Dutton.

"He followed me to the Ardenzy's," she said.

"How flattering."

"He was flirting with me outrageously, right in front of everyone," Anne said, studying Sophia's face. Sophia's face looked peculiarly blank.

"I hope you enjoyed it. I certainly would have."

"What am I to do, Sophia?"

"Why, do as you like, darling. Whatever you like. That is the entire point, is it not?"

And that had been that. Sophia devoted the rest of her energies to Jamie and nearly ignored her. Anne felt, rather righteously, that she had been cast adrift. Was she no longer interesting? Did Sophia no longer care about her long plight with Dutton? Was she to manage him on her own?

She had no satisfying answers to any of her

questions and before she quite knew how it happened, she and Jamie were back upon the cobbles of Upper Brook Street and she accepted Jamie's escort back to Staverton House, but she was a little put out with him, stealing Sophia the way he had. Her problems with Dutton far pre-dated his infatuation with Elizabeth Ardenzy. Far, far pre-dated. Certainly that should count for something.

It most clearly did not.

Jamie was walking very decorously at her side, her footman trailing them, yet she could feel his agitation to get back to Elizabeth, to have Elizabeth. It was most disconcerting. Did no one feel that way about her?

Yes, well, Dutton perhaps did.

That was quite lovely to contemplate. Perhaps Dutton was nearly jumping out of his skin to possess her, the way Jamie was for Elizabeth, and the way Ruan was for Sophia.

The thing was, wouldn't it be better if Dutton were more obvious about it, more clearly on the brink of losing all control?

Yes, that would be much better.

It was as that thought made a cozy place for itself in her mind that they reached the approach to Staverton House and Dutton was standing on the top step, her sorry excuse for a butler standing blocking the portal, when Dutton hit her butler square in the face.

Dutton, darling Dutton, had trounced her own personal dragon.

It was glorious. Perfectly glorious.

Chapter 16

The blasted butler, whatever his blasted name was, fell like a sack of manure upon the marble tiled floor of Staverton House. His blasted nose gushed blood like a fountain. It was most satisfying.

He waited, fists clenched, for the man to rise. Another blow felt appropriate.

Rise, damn you. Get up and meet my fist again.

The man did not rise. The man moaned, put his hand to his face, looked at the blood smearing his hand, and groaned.

Most unsatisfying.

"Get up," Dutton commanded.

A moan was his reply.

Dutton's blood pounded in his ears, in his chest, his fist. He wanted to pummel the man, to smash his face into splinters, to crush his smug face with his boot.

He did none of that. He had enough restraint to do none of that.

If he'd been cup-shot, he'd have done it.

Sometimes it was a burden to be cold sober. He'd thought it often, and never more so than now.

A flurry of steps behind him, he turned his head slightly, not turning his back on the blasted butler, and Anne was suddenly there beside him. She looked flushed and hurried and harried and beautiful and breathless.

"Lord Dutton," she said, breathless, her cheeks pink, her pewter green eyes bright. "Lord Dutton, what have you done?"

Dutton looked over her head to James Caversham standing on the street, watching them. Caversham had a strange, small smile on his face, and then he nodded in apparent approval and walked off. Most peculiar.

Dutton looked down at Anne, expecting to see outrage, some form of concern over her bastard of a butler. She did not appear concerned. She was not looking at her butler. The butler was still moaning, the damned puppy. One blow to the face and this never-ending wail? Damned man should not make disparaging remarks if he could not face the consequences like a man, butler or not.

"I have dealt one paltry blow to this imitation of a man. It was little enough," he said.

"No. Not little enough," Anne said. "Winthrop, go to Cook and she will fix you up. You remain discharged."

Discharged? Perhaps that was why the fellow felt so free to insult his mistress.

"Lord Dutton. You amaze me," she said, laying a hand upon his cheek. The Staverton House door was still open. The butler still lay upon the tiles. There were a few curious people gathered in the street, observing them. "Lord Dutton, you delight me," she said, pressing herself against him, lifting her face to his, her mouth an open invitation to plunder.

Let it never be said that the Marquis of Dutton ignored an invitation to plunder.

It was not a gentle kiss. His fists clenched the fabric of her spencer. Her hat fell off. He bit her lower lip and she scored his neck with her nails.

All the angry energy he had directed at the butler now went straight to her. She met him on equal footing. It was a kiss of blows, of tongues at war, of fists and grunts and torrid shoves.

He kicked the door shut. Or tried to. The butler's legs were blocking the doorway.

"Move your bloody legs or I'll chop them off," Dutton snapped, holding Anne by the scruff of her neck.

The butler, Winthrop, pulled his legs back with a gasp of alarm. Too bloody right. He slammed the door shut.

"Get the hell out," Dutton snarled.

"I gave him the remainder of the day," Anne said, pulling out of his grasp to wrench off her spencer. Her maid stood on the stairs, mouth agape.

"He either gets out this instant or I do," he said, looking at her with the ghost of every dream he'd dreamed of her blazing out of his eyes. He was done with subtlety and foreplay. He wanted her now, had wanted her forever. He was not going to wait one more damned minute.

"You may return for your reference tomorrow, Winthrop," Anne said. "Now get out."

He waited for nothing more. Not the man's removal. Not the maid's departure. Not one damned thing. He swept Anne up in his arms and carried her up the stairs.

"I'm looking for a bed. Direct me quickly or any wall shall do," he said.

Two maids were cleaning the first floor. They pressed themselves against the wall as Dutton passed them, eyes wide.

"Quickly, Anne. I am trying to do what I can to save your reputation."

"My reputation is my own. I do not require aid, Dutton."

"Meaning?"

"Any wall will do," she said.

He had carried her up the next flight of stairs, a long, graciously turned stairway, the landing at the top of the second floor deserted except for a few tables, vases, chairs.

"So be it," he said.

He stood her upon a chair, her soles staining the pale fabric, and he did not care. Her balance was fragile, her eyes slanted, her head back. He lifted her skirts, ripped her undergarments, and he did not care. Her legs were long and white, the skin smooth, her thatch a deep auburn brown glistening with the juice of her passion. He clasped her arse in his gloved hands and kissed her there, his tongue plunging into her. Hot, wet, tight.

She clasped his head in her hands, her fingers tangled, pulling, yanking him closer, her voice a pant of desperate longing.

He flicked her lightly, a mocking of his earlier thrusts.

She swore at him, the curse an echo from the lowest of London streets.

Yes, that. Frustration. Anger. Longing. Defeat.

Power.

Control.

Rage.

Passion.

All of that. Fulfillment and denial. Lust, the pounding demands of lust.

He had no plan. He only wanted to torment her, to fulfill her, to have her and have her and have her.

She kicked him in the chest, her foot planted against

him fully. The kick was not gentle. He stumbled back against the opposite wall. She hopped off the chair, her skirts falling, her eyes shining.

"No. Not your way, my lord," she said huskily, stalking him. "My way. All of this, my way. My desires met. Mine." She pushed him back against the wall, a framed painting two feet away fell off the wall to crash on the wood floor; her hands were on his shoulders, then they were ripping at his cravat and pushing at his coat. She was snarling, snapping, biting kisses along his throat. "Mine," she breathed against his neck.

He grabbed her elbows and pulled her away from him, jerking her so hard that her hair fell down in a glory of red and amber. Her hair reached to the small of her back, a tangle that caught on his buttons. "Yours," he said, "and then mine."

She pulled against his hands, the restraint of his hands on her, her eyes green and hot, her cheeks flushed bright pink. He released her abruptly and she lost her balance, reaching out to him, bracing against his chest with her palms. He grabbed her hands in one of his, pulled her hair back so that her face was lifted to his and devoured her mouth with every bit of hunger that had been building for two years. Teeth nipped. Tongues danced. Moans mingled.

And then he pulled her hair harder, pulling her mouth from his, arching her neck back at an impossible angle, and then . . .

And then he ripped her dress down the front, exposing her chemise from neck to navel.

"My lady?"

The voice came from the stairs, a servant concerned

for his mistress. Not the damned butler.

"Get out!" Anne said. "Naught is amiss."

"Much is amiss," Dutton said. "You're still clothed."

"And you're still talking," she said. "Stop talking. I need no words from you."

She clasped his waistcoat in her fists and pulled it apart. His buttons popped off and rolled in casual disarray upon the floor.

"Perfect," he said.

He picked her up and threw her over his shoulder, her hair hanging down like a burnished flag to touch the tops of his Hessians. He kicked open the first door on the right, the door banging back against the wall with a heavy thud.

The drapes were drawn, the room cold with no fire lit, the furniture covered in sheeting. There was no bed.

He flipped her to her feet, her hair flying down around her shoulders and across her breasts. She attacked him with her mouth and with her hands, standing on the tops of his boots to reach his mouth with hers, kissing him along his jaw and biting his lower lip, her hands pushing at his coat, shoving it down his arms, seams ripping. He shucked off his coat and heard it fall to the floor.

"Get out of your damned gown," he said, ripping the rest of it off her.

"Get out of your damned trousers," she said, pulling at his fall until three buttons gave way.

He pulled her down to the floor, pushing her down upon the disheveled pile of their clothing, grabbed an ankle in each hand, pressed her knees against her chest, and plowed into her with all the finesse of a farm laborer. He slammed home, again and again, home, and home again.

She grunted and pulled his hair, her eyes pouring into his, her mouth tightening in a grimace of passion, of release, of surrender.

She screamed. He grunted, his hair falling into his eyes, her fingers scoring his scalp, her cries in his ears, scoring his spine, his heart, everything in between.

She screamed again, a loud, keening cry, jerking her legs, her feet flexing, her eyes on that far horizon of passion and fulfillment.

He pounded his release into her, a hot rush of aching longing and satisfaction, of victory and power. He had conquered her, conquered it, this obsession that had eaten at him for two years and more. Release. He was released. A flood tide of release.

She slapped him lightly across the face and kicked him off of her, slapping all thoughts of release out of his mind.

"My curiosity is satisfied. Now get out, Lord Dutton. I'm quite done with you."

Chapter 17

She was shaking, but it was only the aftermath of passion, and she was not a novice in the ways and means of passion.

But the violent heart of their passion, that was new to her. She did not dislike it. It was more than satisfying to hit Lord Dutton. She should have done it long ago. Long, long ago. He did deserve it so utterly.

He lay atop her, looking quite the satisfied and sated male, a look which he probably deserved but which she did not intend to indulge. Nothing so simple for darling Lord Dutton. She almost laughed in his face at the plans she had in mind for him.

He would dance so beautifully to her tune; she was quite sure of it.

She slapped him, kicked him out of her, and said crisply, "My curiosity is satisfied. Now get out, Lord Dutton. I'm quite done with you."

His blue eyes narrowed, his brown hair fell seductively over one eye, and his shoulder muscles bunched erotically underneath his linen shirt. Next time, she simply must get him naked. He must look marvelous naked.

Oh, yes. There would most certainly be a next time. His arrogance would allow for nothing else.

He sat back on his heels, his trousers bunched nearly elegantly around his lean hips, brushing his hair back with one hand.

"Are you now?" he said. "And how do you intend to dislodge me when I have every intention of staying precisely where I am?"

And so saying, he grabbed her by the shoulders and hoisted her up off the floor, and then threw her over his shoulder. "I was looking for a bed. I've yet to find it."

"Lord Staverton's sitting room had no need of a bed."

Dutton opened the door and carted her out of it, humming a tune under his breath.

"Is there a bedroom on this floor?" he said.

"Am I to help in this abduction?" She pushed against his back, straining her legs against his chest. He remained unmoved and kept humming.

Dutton opened the next door on the left. It was a small closet with one highly placed window and no bed.

"Still no bed."

"And still no help," she said. "I can have you thrown out, you understand."

"By whom? Your stalwart butler?"

"Put me down, Lord Dutton. I am quite done with you for today."

"No, Anne, you are not."

Anne's gown was torn, her hair was a tangle, and she was red in the face from being hoisted about upside down. She was struggling not to smile. Really, it was quite completely like Dutton to do as he pleased, to disallow any opposition, particularly of the female sort. She simply must do something about that, mustn't she? Something that would make Sophia smile in pleasure.

Anne, her head bobbing, slipped backward just a bit until her foot was just right to . . . and she kicked Dutton right where he most needed to be kicked. He didn't drop her, not exactly, but he did loosen his grip enough so that she could slip down the front of him, push him backward, and run down the corridor her hair flying out behind her.

"Damn you, Anne! You've killed the goose!"

"Of the golden eggs? You put much value upon your goose, my lord. Golden eggs, indeed."

And then she ran into her bedroom and locked the door behind her. It wasn't more than a moment or two before Dutton was knocking on her door, and then pounding on her door. She slipped out of her torn dress, put on a silk sacque, rang for her maid. She ran a brush through her hair, thanking Staverton's grandfather for the stoutness of the doors, and listened with half a smile upon her face to Dutton's increasingly torrid tirade.

"A locked door! Now, when I've breached the keep and tasted---" he shouted, and then, more mildly, "Excuse me." A timid knock, her maid, obviously. Anne opened the door, stood in front of Dutton for a moment, her hair brush in her hand held in only a mildly threatening posture, and once her maid had entered, slammed the door in his face. Dutton, darling Dutton, had looked so completely, so throughly undone. So disheveled and so trammeled, and so very, very well used.

If she were soft-hearted, she'd take him in and spend the day in bed with him. But she was not soft-hearted. A soft-hearted woman would never keep Dutton on the leash, and she did mean to keep him on the leash, and keep him there until he learned to like it.

The maid, Emily Smith, stood looking at Anne with a startled expression and compressed lips. Emily Smith might have become Anne's lady's maid, thereby becoming plain Smith, but Emily Smith was firmly under the thumb of Winthrop the brutish butler and so Emily she remained. Given the events of the day, Anne did think that it was far past time for her to have a true lady's maid.

"Emily, you are aware that Winthrop has been thoroughly sacked?" she said, setting her brush down on the vanity table.

"Yes, m'lady."

Emily was brown of hair and eye and possessed a fine, if unremarkable, complexion. Her frame was narrow and her features regular. She was clearly fond of the first footman, William, though Anne did not think anything had come of that as yet. Or if it ever would. William, as first footman, had his eye on the main chance and a simple housemaid with an unremarkable complexion was not enough to entice him.

Being in mourning and spending much of her time alone had opened Anne's eyes to much that went on in Staverton House below stairs.

"I am restructuring Staverton House," Anne said. "Your position here may remain as it is or it could change. It is entirely up to you."

Emily's eyes widened just a bit. "Are you discharging me, m'lady?"

"Only if you think you would be happier in another situation."

Dutton had resumed his pounding. "Anne! Dammit, Anne! This is a game which leaves us both losers. Open this blasted door!"

Anne looked at Emily and smiled pleasantly.

Emily cast a quick glance behind her at the door, swallowed visibly, and said, "I should like to stay with you, Lady Staverton."

"Then you must remain as my personal maid, Smith," Anne said.

Emily smiled, tentatively, but a smile. "Shall I dress your hair, my lady?"

"No, I need you to find William and Howard and bring them up here, and I want it made very plain to Lord Dutton that he is to leave Staverton House. Can you do that, Smith?"

"I can, Lady Staverton. I most certainly can."

"She threw him out?"

"She had him thrown out. A distinction."

"An unimportant one."

"Lady Staverton actually threw Dutton out of her house."

"You sound surprised."

"I didn't think she had it in her."

"You don't know her as I do. She's vicious."

"Oh, Louisa, you would say that. Just because she stole Dutton right out from under you."

"He was not under me!"

"Not for lack of trying."

Even Jane laughed at that.

Louisa, Eleanor, Jane, and Penelope were in the Hyde House music room, a room particularly favored by them all, and not because of the instruments. It was not so very long ago that their men had engaged in a not-so-minor brawl concerning Jane in this very room.

It was a room to inspire romance of the more violent sort. Eleanor, unmarried and not formally Out, did not have a man of her own, but as she was related to all the men in question in one degree or another, they were hers by connection.

It was highly irregular, or should have been, for Eleanor to be so openly welcomed into such ribald conversations, but as nothing about her upbringing had been anything less than unsheltered, she was welcomed by them all. Well, perhaps not as fully by Jane, who as an American from New York did have some very provincial ideas regarding education.

And this was an education. For a woman not quite Out, a woman on the marriage mart and, if she chose, soon to be wed, it was of utmost importance that she understand all the various ways a man could be a dolt and all the many means by which a woman could bring him to heel. Eleanor, in this company of women, was being exposed to the very best education in the peculiar ways of men.

The Duchess of Hyde, Louisa and Penelope's mother-in-law and a veritable dragon, entered with Sophia Dalby and Elizabeth Grey at that precise moment. The women rose, curtseyed, waited while Molly, the duchess, sat. In the best chair. Let it not be said that Molly, also an American by birth, Boston-born and bred, did not know how to be a proper duchess.

Jane was also a duchess. There was something singularly peculiar about the Americans snatching up all the dukes, but Louisa, as diligently as she made the argument, could get no one to see the oddness of it as she did. She blamed it on willful blindness. People could not naturally be that stupid.

The addition of Molly, Sophia, and the Indian girl changed the conversation instantly.

Or so Louisa thought.

"You were speaking of the events of Staverton House?" Molly asked. Before anyone could do more than nod, Molly said, "Quite rightly. Anne Staverton did to Dutton what half of Town has wanted to do for years."

"And the other half?" Sophia said.

"Have wanted to do what she is reported to have done before she had him thrown out," Penelope said, casting a quick glance at Louisa, which was of course noticed by Molly. Penelope did not have any skill at all at subtlety. As to that, neither did Louisa.

"What did she do to him?" Elizabeth asked.

Elizabeth Grey, who was not truly of their party and not at all of their status, should have kept quiet and looked meek. That Elizabeth Grey was neither quiet nor meek, and that she clearly thought herself not only the equal but likely vastly superior to everyone in the room was one of the most irritating things about her. There were other irritating things. Like her dark beauty, which was not at all the thing but which she managed to make work. She was too beautiful, too exotically beautiful, her beauty a dark and dangerous thing when everyone knew that beauty should be pale and cultivated and fresh. Elizabeth looked as cultivated as a rabid wolf.

"She ravished him," Eleanor said, her freckles looking especially vivid on her elfish features. Really, with freckles like that, how was Eleanor to make a proper match? She was positively spotted.

"Women don't ravish men. They are ravished by them," Penelope said primly.

"Is that what happened in your greenhouse, Lady Iveston?" Louisa said.

Penelope did not blush, but she did look down at her cup. Her mother-in-law was in the room, after all. What Penelope had done to Iveston in her greenhouse was not something one discussed in front of the mother of the man upon whom it had been done. But she had ravished him. Everyone knew that.

It was a quite a good bit of work as far as Louisa was concerned. She had come close to ravishing Blakes, after all. She understood what these Blakesley men required to be brought to heel and to altar.

"I'm sure Elizabeth would benefit from hearing about the courtship practices of the ton," Sophia said, her dark eyes glittering, "and I'm equally sure she would benefit from practicing some of their finer points herself. As she is not marriage minded, I do think this conversation is lost on her."

"I'm not lost," Elizabeth said, her dark eyes flat with menace and ill humor.

"Aren't you?" Sophia asked, stirring her tea.

"Lord Dutton and Lady Staverton," Eleanor said, cutting against the tension between the two women, "have been---"

"Have been," Molly said, cutting off Eleanor, who probably should not say what Dutton and Anne had been doing out loud, "engaged in a very vigorous and somewhat violent courtship."

"Courtship?" Jane said.

"Of a sort," Molly said.

"A violent sort," Jane said, smiling.

"Precisely," Molly said. Molly was Jane's aunt, sister to Jane's mother, and the two women had an easier relationship than, say, Louisa or Penelope did with her.

"I was not aware that their relationship was that serious," Jane said.

"Serious?" Penelope said. "They are engaged in a rough and tumble---"

"Tumble," Sophia cut in with a quick smile. "Though I don't see anything coming of it. Anne has no serious intentions where Lord Dutton is concerned. Certainly that was made perfectly plain when she married Lord Staverton."

"Lord Staverton is dead," Penelope said, "and I do think that, given the length of their acquaintance and the obvious strength of their attraction, they may well end up married to one another. Which would be a good thing. Wouldn't it?"

"I don't see how," Sophia said. "Anne married well in marrying Lord Staverton. She is now well-widowed. What has she to gain by marrying Lord Dutton?"

"A husband?" Louisa said.

Sophia smiled and set down her cup on the table to her right. "What need for a husband? She has all that a man can give, his title, lands and money, and can want for nothing. Nothing that a simple lover cannot provide."

"Is there such a thing as a simple lover?" Eleanor said.

"And could Dutton ever be such a thing?" Louisa said.

"I think you must ask Anne about that," Sophia said.

"I should never want to marry such a man. He is known to be intemperate and volatile, a man of extremes," Molly said. "Whatever Lady Staverton decides to do with Lord Dutton, I am quite certain he deserves every bit of it."

"Sharing his bed is what he deserves?" Elizabeth asked. "This serves him. Not her."

"That, my darling Elizabeth, depends entirely upon the man," Sophia said. "I do think that is one lesson you should endeavor to learn before returning to New York."

Jane gasped. "What lesson?"

Sophia laughed. "Now, Jane, you put too much upon me. I simply meant that my niece should learn that not all men are created equal, not in certain things, and that it is a woman's pleasant duty to test his mettle in the ways that most matter to her. That is all."

"And what ways matter to her?" Eleanor asked.

"That, my darling girl, is not for me to say. Each woman must make her own determination."

"Without question," Molly said, looking at Elizabeth in a highly critical fashion. Louisa enjoyed it immensely. "What matters to you, Miss Grey? Hunting skill? Tracking abilities?"

Elizabeth lifted her chin and, staring straight into Molly's gunmetal blue eyes, said, "Yes. Of course. A man who cannot hunt and cannot track is not a man. A man must have knowledge of many things."

"Most certainly. Many, many things," Sophia murmured, looking at Elizabeth pleasantly. Louisa's skin prickled. When Sophia was so obviously pleasant, something most unpleasant was about to befall. Right on Elizabeth's arrogant head, one hoped.

"Of women, I should think," Louisa said.

Elizabeth gave her a scathing look. Louisa returned the look in double measure. Such arrogance from this . . . this Indian!

"That is an English thing, I am coming to learn. The man I choose need only have knowledge of me."

"And how is he to come by that knowledge?" Sophia asked. "Will he track you and then hunt you and then know you?"

"It is the normal way of things," Elizabeth said.

"That's true," Jane said. "That is the way of things the world over."

"To hear men tell it, that's the way it is," Louisa said.

"Quite right," Molly said, straightening her already straight spine. "Men may track, but the woman sets the trap and springs it. Normally, even the best of men is so blind that he doesn't even know he has been caught. Even more, he thinks he has done the hunting and the trapping. It's quite comical of them and equally endearing. A harmless delusion, to think themselves in charge of the whole affair."

Naturally, Louisa agreed with her completely. She had seen nothing, absolutely nothing, to convince her this was not true. Penelope was nodding agreement in a most vigorous fashion. Jane smiled at Sophia in some sort of secret joke. Eleanor giggled. Elizabeth scowled, clearly confused.

The woman truly was as ignorant as a savage.

"That may be true. Of Englishmen," Elizabeth said. "Is this what Anne Staverton is doing with Lord

Dutton? Trapping him?"

"If she is, the trap is sprung," Sophia said. "Anne, as is well-documented, has no interest in Lord Dutton beyond the most obvious and most temporary. She is a widow, free to do as she pleases. If it pleases her to dally with Lord Dutton, and if Lord Dutton, as he is rumored be, is willing to be dallied with, well then, what harm? She will never marry the man. He must know that. All of London must know that by now. He has pursued and she has allowed him to catch her. For now. When she is tired of the game, she will release him. 'Tis a simple enough game and no one will be hurt by it."

"Not Lord Dutton?" Elizabeth asked.

"How so? If it is as you believe, that men pursue and track and catch, then darling Lord Dutton is exactly where he wishes to be," Sophia said sweetly, her eyes glimmering. "I, certainly, would wish him nowhere else."

Louisa felt a shiver run down her spine. If she cared a fig for Lord Dutton, and she did not, not truly, she might have felt a niggle of trepidation on his behalf. But she didn't. Especially not in front of her mother-in-law.

"In front of the staff? The entire staff?" Lord Raithby asked.

"In front of her maid and most of the footmen," George Prestwick answered. "Not the butler. The butler had been sacked at that point. I believe. I'm not sure about that bit. Seems the butler comes in and out of the tale."

Raithby and George were riding in Hyde Park, the sunlight having beaten back the rain for the past hour. They had begun in a drizzle, hardly caring, and were finishing in sunshine. It ought to be a metaphor for something, but George could not think what, certainly not for the horror that was the the thud heard on St. James.

"He actually hit the butler?" Raithby asked.

"Square in the face. No one disputes it. The man fell down on his arse like a stone. Apparently it was well-deserved."

"Possibly," Raithby said, "Still, to hit an inferior."

"I heard from Jamie Caversham that it was the fact that the man was acting far beyond his reach, and therefore, entirely well-deserved."

"Caversham? Aldreth's bastard?"

"Yes. He witnessed the entire thing. Apparently had a good laugh out of it, too."

"Odd sense of humor," Raithby mumbled.

They urged their mounts into a gallop, Raithby's mount far superior to George's. George caught up with him under a linden tree.

"Why do you think she threw him out?" Raithby asked, adjusting his glove.

"Annoyed with him, would be my guess."

"After bedding him? Dutton's reputation does not lead in that direction, does it?"

George looked at Raithby, at the scar that marked his passion for horses and racing, at the lean cut of his cheeks, the puzzlement clouding his eyes, and knew that his puzzlement did not concern Lady Staverton and Lord Dutton. But he could say nothing of that. Entirely inappropriate at this point, perhaps at any point. A man did not make comment about another man's romantic failings, at least not to his face.

"Quite the opposite, but when did reputations ever matter when dealing with women?"

Raithby grunted in assent.

It was then that Dutton rode up in a fury of horseflesh, sweat, and flying clods of wet earth. Dutton lifted his crop as he approached and George called out to him in a burst of he-knew-not-what. Dutton slowed his mount and slowly circled back to them, his brow furrowed in question and ill humor.

Getting thrown out of a woman's bed would do that to a man.

Having everyone in Town aware of it might push a man to a discreet suicide. Everyone in Town knew that Dutton was not a man to do anything discreetly, so George had no worries about suicide.

"Good morning," Dutton said crisply, looking quite self-possessed for a man thrown out of bed.

"Good morning," George said. Unlike many in Town, he had never had the occasion to hit Lord Dutton. The list of those who had was reputedly quite long.

"Morning," Raithby mumbled. "Heard you did a bit of work on Staverton's butler."

"A good bit of work, according to Caversham," George amended.

Dutton grunted and whirled his mount around. "Gossiping, ladies?"

"Call it an admiration society. According to Caversham, the man deserved that and more," George said. "A bit of chivalry, to hear him tell it. A knight, fair damsel, fire-breathing dragons, the whole bit."

"If butlers can be dragons," Raithby said. "A stretch, isn't it?"

"You've not encountered Fredericks? Lady Dalby's butler?" George said.

Dutton grunted a laugh, his eyes lighting up for a brief second. "There's a butler who'd burn you in your bed and warm his hands in the blaze."

George laughed. "A perfect description of the man. I never look directly in his eyes when I call at Dalby House. The fear of a Medusa reaction. I'm too young to be turned to stone."

Raithby and Dutton both laughed at that, the ice melting just a bit.

"What did the man do?" Raithby asked, his mount perfectly behaved. Dutton's mount continued to sidestep. George's mount kept jerking the reins. George had decided long ago that if he were to continue to ride with Raithby, he simply could not afford to make comparisons. It was too disheartening otherwise.

"Insulted Lady Staverton beyond all measure," Dutton said hoarsely, his voice as close to a growl as George had ever heard.

"In your hearing?" George asked.

"To my face," Dutton said. "Drawing and quartering would have been my preference. As it is no longer the fashion, I had to make do with merely knocking him to the floor."

"And Lady Staverton's reaction?" Raithby said. "She

was not upset?

"No," Dutton said, turning his mount in a fury-tinged circle. George began to suspect that the mount was merely responding to a rage that was coursing through Dutton down through the saddle and reins.

"She was likely relieved to have a rescuer so close to hand," George said.

"Yes. Perhaps," Dutton said. "Lady Staverton's business is her own. I happened to be on hand to help her discharge the man. I am certain she did not need any aid, but as I was there, I was pleased to offer it. Now, if you will excuse me."

He rode off before they could bid him good-bye.

"He does not speak like a man thrown out of Lady Staverton's bed," Raithby said.

"Very chivalrous. I do begin to wonder what will happen next," George said, though he thought what would happen next was rather more obvious than not.

Dutton knew what would happen next. The Town would talk, titter, speculate. He would see Anne and he would seduce her.

Such a simple list.

The list never varied. No matter the players, the event, the Season, the list never varied. Talk, gossip, a raging fire of gossip, seduction. More gossip after that, he supposed. He never cared about the gossip, either before or after, but now he was sick to death of it.

Seduction, pure seduction, no gossip and no

speculation. Just Anne. Seducing Anne. Having Anne.

Again and again, having Anne.

It had not been as he expected. Two years of expectation and it had not been as expected, not one moment of it. It had been . . . better. Richer. More dangerous, more volatile, more unpredictable.

She'd thrown him out, standing in her silk robe, her hair shining like red fire down her back, she'd pointed to the door and had her men throw him out. She'd been smiling as she did it. Smiling, so amused, so playful, so entertained.

It was a move, a move upon a chessboard, and he knew what the next move was; he was to pursue her, to hound her like a lovesick puppy and beg her to take him back.

Well, he wouldn't do it. Or, he might. If he felt like it when she beckoned. The point was, she was not going to control him. She was not going to control *this*, this raging passion that still raged when it should have been tempered, if not extinguished.

The sound of hooves coming up behind him, a single horse, not Raithby or Prestwick catching him up for more gossip, and it had been gossip, and he had not been amused.

"You look none the worse for it," Lord Ruan said, coming up beside him on a magnificent black gelding. "Not even cup shot, were you? Done in complete sobriety."

"Ruan," he said in greeting.

"Was it worth it?"

"He deserved worse," Dutton said. He was not going to speak about Anne, not about that. "Far worse."

Ruan nodded, his green eyes enigmatic. "I don't doubt it. I was exposed to his brand of service earlier in the day. Lady Staverton is well rid of him. In fact, I advised her to sack him moments after seeing how he comported himself."

"Seems she took your advice," Dutton said, feeling an odd sense of discomfort that Ruan had intruded upon Anne's domestic affairs before he had. "The man was given the end of the day and chose to use it poorly."

"He didn't give the impression of great intellect."

"Perhaps I beat some sense into him."

"A good job, if you did."

The two rode in companionable silence after that, the sun losing ground to thickening clouds, turning the sky to lavender and pewter, which had the odd result of reminding Dutton of Anne's eyes and the pale glow of her bare skin.

"Did you achieve what you intended?" Ruan asked, keeping his gaze on the track in front of them, the soft footfall of their horses a comforting, solid sound.

He meant Anne. He had intended nothing for the butler but knocking his teeth down his irreverent throat.

He was not going to discuss Anne. He was not going to take whatever it was between them and turn it into fodder for the Town mill.

Yet Ruan was no tattler. Ruan had, tentatively enough, tried to help him. Ruan believed Sophia to be the root of all his Anne trouble. Well, he had no more Anne trouble.

Except that nothing had been resolved, even though he'd had her, and that was trouble of a sort.

Yes, he supposed it was. Trouble of a very peculiar sort.

"Perhaps," he answered, patting his mount on the neck, the dust rising into the soft air at the action.

"What was it you wanted to achieve?" Ruan asked.

Dutton grunted. A fair question. What had he hoped to achieve? Deliverance, of a sort. Relief. Satisfaction. He had that in part, but not complete.

She'd thrashed him, taken him, rejected him, delighted him.

She had not delivered him of this obsession. He had no lasting relief. He had not been satisfied for long.

"Anne," he said. And that was true enough.

Ruan smiled, a mumbled sound of agreement or understanding in his throat. "'Tis a hard thing, to catch a woman."

"I've caught her."

"Have you?"

No, perhaps not. He should have done. The act was done. He'd taken her, possessed her. Yet she was in no way possessed.

It was confounding.

Dutton shrugged. His mount took a piss. That seemed to punctuate his feelings nicely.

"There's nothing of Sophia in this," he said. Ruan cared only about Sophia Dalby; Dutton knew that without question. Ruan's interest in Anne Staverton could only relate to his interest in Sophia, and Sophia had not been in that room with them. "Your interest in my affairs continues to confound me."

"Sophia? Likely not," Ruan said.

"Definitely not."

Ruan nodded his acquiescence. "As you say. Anne was in that room, a room without a bed, so it's being said, but when did a man and a woman ever require a bed?"

Dutton said nothing.

"Anne is a mature woman, experienced in the ways of the world, accustomed to dealing with men of a certain disposition."

Dutton felt his hackles rise. He was not aware before this instant that he possessed hackles.

"A certain disposition?"

"Amorous," Ruan said. "Did you think she would not be able to manage you, Dutton? Did you imagine this twice widowed woman, a woman with her unique upbringing, would not know how to play the game of grunts and thrusts---"

Dutton kicked his horse into a sideways blow against Ruan's mount, crushing their legs between the beasts. Ruan kicked his horse sharply, and his mount jumped forward, opening space between them.

Ruan turned his mount to face him. "She does not need Sophia for this, Dutton. She was born to this. It was in refusing you that she needed guidance and counsel, which Sophia provided, doubt it not. But to fumble in the dark with you? She can do that all on her own."

Ruan spurred his horse and was out of range within moments. Dutton watched him go. Inanely, his only thought was that it had not been dark and that neither one of them had fumbled.

Anne fumbled in her greeting for only a moment. She was delighted to see Sophia, less so to see Miss Grey. Far, far less so. The Indian woman looked at her in a most peculiar manner. Anne did not think it was her normal facial expression, though she could not be completely certain of that.

"Sophia, how wonderful. Just the person I most wanted to see. How nice of you to come. And you as well, of course, Miss Grey," she said, finding an odd joy in being cutting to Miss Grey.

Truly, her violent encounter with Dutton had unleashed something dark and wild in her. She quite liked it.

Had she ever conceived of such a wild attack as that which had occurred between them yesterday?

Of course she had. She had imagined it a thousand times. She had also imagined their coming together gently, with hushed tones and ardent speech. She had imagined them coming together silently, their bodies entwined in dewy splendor with nothing but the sound of their moist bodies making contact to mark the moment.

In short, she had imagined everything possible and excluded nothing at all as improbable. It was all possible and all probable. She put nothing beyond Dutton, that was certain, and she knew that nothing was beyond her.

Her childhood had been most singularly instructive. Caroline, Sophia's daughter, had been protected and sheltered. Anne had not. Her mother had not possessed the means, even if she had possessed the talent for protection.

She had consumed Dutton yesterday. She had burned him up and thrown him out. Oh, that had been delicious. She had been a virago, a firebrand, a tempest. When she had supped of him, ravaged his body, she had tossed him out on the street.

He would have hated that. And that was precisely why she had done it.

Men like Dutton . . . well, there were no men like Dutton, but men of his general type, the type who seduced by simply walking into a room, leaving heaving bosoms and crushed dreams in his sensual wake, quite truly believed that they could taste at their leisure and leave when their appetites had been satisfied.

No, and no again.

She would not be tasted. She would be devoured and would devour in turn. And then she would demand to devour that particular dish again. Dutton would simply have to make himself available to her, upon request, as it were.

He would loathe that.

And he would love that.

And so she would destroy him.

She couldn't wait.

She was hungry for him already.

"Darling, you're glowing," Sophia said. "Something certainly agrees with you."

"Doesn't it?" Anne answered, showing Sophia to a chair in her salon. Then she turned her head and smiled at Miss Grey and waved her to a small and uncomfortable chair. Miss Grey sat on the settee, her eyes cold black pits of superiority.

"It?" Miss Grey said. "Not he?"

"Miss Grey, as you are a unmarried woman and, one assumes, profoundly innocent, I did hope to shelter you," Anne said, who hoped no such thing.

Sophia smiled and dabbed at her nose with a lace handkerchief she pulled from her embroidered reticule. Sophia was dressed in white muslin with an elaborately embroidered hem in rose red thread and a matching rose red cashmere shawl. She looked the picture of elegance. She wore dangling pearls at her ears and a massive pearl set in gold on her right hand.

Miss Grey wore pale blue. It did not suit her.

"I do not require protection," Miss Grey said in her surly fashion.

"It's quite true, darling," Sophia said as a tray of coffee was brought in by Smith, not quite the duty of a lady's maid, but Anne was still getting her house in order and there were many positions to fill. "Elizabeth has benefitted from a different sort of education than the typical English girl. We may speak relatively freely, I assure you."

"Yes, one can see at a glance that Miss Grey has not been the recipient of a normal education," Anne said, giving her a dismissive glance. "Coffee, Sophia?"

"Thank you, yes."

"Yes," Miss Grey said, her black eyes burning like coals. "Black."

"Black. Of course," Anne said, passing the coffee to her guests.

"Now, tell us everything, darling. The entire Town is

mad for news of the fevered encounter between Lord Dutton," Sophia said, eyes twinkling, pausing to add, "and your unfortunate butler. Did the man lose a tooth? Someone on Green Street is positive that he lost a tooth in the melee and is spreading it about that Lord Dutton is having it strung and will wear it on a fob."

Anne burst out laughing. She had never, not in a decade at the very least, been in such a good humor.

"I saw no lost tooth."

"Did you look?" Sophia asked.

Anne grinned. "No. I did not."

"You were otherwise engaged," Sophia said.

"I was. Most fully engaged."

They shared a grin, a warm, effusive grin.

And then Miss Grey spoke.

"Would you wear the tooth? As a token?"

Now that was surprisingly cordial. Anne almost couldn't credit it.

"A war token, perhaps," Sophia said. "Like a scalp."

"Yes, very like that," Elizabeth Grey said.

Anne had no use for scalps or teeth. This was becoming entirely too bloodthirsty.

"He fought for you, would have bled for you," Elizabeth said. "This is worthy of him, and worthy that it should be done for you. A man should bleed, should fight, should--"

"Strive," Sophia interrupted. "What's a little blood? When a man wants something, why shouldn't he bleed for it?"

Or perhaps not too bloodthirsty at all.

"Bleed? Metaphorically?" Anne said.

Sophia shrugged. "If necessary. Sometimes

metaphorically is the best one can hope for, though in Lord Dutton's case, I do think you might do better than metaphor. Still, what must he still do, Anne? Something, surely. You are not a woman to fall meekly into a man's lap."

"A woman who falls meekly is no woman. She is a child," Elizabeth said.

"I can promise you that meekness has not yet played and will not play any part in this," Anne said.

"I'm delighted to hear it, darling. You clearly have something in mind. Might we be privy to it? I can assure you that your strategy for bleeding Lord Dutton will go no further than the walls of this room."

And so she told them. Miss Grey was struck quite speechless. Anne could not have been more delighted.

Chapter 18

Lord Dutton did not call at Staverton House that day. Anne had not expected him to. No, she knew full well that darling Dutton was now counting on her to be insecure, needy, and desperate. And that he expected her to fall into his waiting hands when she next ran afoul of him.

She was none of that, and none of that was going to happen.

Something had happened to her upon firing Winthrop yesterday, some great sea change in her outlook and deportment. She had been afraid for so long. Her childhood had been one of fear and crushing need, physical need. The very roof over her head had not been secure. Her mother had struggled in the demimonde, as most women did. She had beauty, but not brains, and sweetness without a hint of ruthlessness. All very well and good for the men she tumbled against, but not so very good for her. Or for her young daughter.

Emma's fall had been long and dreary. Like Sophia, Emma had been taken up and ill-used by the 7th Earl of Westlin. Unlike Sophia, Emma had managed to remain in his good graces for only a few months. She had been dismissed and then discovered she was with child.

Anne was that child.

It was a not exactly common knowledge that she was the 7th Earl's natural child, but it was not exactly a secret either.

The 7th Lord Westlin was dead now, as was Emma, and Sophia's daughter was married to the 8th Lord Westlin. No one who knew Sophia believed that to be anything but the most well-orchestrated revenge ever exacted upon anyone.

Being the bastard child of a struggling courtesan was not an unusual circumstance in a town such as London. Being the budding beauty bastard daughter of a failing courtesan, a courtesan who was moments away from plying her trade upon the streets of Covent Garden, also bore certain natural consequences.

Her mother had, with many pointless tears, sold Anne's virginity to a Russian princeling's son. She had been fourteen. The Russian had been sixteen. It was not as unpleasant as it might have been. She had never imagined herself in love with the Russian, though their affair had lasted for more than a month; she was too much a child of the streets and the sheets to delude herself that passion and love were one and the same.

Just as she was not holding onto any delusions about Lord Dutton. Dutton was lust, not love. She well knew the difference.

But when the Russian had left her, her future as a courtesan seemed set in the very stars. And that's when Sophia had rescued her. Russian princelings and fourteen year old red-haired virgins, a virgin who was reputed to be the natural child of an English Earl, for that had added to her appeal to the Russian, were not thick upon the ground, not even in London, and Sophia had swiftly deduced who was whom and what was what and she had acted accordingly.

She had found Emma with little difficulty, taken them both under her wing, and provided Anne with the first secure home she had ever known.

Emma had not stayed secure. Emma, sweet and

pretty, stupid and gullible, had wandered into another man's bed, and then another's, and then she had been taken to the Continent and had not been heard from until a final letter before her death next to a stinking canal in Venice.

Anne had vowed often and violently to be like Sophia and not like Emma. She would be no man's toy and no one's fool. She had married a naval officer, a quite respectable marriage, and when he had died, she had mourned and continued on as a respectable, forgettable widow.

It was during her respectable widowhood that she had been exposed, as one is exposed to the pox, to Edward Preston, 3rd Marquis of Dutton. He had treated her like a, well, like a treat. A woman who was his for the asking, and his for the discarding. Even with all her experience, her lifelong exposure to men of his sort, a miserable exposure, to be sure, she had been nearly helpless before his allure. Nearly, but not completely. That, and Sophia's counsel, is what had saved her.

She had married Lord Staverton, a truly kind and lovely man, and in so doing had been elevated to the peerage and there she remained. No one, now, could take her security away from her. Not even Dutton. Especially not Dutton.

She could do as she wished now. She had the freedom, the means, and most importantly of all, the knowledge. She was not a courtesan's daughter for nothing. All those old lessons, so bleakly learned, could be used now.

And on such a perfect target.

"Did you find the pearled reticule?" Anne asked Smith.

Smith, after only a day as her lady's maid, held herself more proudly and was dressing her hair more elegantly. Amazing what a change of status could do for a woman.

"Yes, m'lady," Smith said, handing her the reticule, a fine cotton handkerchief was tucked into the top of it. "You look lovely, my lady."

She did, didn't she?

Anne was wearing white silk shot with silver thread, a delicate train with a crystal beaded design, long white gloves, and a white feather in her upswept hair. At her ears were the pearl and emerald earrings Lord Staverton had given her on the first anniversary of meeting her in the Dalby House white salon.

"Thank you, Smith," she said. It was going to be quite a night. She did not expect the beaded train to survive it.

The dowager Countess of Lanreath, Antoinette, did not entertain as much as she should have done, but that was the fault of her disposition and not of her accommodations. Her home, on Berkeley Square and Bruton Place, was entirely lovely and of a decidedly French and overtly feminine style. She could take no credit for the design and decor as it had been the work of her late husband's uncle. Nothing had been changed, and did not require change, and, indeed, could not be changed by her since her late husband's eldest son by his first wife was in charge of the house, even if he had no interest in taking possession of it until he married. As he had been the heir for years and was still unmarried, it was becoming something of a topic of gossip about the Town. Had he no interest in protecting his legacy and the doing his duty by his family?

Has it happened, he did not.

As Antoinette knew the son only distantly and therefore was on quite cordial terms with him whenever they had occasion to interact, which was extremely seldom, she did not concern herself with his marital status. She was also not at all concerned about her marital status. She had married a friend of her father's, and a bit older than her father, at his direction. She had been widowed, childless, and now she was quite content to live her life quietly and simply. Simply, in that she lived with a very comfortable yearly income and in one of the best houses on Berkeley Square. She had nothing of which to complain.

And she did not complain. Not at all. But she was, sometimes, on the odd rainy day or still winter's eve, lonely. Life was very . . . quiet. Peaceful, certainly, but so very quiet. She liked a quiet life. Helston had not been a quiet sort and he had quite pushed her to the end of her patience and forbearance, but then he had died and she had been able to indulge her love of quiet and order to her heart's content.

Her heart was quite well contented. Perhaps too well contented. Or too quiet. She was not certain. She only knew, or rather suspected, that something must change.

It was for that reason alone that she was hosting this evening. The last time she had hosted an event at her home on Berkeley Square had been during the 1802 Season, the Season in which so many unexpected marriages had been arranged. By Sophia Dalby.

Oh, there was no secret as to her involvement. Antoinette thought it quite amazing as accomplishments went, and certainly the parties who had found themselves so suddenly and violently wed were the last ones to complain of either the suddenness or the violence of their matches. No, quite the opposite. They had seemed, and still did seem, to be nearly deliriously happy.

It did make her think that, perhaps, a quiet, ordered life might not be as satisfactory as she had once supposed.

She did not wish to marry again. Hardly that. She had been married and she had no wish to repeat the experience. But taking a lover, someone to rattle the edges of her life, might be something worth doing. She had thought to take George Blakesley to her bed, and had intimated that she would be very receptive of such a proposal from him.

That had not gone well at all.

For the third son of a duke, he was far more obtuse than she would have believed possible. Of course, it was equally possible that he simply found her unappealing.

On those odd rain-soaked afternoons and silent snowy nights, she did hard battle against just that thought. She was not desirable. She was beautiful, she knew that, but not desirable. It was possible, she just knew it. Certainly Helston had never been more than tepid in his reaction to her.

Yes, he had been old, but was any man *that* old?

After George Blakesley's rejection, his bland rejection, she had retreated to the normal routine of her life and the normal expectations of her quiet, quiet days. She did not know if George had been London since the 1802 Season. She did not care to know. If he had come to see his mother, the Duchess of Hyde, and not made any attempt to see her . . . no, she did not want to know.

Antoinette walked the rooms of the first floor, checking the gleam of the silver, the glow of the floors, the glitter of the many crystal chandeliers. The servants were very reliable, of course, but she liked to see that all was ready with her own eyes. She was a very careful sort of person, too careful according to her sister, Bernadette, but she could not help being careful. Indeed, being careful had served her very well in life, and so she walked from room to sumptuous room, straightening a candle here, moving a flower there, knowing that she looked lovely as she moved through the rooms of her house, knowing that she had chosen the right gown and the perfect jewels to augment her beauty in this beautiful house, the soft whites and creams of the rooms working beautifully with her cream silk gown with its pale green beading at the hem and sleeves. Her jewels were magnificent. Her skin glowed and her eyes sparkled. She was a careful sort of woman; she carefully paid attention to each and every detail and she did not, ever, fail to appear and behave at her absolute best.

And she slept alone, dined alone, walked alone.

There was something very odd about being so very perfectly careful and having such a perfectly uneventful life. Bernadette called it dull. Antoinette called it safe, and only occasionally dull. Being safe was worth the dullness, the stillness, she was sure of it. But not quite as sure as she had been before.

The Marquis of Dutton arrived at Helston House in a foul temper, a roiling temper, a volcanic temper. All because of the Marquis of Ruan, who met him by chance at the bottom of the stair leading to the door. Dutton assumed it was by chance. With each additional word, he was less certain. Ruan seemed to have very much to say about something that was none of his concern, namely, Lady Staverton.

"You must know that, whatever happened as a result of that altercation with her butler," Ruan said, casting Dutton a speculative glance, which Dutton firmly ignored, "that, consequently, you have both been thrust into as public a dance as this town has seen since 1802. Are you quite prepared for that?"

He wanted to answer that he was prepared for anything. He said, "I am going to a rout at Helston House. For what should I be prepared?"

"Anything," Ruan said. "Everything."

"I have complete trust in my valet. I'm quite certain I am adequately prepared, Lord Ruan. I do appreciate your concern, though I am bewildered by it."

He had taken Anne, had her, possessed her. And he had not maintained possession and felt nothing so much as that she had sampled him and found him wanting. Unacceptable. Inconceivable. Inexplicable.

But it was not a dance and it was not public. It was private, intensely so, and he did not appreciate Ruan saying it was anything but.

"Being bewildered may become your personal state if you are not on your guard," Ruan said. "I will leave you to it, Lord Dutton. I wish you the best in your battle."

"There will be no battle. There is no battle," Dutton said stiffly. "But if there were, I would be found the victor."

"All hail to thee, Victor," Ruan said, smiling in a most mocking manner. With no more words spoken between them, they entered Helston House together.

The crowd was not yet a crush, for which Dutton was thankful. He was looking for Anne, had only come to see Anne, and would not be content until he had found Anne.

What was not public knowledge, he was quite certain, was that he had called at Staverton House during the normal hours for callers and not been received. He blamed that on the lack of a butler. Certainly Anne would have admitted him had she known he was calling on her.

On the other hand, why had she slapped him and had him thrown from the house?

Women were normally more predictable. Anne Staverton had never once behaved according to prediction. He could not quite fathom it. He was intrigued by it.

Dutton snorted. One could almost imagine that she was being unpredictable on purpose.

"One hears the most remarkable tales regarding butlers these days."

Dutton turned, knowing the voice and the man. The Duke of Calbourne stood at his elbow, smirking down at him. Yes, down. Calbourne was annoyingly tall. He was a duke, he was not hideous to look upon, he was a widower, and he had his heir tucked away in the country. Calbourne, in short, had everything a gentleman could wish for.

"One should never listen to rumors."

"Then one would never hear a single thing of interest," Calbourne rejoined. "I've come to the source, you must credit. Is it true? Did Lady Staverton's butler truly spit on your shoes? And did you truly knock out three of his teeth? How many blows did that take? I've heard one, which would be impressive, Dutton, and I've heard four blows to his three teeth, which is still impressive, but not nearly as much, you must admit."

"No teeth were lost. Neither his nor mine," Dutton said.

"Not yours, surely. He did not land a blow, did he?"

"No."

"You got off the first punch. Good man. First punch wins the fight, or so I found whilst up at school."

"There were no teeth, no spittle, nothing upon which to whet your appetite for scandal," Dutton said.

"No blow? No fall? No Lady Staverton swept up in your manly arms and taken up to her bed to recover?"

"If the rumor is that Lady Staverton fainted, that is entirely false. She is made of sterner stuff."

"Yes," Calbourne murmured. "I had heard that as well. Things going well there, I assume?"

"You assume much if you think I shall discuss Lady Staverton with you," Dutton said.

"No insult intended."

Dutton nodded curtly. This damned business, everyone tittering about his private affairs, about Anne, about that damned butler, about matters that were entirely and completely private.

"And there she is. Looking rather lovely, I must say," Calbourne said.

He did not need to say, but Dutton held his tongue. He was feeling increasingly possessive about Anne, and he did not enjoy the sensation in the least.

Dutton turned in the direction Calbourne was facing and saw her instantly. The room seemed to still upon her entrance, and he did think he must be imagining that. The room also seemed to turn to him, to gauge his reaction to her entrance, and he was damned certain he was not imagining that. He kept his face blank. His heart raced.

She was a damned vision. White, silver, bosom, red hair, glowing pearly skin, bosom again, sparkles at her ears, a throat like a swan, shimmering, glowing, gleaming with femininity and sexuality and elegance.

She scanned the room with a cheerful and expectant expression. He fully expected her to ignore him. She always ignored him. He had, he was forced to admit, enjoyed rattling her cage when she attempted that. Ignore him? Never. They both knew that.

He was fully prepared to play the game that was well established between them. Indeed, he considered it rather gallant, even noble, of him to do what he always did; a sidelong approach, a quiet conversation in which he promised to seduce her, a rapid and heated exchange resulting in her speedy retreat.

Anne, unfathomably, broke all the rules. Their eyes met. Across the room, through the throng of twenty or thirty between them, she smiled at him. A full, beaming, triumphant smile. A smile of recognition and delight and anticipation.

In front of the whole damned room!

How the devil was he going to shield her reputation if she smiled at him like that?

"Things *are* going well," Calbourne said, his voice dripping with wicked amusement. Damn Calbourne and his wicked amusement. "I've always thought Lady Staverton to be quite a beauty, naturally, and of a very pleasing temperament, but I never realized before this instant just how . . . charming, how warmly charming she was. How clever of you to have seen the true woman beneath the civilized veneer."

"It's no veneer," Dutton snarled.

"Isn't it? Well, I suppose you would know."

Dutton had never, at least not since yesterday, wanted to hit anyone more intensely in his life. Fortunately, or unfortunately, he could not quite work it out, Anne made her way directly to him. Directly, with no subtly whatsoever. Ten people, at least ten, stared at her as she passed them. She did not seem to mind. That was not at all like Anne. Anne was always, ever and always, circumspect.

What on earth had happened to change her?

"You truly have worked wonders with her, Dutton," Calbourne said when she was not five feet distant. "Unleashed the wanton, haven't you?"

Dutton had no time to do more than clench his fists before Anne joined them.

"How lovely to see you, Your Grace," she said.

"Lady Staverton," Calbourne said, dipping his head. "You outshine every woman in the room. I, for one, am glad to see you back in Society. But I doubt the women of the *ton* can feel the same. Beware of a dagger at your back."

"Your Grace," she said lightly, her green eyes sparking to match the emeralds at her ears, "you are a rumor-monger and a scandal hound. I shall not heed you in the slightest degree. Besides," she said, casting a playful glance at Dutton, "who says I might not enjoy a dagger at my back?"

Blast and damn. Too ribald by half. She'd have Calbourne dragging her into a Covent Garden side street if she kept this up.

"Lord Dutton," she said before he could say a word, or even think of the appropriate word to say. *Damn* was the only word he could seem to think. "What a pleasure it is to see you again. You look remarkably refreshed considering the week you've had. I was so hoping that your activities at Staverton House had not worn you out too terribly." Calbourne looked ready to have an apoplectic fit. "You may not be aware, Your Grace, but Lord Dutton did me quite an unexpected service."

"Did he?" Calbourne managed to say.

"Oh, certainly," she said. "Don't say you haven't

heard?"

"I had heard something, unsubstantiated," Cal said.

"Allow me to substantiate it fully. Oh, so very fully," Anne said, looking at him again, sparkling all over him.

Damn.

"It shames me to admit it," she said, and he was horrified to realize he had no idea what she was about to admit and what, precisely, caused her shame. Not their affair. No, it could not be that. "But I had lost, if I ever truly had, all control of my butler. He was Staverton's, you see, so fully Staverton's that I could not make him my own. He was terribly volatile and quite uncontrollable, and I was truly reaching a desperate state. Anyone could see what I had to do, and indeed, the Marquis of Ruan told me in very precise terms exactly what I should do not hours before I did it."

Ruan told her to do what? Sack the butler or take Dutton to bed? Dutton was not entirely clear upon the point. But, damn it all, he should have known Ruan would have had a hand in this somehow. The man had an unnatural interest in Anne Staverton, the direct result of his unhealthy obsession with Sophia Dalby. No matter. It was all excessively uncomfortable.

"Lord Ruan is a most observant, most reliable man," Cal said, nodding down at Anne like he meant to eat her up.

"Something of a busy body," Dutton said.

"Sometimes what a woman needs most is a man who is, who has, a busy body," Anne said. "Would you not agree to that, Lord Dutton?"

"I could not say," he said, sounding like a veritable prig with a stick up his arse.

Anne grinned at him. Cheeky girl.

"But as I was saying, Lord Ruan did lay it all out for me, and his advice seemed so wise to me and so I acted upon it. Or I was intending to, but Lord Dutton got there before me. He did me quite a good turn, I can assure you. My staffing problems are quite at an end. Well, except for needing to engage another butler. Do you have any recommendations, Your Grace? Your home is so famously well run."

"Why not ask Lord Ruan?" Dutton said. "He seems to have all the answers."

"Why, what a splendid idea! Thank you, Lord Dutton. Your Grace." And with a sweet smile, entirely too innocent to be genuine, and a dip of her red head, Anne turned on her heel and left them standing there. Dutton was quite afraid that his mouth was open.

"Tired of her so soon, Dutton?" Calbourne said. "You do seem to be pushing her at Ruan."

Calbourne shook his head sagely and walked over to the Earl of Quinton and Lady Lanreath before Dutton could think of a response.

Then again, perhaps there was no response to such insanity. Dutton followed Anne's path through the room, running her to ground as it were.

Precisely that, in point of fact.

"Lord Ruan, how timely your arrival," Anne said.

"Lady Staverton, I can think of no finer compliment than of being timely," Ruan answered, his mouth quirked into the smallest and most amiable of smiles. "How may I assist you?"

"You certainly have heard that the appalling Winthrop has been sacked, just as you advised."

"I certainly did not advise you to beat the man off the premises but if that was what required then I can only applaud that you found a man to do such service so swiftly," Ruan said.

"Lord Ruan, I do believe you are being coy," Anne said, laying a hand upon his arm, smiling up at him.

"Lady Staverton, is that an accusation or an insult?"

"A compliment, most truly," she said, laughing.

"Or a performance? Truly, most truly that," he said with a smile. "Still beating poor Lord Dutton from pillar to post, are you? If you require assistance, I shall do all I can."

"You are more than gallant."

"Accusation? Insult?"

"Observation."

"Worse and worse," he said, looking over the top of her head.

Anne turned and saw that Sophia had entered the room, Mr. and Miss Grey with her. Mr. Grey looked dangerously handsome as he surveyed the room, his dark eyes gleaming. Miss Grey looked seductively beautiful as she blatantly ignored everyone in the room, her dark brows lowered. It was most dreadfully annoying of her. But she was glad to see Sophia.

"Lord Ruan," Anne said. He looked down at her again, ignoring Sophia for the moment. It would always be for the moment; Lord Ruan was as fully caught in Sophia's net as it was possible for a man to be. She risked a glance at Dutton; he was scowling at her and paying no heed to the Duke of Calbourne, who was talking animatedly, as was his fashion. "Dear Lord Ruan," she said.

His brows raised. The Marquis of Ruan was not the sort of man one treated with easy intimacy; he was a forbidding, secretive man by every measure, but he had for so long now been a tender ally in her battle with Lord Dutton and he was so clearly devoted to Sophia that she could not but care for him in a nearly maternal fashion.

"She is a woman worthy of every consideration, every tenderness," she said.

"And she makes no secret of it," he said.

"She does not. Should she?"

"Perhaps not," he said, "but we were speaking of you and, of course, of Lord Dutton. Things have progressed, have they not? What more need could you have now? Is he not caught?"

"Lord Ruan, such plain speaking."

He smiled and waited.

"He is not caught. Not as I wish him to be."

"Ah. That explains all."

She did not care for that observation at all. She was quite certain that a single remark could not explain all, all the turmoil and tension of what she felt for Dutton, especially as she could not explain to herself what she wanted and why she was not satisfied. But she was not satisfied and she wanted . . . more. Just a bit more.

"Does it? How odd," she said, sounding very much like Sophia, and liking it. "You have done it, Lord Ruan. Simply speaking with me, being easy and comfortable in my company, smiling at me, this is how you've aided me. I do think that Lord Dutton does not like to think that you advise me, that we are on such easy terms."

"No, he would not, I shouldn't think."

"And so I thank you, Lord Ruan."

"You are very welcome, Lady Staverton. Any time you wish me to smile at you, just ask."

"You speak as if your smiles are granted often and freely, Lord Ruan. You must be aware that they are not."

"And why do you think that is, Lady Staverton?"

He looked so alone in that moment, so severe and lost beneath the expensive coat and the crisp cravat, that she said spoke from the heart, which was surely not a wise thing to do in such a setting.

"Because you have suffered something dreadful, my lord, and are, I suppose, suffering still."

Ruan did not so much as blink. He lifted her hand, kissed it briefly, his eyes looking into hers, and then left her. He moved through the room like a panther through the trees. He did not move toward where Sophia stood with her niece and nephew.

Anne's heart broke for him then, just the tiniest bit.

"There is the man who wants you," Elizabeth Grey said. "Will you let him have you?"

"I have not yet decided," Sophia answered mildly, watching Lord Ruan cross the room.

Elizabeth gave her a hard look; she had intended to

offer an insult by her remark. That Sophia had not taken the matter of her choice of men as an insult spoke to her niece's inexperience of the world, and of men, something John thought should be remedied, and so he had sent his daughter nearly kicking and screaming into the barbarism of English high society, much as Sophia had sent her slightly spoiled and very ignorant son into John's keeping two years ago.

Children could so easily become so entirely certain they knew everything worth knowing when they did not know much of anything at all. It was the duty of a parent to see to it that their children learned hard lessons in controlled situations. It was the only way to keep them alive, to be perfectly blunt.

Naturally, one was never perfectly blunt with children who believed they knew everything about anything.

She did have the satisfaction of knowing that Mark was not at all the same sheltered, ignorant, soft man she had given to John so many months ago. No, Mark had matured nicely. He should be ready to take over the duties of his title very soon now. Prying him away from the rugged freedom of the North American continent would be the next trial she would face. Who would prefer the strictures of English Society after that? Certainly Elizabeth was having a most difficult adjustment.

She did look the part, however. She was a stellar looking girl, tall and dark and proud. Elizabeth was the antithesis of what the English believed they wanted in a woman; naturally they were completely wrong in their beliefs, which was not at all out of character for them as a nation.

"Are we not here tonight to watch you seduce some man?" Elizabeth said. "Is that not the purpose of my being here? To watch and learn?"

"You are a clumsy, careless opponent," George said, his voice a rumble of anger.

Elizabeth bristled and lifted her chin.

"Darling, you are here in obedience to your father. Are you as willful as all that?" Sophia said, flicking open her fan with a snap of her wrist. "Do you believe that only Mark is lacking in knowledge of the world? This is the world, Elizabeth, a world you have yet to master and have not begun to comprehend. You may be comfortable in your ignorance. Your father, my brother, is not."

"Well said," George murmured, lowering his gaze.

Elizabeth stared directly into Sophia's eyes, her emotions well concealed. Still, Sophia could see the trace of shame and hurt that flashed briefly behind her eyes as swiftly as a crow disappearing into the pines.

"I am not as willful as all that," Elizabeth said, dipping her head slightly.

"I was certain you were not," Sophia said, turning to gaze out into the room. "Shall we greet our hostess? A most lovely woman, the daughter of one earl and the widow of another. Lady Lanreath, who does not entertain as often as she should."

"As often as she should?" Elizabeth said.

"A woman who does not entertain, who does not go out socially in this Society, disappears. She loses her standing," George said.

"Precisely," Sophia said as they reached Lady

Lanreath. "Darling, how marvelous you look. You should show London how radiant you remain once a week, at the very least." Antoinette, Lady Lanreath, did not so much as blush and she certainly did not lower her gaze like a skittish virgin. All to the good. There might be hope for Antoinette yet. "May I introduce my niece to you? She is the twin sister of George, whom you already know. This is Miss Elizabeth Grey, recently of New York."

Elizabeth dipped her head and tucked her knee, the closest thing to a curtsey she would deign to give. Antoinette smiled and said, "How lovely to meet you, Miss Grey. Your brother is quite popular among the younger set; I'm certain you shall be as well."

"The younger set? Am I to be sent to the nursery at some point this evening?" George said, kissing her hand, lingering there.

Antoinette started slightly. And then she smiled as fully as Sophia had ever seen her do.

Well done, George.

"I meant no insult, Mr. Grey," she said.

"And I will take none. If you will consent to be my nursemaid," George said, winking.

Antoinette, the lovely, remote, cool Lady Lanreath, chuckled.

"You and my brother are acquainted?" Elizabeth said. Antoinette resumed her placid composure instantly.

Ignorance at its finest. Ah, well, Elizabeth would learn. Eventually.

"Only very slightly," Antoinette said.

"And very pleasantly," George said.

"How kind of you, Mr. Grey," Antoinette said, "but don't let me keep you from your friends. I believe Lord Raithby was asking for you."

George bowed, his dimple winking and his dark eyes sparkling, "I do not need to be strongly encouraged to seek my pleasure from my friends. I do hope you consider me a friend, Lady Lanreath?"

The lady blushed. The lady was entirely deserving of a feminine flush of pleasure.

Really, something must be done about these four Helston girls. One was buried in propriety and solitude, one was flaming through Society like the veriest wanton, one was unable to make a mark on Society that created any lasting impression, and the youngest was being hidden away in the nursery long past her time to be out in Society. Lady Helston, who had quite a chilly relationship with Lord Helston, was not doing her best by her four daughters. Something simply must be done.

There was always so very much to be done. How fortunate that she was endowed with remarkable stamina.

"George, don't feel you must hover over us. I'm certain Lord Raithby would welcome your company." Lord Raithby was standing in a far corner of the room, alone, looking quite lost.

"Lord Raithby," Elizabeth said. "His title?"

"And his name," Sophia said. "He is the Earl of Quinton's heir. Humphrey, I believe, is his Christian name."

"Humphrey," Elizabeth said, smiling in black humor. "What sort of name is Humphrey?"

"A French name, darling. Now, shall we mingle? I do

think that you should meet Lady Helston, Lady Lanreath's mother, who is not a widow but one would never know it by how she conducts her life."

"She is amoral?"

"Darling, such a dour cast of mind you have. No, she behaves freely, a woman who answers to no one. When one is the English wife of a very English lord, that is a highly unusual state of affairs. Now, put on your most stern expression when I introduce you to Lady Helston. She will most appreciate it. She quite enjoys sternness and dourness. I do think you will get on famously."

Elizabeth swallowed a reluctant smile at Sophia's jab and it was thus that she was introduced to Yvonne, the Countess of Helston.

Yvonne was far older than Sophia, by fifteen years at the very least, and she had been married and in Society when Sophia was a girl in first France and then England. That Yvonne was French and that they had, by pure chance, some of the same connections in both France and England was not something she enjoyed. Yvonne had married for duty and to improve her family's situation. She had done what families require of daughters. It did not suit her nature that Sophia had achieved the same result without the same strictures of duty and protocol.

Some women could be so very petty about the most inconsequential things. What did it matter how one came to the desired result as long as it was the result which one had desired from the outset? Surely Sophia's success did not render Yvonne's success as any less desirable.

"Lady Helston, may I present my niece, Miss Elizabeth Grey?" Sophia said.

Yvonne looked quite lovely, as she always made it a habit to do, which was so very pleasant of her. She had gone gray quite early in life and the result was not dreary in the slightest; her hair was now a pure white, looking almost powdered and quite elegant, her blue eyes more pronounced against her fair hair. As a younger woman her hair had been a quite unremarkable shade of brown. White was a definite improvement and she was clever enough to know it. Her gown was of the palest shade of blue silk and her jewels were deep purple amethyst that did quite wonderful things to her light blue eyes. Yvonne had always known how to dress to her best advantage, which was one of the finest things one could say about the French.

"How do you do?" Lady Helston said politely. Also, chillingly.

Elizabeth made no response. Yvonne was not pleased by that.

This was going to be just as much fun as Sophia had hoped.

Chapter 19

Anne was having just as much fun as she had hoped. Dutton was, quite simply, confused, miserable, and angry. And she had done it all by herself.

Could life get any sweeter?

Oh, surely, yes. Most definitely, yes. She knew just how to do it, too.

Dutton was staring at her, trying not to, clearly, and failing, just as clearly, while she chatted with exaggerated animation with the third Helston girl, Camille. It was a bit odd that the Helston's had named their four daughters in alphabetical order but it was also easy to keep them straight in one's mind. Perhaps that is why they did it. Lady Camille was a very pleasant girl, a bit vapid perhaps, but girls with no experience of the world could hardly help being vapid.

Oh, she was beginning to sound more and more like Sophia. How delightful. She supposed dangling Dutton by a silken thread, a silken thread edged with spiny fish hooks, was responsible for her new perspective.

It was so very hard not to laugh out loud. But that would never do, would it? No, she must keep him guessing. In fact, she must keep them all guessing. Being obvious never served anyone well.

"And you still have no butler?" Camille said. "I don't know how we should survive without ours for a single hour."

"It is difficult," Anne said. "But having a disastrous butler is even worse. I am going to hire the future butler of Staverton House very carefully, I can assure you. I don't suppose you could recommend anyone?"

"I could ask Taylor, our butler, I suppose. Would that help?"

She did not see how. Camille, as pretty as all the Helston girls were, was as sheltered in her outlook and careful in her propriety as virgins were expected to be. She did not disappoint. She, also, did not inspire.

Dutton wouldn't give her a second glance. Not even a first glance.

Yes, it was very difficult not to laugh out loud.

"Would you? That would be most kind," Anne said. "Enough about my troubles. How are you enjoying the Season? It is not your first I seem to recall."

"No," Camille said, her expression dimming. "It is not my first. I cannot say if I enjoy it less each year or more. The giddy anticipation of the first? The lack of nerves when facing the second? I suppose it matters little whether I enjoy it or not. It is required, isn't it?"

"I suppose it is," Anne said. "Certainly the round of parties is enjoyable? The clothes? The food?" Anne said on a chuckle.

Camille smiled brightly in response, a moment that was all the sweeter for being unexpected. Why, she was a sweet girl. Being vapid was hardly her fault. She had been educated to it.

"I do enjoy riding," Camille said. "Horses, however, are not on my mother's list of events." She cast a very surreptitious glance at Lord Raithby, famously horse mad, and then looked blandly into Anne's eyes again. It had been quite, quite subtle, but as Anne had watched Lord Dutton in just such a manner for more than two years she recognized the signs quite well.

"Perhaps she will allow you to add an event or two of your own? If you are very, very compliant and talk to very, very many eligible men?" Anne said.

More and more like Sophia. What was she doing, encouraging this slip of a girl, her inexperience and timidity shining out of her like a bonfire, to manipulate both her mother and whatever eligible men she could snare, however briefly?

"You do not know Lady Helston as well as I do," Camille said, showing the first glimmer of spark.

"No, I'm certain that's true," Anne said, "but it is a truism that if you can please her then she will be more ready to please you."

"That does not work quite the same with horses," Camille said in a musing tone.

She was quite a pretty girl. Certainly some man could be made to pay attention to her, in full view of the redoubtable Lady Helston.

"What have you to got to lose?" Anne said.

"Nothing I care to keep," Camille said brightly, her chin lifted, her lovely eyes sparkling.

Oh, dear. That sounded nearly dangerous.

"Lady Camille, I am not encouraging you to any dire deeds, to anything that will harm your reputation. You must guard your reputation. It is easily damaged and . . ." Anne couldn't think what to say after that. She was no Sophia. A little push to help the girl enjoy her Season and she'd somehow shoved her into a Covent Garden byway.

"Please don't worry," Camille said, laying a hand briefly on Anne's arm. Anne could not possibly have been more alarmed. "I shall do nothing that causes me a moment of regret."

That was not quite reassuring.

"Lady Camille," she said.

"Yes, Lady Staverton?"

"It is . . . that is, the world is not safe."

"My world *is* safe, Lady Staverton. Too safe, I begin to think."

Oh, dear! Worse and worse.

"I do think I've mislead you somehow," Anne said. "I should hate to see you come to harm as a result of a very innocent, perhaps ill-conceived conversation."

"Lady Staverton, I am hardly so imprudent." Camille's beautiful green eyes looked as hard as jade.

"Of course not," Anne said, not believing a word of it.

"If you will excuse me, I must say hello to my sister."

"Of course," Anne said, not bothering to ask which sister. All four were in attendance, even though the youngest, Delphine, was not yet *out*. It was only a rout at her sister's. She need not be *out* for that.

As soon as Camille had moved across the room, Anne looked for Sophia. She simply must have help. She had pushed when she should have pulled, spoken when she should have kept silent, urged when she should have cautioned. Sophia must undo what she might have done.

She was just managing Dutton. How did she think herself capable of managing more than that? She couldn't even manage to acquire a competent butler!

But she did not see Sophia. She saw Dutton, standing not ten feet from her, talking to Bernadette Paignton, the second of the Helston daughters and quite, quite indiscreet in her many, many affairs, and to Mr. George Prestwick, who was always so very, very pleasant.

Anne had no desire to speak to any of them. Not even Dutton. Not speech, certainly. But she did have something she wanted of Dutton, the precise thing, and she had come prepared to get it. She was in the exact state of mind to require it right now.

Anne moved a foot or two closer to the arrogant Lord Dutton, caught his ever wandering eye, reached into her pearl reticule and drew out a button. His button. One of the many buttons she had torn from his waistcoat earlier. She had such lovely plans for his buttons. Each one was to be her calling card, her reminder and her command.

She held the button up between her fingers, saw his eyes widen slightly, and then she dropped the button so that it rolled toward him. With not so much as a lifting of her brows or the shadow of a smile, she walked out of the room toward the door that led to the stair hall. She knew he would follow her. His very blood would demand it.

The hall was formal and large, marble and filigreed iron. It was colossal and quite public. Candlelight made pools of warm gold, shadows were dark fingers that touched golden light, and the hum of conversation reached upward and downward. No dark corners, no seclusion.

Perfect.

She crossed the marble, walked up the steps until she stood beneath a massive candelabra, the light bathing her, her shoulders resting against the wall, her expression as bored and her posture as casual as the lightskirts she had seen throughout her childhood. This was a pose she knew. This was a game she knew.

Dutton, dear, predictable Dutton, opened the door and nearly slammed it behind him, his hard blue gaze piercing her instantly. He held the button up between his fingers. She lifted one shoulder lazily, staring at him boldly.

"What game is this?" he snarled, walking toward her with long steps, his thigh muscles outlined against his trousers. She would not allow herself the pleasure of a sigh of appreciation nor of anticipation.

"You know this game well, my lord. Do you dare to pretend otherwise?" she said, her voice icy with both contempt and indifference. She spread her legs slightly, balanced upon the stair, knowing that the light lit her hair like a torch. "Come. Do as you are bid. I have paid you. Now tender your service. I do not like to be kept waiting."

He took the stairs two at a time, his hair falling forward over his exquisite brow, the button clenched in his fist.

"You play the bitch in heat and I am to be your rutting stag?"

"Not difficult duty, is it? Have you not played this part for years?"

He took her face in his hands, lifted her face to his. He was not gentle. She did not need gentleness from him. Not now.

"Bitch," he said, kissing her brutally, an invasion of heat and tongue and fury.

She pushed him away with both hands. "Is that meant to insult me? You must try harder than that."

He took a step back upon the wide marble stair, his

blue eyes a flame of passion and rage.

"Stand and deliver. That is all I require of you," she said. "Now. Upon this moment. Can you do it, Lord Dutton? Can you give me what I want?"

"I'll be taking what I want. I always get what I want. You know that by now," he said.

Anne lifted her skirts to her knees, a casual jerk of her wrists, her face impassive. "You will tell yourself what you must. Be quick about it. I don't have all night. There are people I want to enjoy a pleasant conversation with."

She did not say *you are not one of them*, but it was in the air between them, all the same.

He yanked at the buttons on his trousers, lifted her skirts to her hips with one hand, and pushed her left knee out with the other. He lunged into her with all the finesse of a fourteen year old boy with his first woman, all banging motion and grunting breath, brutally losing himself in her in the act of possessing her.

He gave himself to her. He took nothing she did not take twice-fold from him.

She said nothing. She closed her eyes, silently, invisibly savoring the moment. She had dreamed of this for years. This, and more. More she might not have, but she could have this. She would have this. For as long as she wanted it. She would not let him control their affaire. She had started it when she wanted to and she would end it when the time came. She, not he. She would not relinquish control, not to him. He was too dangerous for that.

"You are mad," he said, his breath against her cheek, his voice hoarse and low. A shiver of longing, even now,

now when he was still buried in her, coursed through her blood. "Do you want people to think you a common whore?"

She pushed against his shoulders and he slipped out of her. "I am Lady Staverton. I am neither common nor a whore. I am a lady of the peerage seeking her amusement with a peer of the realm. How could you possibly be confused about that, Lord Dutton? Now, if you will excuse me." Her skirts had dropped down to her ankles, her hair had not been mussed in the slightest, not even the seams on her gloves had been turned. She looked as untouched and unaffected as possible. He would positively loathe that.

Perfect.

He was buttoning his trousers, his hair a shock of gleaming brown over his brow, touching his arched eyebrow like a caress, when a voice from the wide hall at the bottom of the stair said,

"Anne? Anne Chester? Can it be you? You are just as I remember you."

That voice. She knew that voice. She looked down the stair and saw a man and in her mind saw the youth he had been. The princeling who had been sold her virginity.

Why did nothing, ever, go as planned?

⁂

To be interrupted, now, was not to plan.

Dutton looked down the stair to that unwelcome voice. Know it? No, he did not know either the voice or the man. Unwelcome it still surely was. He had not quite finished with Anne, Anne with her harlot games clothed in aristocratic iciness. It was a game and he was being drawn into it, even if he was not the sort of man to be played, and especially not by a woman. But who was this man who interrupted them, and how did he know Anne, and what, by God, did he mean by that *just as I remember you* remark? Anne looked exactly like a woman who had just been tumbled, hard.

"Vasily," Anne said, her green eyes shining, her cheeks pink. Dutton was certain her shining eyes and pinked cheeks were the result of his attentions, not the mere name *Vasily*. "Prince," she added, walking down the wide marble steps like a queen greeting a courtier. "What an unexpected pleasure. What brings you to London?"

"The weather," he said with a smile that crept from one side of his mouth to the other. It was a damned annoying smile.

Anne laughed and held out her hand. Vasily kissed it. He did not kiss her hand like a courtier. "Yes, I remember well how fond you are of London weather."

The moment was awkwardly intimate. Dutton would bear not an instant more of it.

"We have not had the pleasure," he said, bowing crisply. "I am Lady Staverton's escort for the evening."

"Excuse me. My manners were quite overwhelmed by my surprise," Anne said, brushing her hand against his arm in something quite near to a blow. "The Marquis of Dutton. Lord Dutton, Prince Vasily Borisovich Yusupov."

"Lady Staverton?" Yusupov said.

"Prince?" Dutton said in the same instant.

"Prince Vasily is an old acquaintance," Anne said.

"Certainly more than that," Yusupov said in an tone of voice Dutton did not care for in the slightest.

"Lord Dutton is also an acquaintance, Vasily," Anne said, her eyes twinkling. "I married Lord Staverton, loved him devotedly, and am now his lonely widow. You know what is said of lonely widows."

"That they are not lonely long," Yusupov said, quite slyly, too.

"Just so," Dutton said. "If you will excuse us?"

"Oh, we can't abandon Vasily so ruthlessly, Lord Dutton. Shall we all not walk in together?" And so saying, she linked her arms through both of theirs, Dutton tugged along most harshly, Yusupov sailing along quite effortlessly, Anne smiling broadly.

A true bitch, this one.

Dutton could not help but smile in wry appreciation.

Sophia smiled in appreciation when she noted Anne entering the salon with both Lord Dutton and Prince Vasily Borisovich Yusupov on her arms. She remembered Prince Vasily from his first trip to London, and of course, from Anne's confession of what her mother had done to earn a few more pounds to see her through another month. It had not been well done. Emma Chester had not had the iron will and fortitude required to make the best of mothers, or the best of women, as to that. She had been lovely, but so weak. So very weak, so easily distracted, so pleased by small and fleeting things, and that did not lead a woman into any sort of pleasurable situation. Could she not have requested the deed to even one first rate property in return for Anne's innocence?

Ah well. Some people really did not possess a good head for business.

"Who is that?" Lady Camille said.

"Prince Vasily Borisovich Yusupov," Sophia said. "A Russian prince of immense wealth and lineage. His ancestors were Khans of Russia."

"He is married?" Lady Delphine said, coming very close to licking her lips. Clever girl. Vasily was an astoundingly handsome man.

"I don't believe so," Sophia said.

"How does Toni know *him*?" Camille said.

"There is your answer," Sophia said, smiling in pure amusement. What an interesting evening this was developing into.

"Is that . . . why, I believe that's the 4th Earl of Lanreath," Delphine said. "Isn't it? I haven't seen him since I was an infant."

"You were twelve," Camille said.

"Nine," Delphine said. "Perhaps ten."

"That's impossible, Del!" Camille snapped, lifting her bosom to lovely heights. "Toni married the 3rd earl in 1795 and you were, well, yes, you were ten. Still, hardly an infant."

"As far as he was concerned, I was," Delphine said with an appreciative sigh. Sophia had difficulty not laughing outright.

Camille did laugh. Softly, delicately, but she did laugh. Camille looked more like her mother than Lady Helston's other daughters. Camille at twenty-two had the blue eyes and brown hair of her mother, but an intensified version. Her eyes were deepest, darkest blue and her hair was just a shade away from black. She had the classical beauty of Antoinette and something of Antoinette's subdued serenity, but perhaps not the deliberate obedience of Antoinette? How else to explain why the girl had not yet married? Antoinette had married where her father directed her, a girl of eighteen marrying a man with a son and heir who was nineteen. It was done, and not uncommonly, but was it desirable? A young man and a young wife, thrown together in the same household, an aging man standing between them.

But Robert Donnington, the 4th Earl of Lanreath, had not been in the same household. As Sophia remembered it, he had moved out a week before the 3rd earl's marriage and not been back since.

Until now.

"Perhaps he will see you differently now," Sophia said. "It seems quite obvious that he has come to Town to find a wife."

The two younger Helston girls did not preen, which would have been quite logical, even exemplary. No, they shrank inward.

"But what about Toni?" Camille said.

"He can't do that to Toni!" Delphine said in the same instant.

"Lady Lanreath must find a new home," Sophia said. "I'm certain she cannot have imagined she would stay at

Lanreath House indefinitely."

"She likes it here," Delphine said.

"And who would not?" Sophia said. "Yet it belongs to Lanreath and his future wife, as it should, would you not agree?"

They said nothing, the pair of them. They did look at Lanreath with looks of both speculation and disapproval.

"Do you believe Prince Vasily is in Town to find a wife as well?" Delphine asked.

"I can lay claim to no special knowledge of their plans," Sophia said. "However, I can't think why either man should not marry, and it is the Season, and they are both highly eligible."

"And he is handsome," Delphine said. Sophia was not certain to which man she was referring. It hardly mattered as both were very handsome indeed. And available.

Lanreath was darkly handsome; tall and lean with dark brown hair falling in very loose waves around his ears and neck, a windblown look which suited his fine features and dark brows. His eyes were almond shaped and of the deepest brown. He looked a man of field, wood, and horse, and so he was, by every rumor of him.

Vasily's hair was also of the windswept style, but of the darkest blond and of a more definite wave. His brows and eyelashes were brown, his nose of the most regal shape imaginable, and his eyes were slices of frigid ice blue.

Lanreath was a man to make a woman sigh.

Vasily was a man to make a woman gasp.

"He's very well-endowed," Sophia said.

Camille gasped and Delphine sighed. Well, what to make of that?

"His worth, of course. He is quite well off," Sophia said.

"Lanreath or the prince?" Delphine said.

"Both," Sophia said. "And isn't that convenient? Now all that's left is for you to choose. Not a simple choice, I grant you. They are quite a remarkable pair. But then, so are you."

"Which?" Camille said, her dark blue eyes shuttered. "Which of us?"

"Both, darling. Both of you. Isn't it obvious?"

"I'm afraid not," Camille said.

"I'm afraid I don't know him," George Prestwick said to Elizabeth Grey.

"The taller man is the 4th Earl of Lanreath. The other man is one of the Yusupovs, I believe, though I can't determine which one," Ruan said.

"Lanreath," Elizabeth said. "A relation of our hostess?"

"Her late husband's son and heir," Ruan said.

"Her son by marriage," George Prestwick said.

"They are of an age," Elizabeth said.

"Yes," Ruan said, his face a mask of bland urbanity.

Elizabeth shrugged lightly and turned away from the two men, away from Lady Staverton and Lord Dutton, who had entered the salon at their side. Lady Staverton looked as she always did, perhaps a bit pinker. Lord Dutton looked like a warrior facing a hated enemy with a broken knife. Whatever was happening between Anne Staverton and Dutton, Anne was winning. She could not help but be cheered by that.

This society, this English Society, was weighted in every possible way toward the man. She did not like it. She did not see any reason to pretend to.

"I think no ill thoughts," she said. "A man and woman may be of an age and not seek to share a bed. You and my aunt are proof of that, are you not?"

Ruan, who did have the face and manner of a warrior, did not flinch, blink, or smile. He did not react in any way at all. A good warrior. A stout warrior's heart. She liked that about him. Sophia probably liked that about him as well.

Why were they not together? Sophia was not particular, that was obvious, and Lord Ruan was interested, though not obviously so. Even so, she could read the signs. And George had told her a few things in private. That had helped separate the wheat from the chaff.

"You are a stranger here, Miss Grey," Ruan said. "I would advise you to learn the ways of the land you inhabit."

"Or?" she said.

"Or you may not survive," he said, his green eyes as sharp as honed steel.

The moment stretched out between them, a moment of silent and humming hostility. She did not mind it. She sensed he did not mind it. Mr. Prestwick did.

"Have you had to adapt to a foreign land, Lord

Ruan?" Prestwick asked, his dark eyes shining with aggressive merriment.

Ruan nodded and looked away, his gaze skimming to where Sophia stood talking to the young Lord Lanreath and the woman who shared his title and his house. Sophia did not so much as twitch her fan. Still, Elizabeth knew that Sophia was aware of Ruan's attention. It was in the air between them, like smoke trails from a hidden fire.

"I have never yet been out of England, though I did once come close upon the border to Wales," Prestwick said. "I think that should count for something on the topic of foreign lands and adaptability."

Ruan smiled and said, "And how did you adapt?"

"I learned a few words of the language," Prestwick said. "A most complicated language. So very many consonants."

Ruan laughed. It transformed his face. His eyes, his hard green eyes, stayed hard and sharp, the gleam of humor washing over them like water over stone.

She could understand, grudgingly, why Sophia was drawn to this man. He was a man tested, forged and hardened. A man at home in this world, at the top of the hierarchy in this world, and yet she could see that he would rise in any world, any place. He was a man who would fight and win. A man who would fight even when losing. A man who could laugh in both victory and defeat.

A man such as this one did not come often into the world.

This was a man to mark.

Why did Sophia not take him? He was hers for the

taking.

And why was that? Why did Sophia have the power to take any man, this hard and experienced man, when other women did not?

She had a power, a strange power, and Elizabeth did not understand where it came from, how it was wielded and the circumstances when it was not. Such power was a weapon. All weapons must be used in their proper way, in their ideal time.

And that was when she understood for the first time what her father had wanted her to learn.

How to wield a woman's weapon, when to unleash and when to curb a woman's power.

Elizabeth took a deep breath and smiled. Now she had only to choose her sparring partner.

Chapter 20

"I am not going to spar with you about this, Mama," Antoinette said in an undertone. "Certainly Lanreath may use his home any time he wants."

"And if he does, where does that leave you?" Yvonne said.

"It is a large house."

"It is unseemly. You are too well-matched in age."

"You forget, I am above reproach," Toni said. It was said with some despair, though she knew her mother would not hear it.

"You should marry again and then you would not find yourself in this position."

"The only position I find myself in is that I have two extra men at my rout. I hardly find that onerous."

"I've heard of the Yusupovs. Fabulously wealthy, and known collectors of the better things in life."

That sounded so like her mother. Yvonne had been born to the French aristocracy, of one of the best and first families, in the precisely wrong time in French history. Her family's fortune had been consumed by the revolutions in America and France and the title, if one dared to use a title in France today, had become more burden than benefit. Her family, wisely by every account, had married her out of France and into England by way of Helston. That should have made Yvonne very happy.

It had not and it did not.

Since Antoinette had been married to suit her family and its goals, her own goals having been considered quite meaningless, she was sympathetic to her mother's general dissatisfaction. In fact, on her worse days, she feared she was coming to resemble her mother greatly.

She did not wish to resemble her mother in any meaningful fashion.

She did not want to be dissatisfied, disagreeable, or disapproving. At the moment, she was only despondent and despairing. Oh, yes, she recognized that much about herself. She knew the problem; it was only that she could not enact the solution.

She simply must take a lover. If it became absolutely necessary, a husband.

She did not imagine it would ever become necessary. A comfort, that.

"He's quite remarkable looking, isn't he?" Toni said.

"Isn't he just?" Sophia said, stepping into their small circle of conversation.

"How a man looks is the least of his accomplishments," Mama said.

"Darling, you are not as old as all that, are you?" Sophia said with a sly smile.

Toni swallowed a smile.

"I should hope I am wise enough to measure a man's worth by more than the breadth of his shoulders," Mama retorted.

"Oh, you noticed that, did you?" Sophia said. "He is quite broad through the shoulder, isn't he? And so deliciously narrow at the hip. And those eyes, like an arctic wolf, aren't they? He almost makes me shiver."

"But, of course, you would never do anything as coarse as that," Yvonne said.

"I am a woman, Lady Helston. I would be a fool to deny myself a simple erotic shiver, wouldn't I? Not one scandal was ever made over a shiver," Sophia said, looking at Toni encouragingly.

Antoinette was quite certain that Sophia was encouraging her to have an affair with Prince Vasily.

Well, and why not?

She walked over to Lanreath and Prince Vasily, to greet them, of course, Mama and Sophia trailing her like a pair of hounds. Let them trail. It was her house and her party. She was the hostess. She had to greet them, didn't she?

Of course she did.

"Lord Lanreath, what a pleasure to see you again," Antoinette said. "It has been too long."

"It has," he said. The 4th Earl of Lanreath was quite like his father in that he was a man not given to gushing conversation. He was unlike his father in every other respect. "I hope I do not inconvenience you?"

"Hardly that," she said. "This is your home. I am your guest. I hope, in coming home to a houseful of guests, that does not inconvenience you?"

How careful she was being. It was habit, surely. She had met Robert at her wedding breakfast, her husband's head bent over his plate, talking and spewing bits of egg and beefsteak out upon the gleaming walnut table. She had avoided looking at her new husband, his balding head pink with either the joys of gluttony or the joys of marriage. Gluttony, she came to believe. She had, after her first look at Robert, so slim and dark and solemnly handsome, avoided looking at him as well. It would never do to create an impossible situation with one's son by marriage.

"Hardly that," he said, echoing her. "May I introduce Prince Vasily Borisovich Yusupov."

"Prince," she said, dipping a curtsey. "My mother,

Lady Helston. And this is Lady Dalby."

Prince Vasily bowed crisply, dipping his dark blond head, and upon raising his gaze, his pale blue eyes shone at Sophia. Of course they did. For Antoinette, staid and respectable Toni, barely a glance.

Truly, something must be done. Immediately. She was far too young to be overlooked, and in her own home, too. Her borrowed home.

Mama might have a point. Something must be done about that as well.

"You host a sparkling gathering, Lady Lanreath," Vasily said. "I am honored to be included amongst their number. Even accidentally."

The prince spoke English flawlessly, the result of a stellar education, no doubt. His manners were perfect, perfectly English, as well, yet there was something about him that whispered of the exotic. Perhaps it was merely his honey gold tossed hair and chillingly blue eyes. Toni, not given to erotic speculation, had an instant's vision of him lying upon the sheets of her bed.

She shivered.

"Perhaps it is not so much accident as destiny," Sophia said, nearly purring.

Vasily's eyes, and Lanreath's, shifted to Sophia. "Do you believe in destiny, Lady Dalby?" Vasily asked.

"It is a romantic notion," Lanreath said. "I had not thought Lady Dalby to be a romantic."

Sophia smiled, a dark smile full of mischief and seduction, her black eyes sparkling. Toni simply must teach herself how to smile in more than mild and forgettable pleasure. She quite clearly had no layers, no nuance. It was inexcusable. Still, neither her father nor her husband had wanted nuance from her. She might be excused for a lack of encouragement in pursuing the art.

"You had not heard that Sophia Dalby is not all things to all men?" Sophia said. "You really must leave the wood more often, Lord Lanreath."

Lanreath, whom she had never seen smile, let alone laugh, chuckled and encompassed Sophia, and only Sophia, in his warm, dark gaze.

Toni felt as sexless, as invisible, as a pine plank floor.

She could feel Mama's displeasure at the turn in the conversation, and that Sophia had, by a word, become its focal point, and so, before Mama could say something harsh and before she could heed caution, her constant companion, Toni opened her mouth and said, "Yes, truly, you must and should, Robert. You have been much missed. In Society," she added, caution have caught her by the heel and demanded compliance.

Robert, the Earl of Lanreath, whom she had never called by anything other than his title, lifted his dark brows slightly, so very slightly, and looked at her in something not unlike amazement. Well, really, she did know his name. And they were family, after all. She might call him by his given name and not be thought ill-bred.

"To be missed," Sophia said. "Is that not the most intimate of experiences?"

"The most intimate? Surely not," Vasily said, quite inappropriately. Perhaps he had not been beautifully and flawlessly educated in the English manner after all.

"Prince Vasily," Sophia said as Mama was opening her mouth to speak, "you are far too literal, I fear. Or perhaps I hope. I have not yet decided which." Her tone was a bit severe, but her smile was the precise opposite. Toni simply *must* do something about the limitations of her smile. "How did you and Lord Lanreath meet? Not in the hunting field, I shouldn't think. You don't seem the sort of man to spend hours alone with his weapon."

It was quite saucily said. Mama looked quite red in the cheek.

"Yes, where did you meet?" Toni said. "At school?"

Lanreath blinked. It was a very direct question and was surely no one's concern, yet something must be said to hold Mama in check and to keep Lanreath and Vasily at her side. Yes, that was her goal. It was quite bold of her to admit it, even if it was only to herself.

"Not the hunting field, as you surmised, Lady Dalby," Lanreath said. "Though Vasily is a most accomplished hunter."

"No doubt of that," Sophia said suggestively.

"Not at school," Lanreath said.

"Because one of you spent so little time in study. We shall not embarrass either of you by guessing which," Sophia said. Why, she had turned Toni's rude question into a game of sorts. How lovely of her.

"At the Museum?" Toni said. "Appreciating the art?"

"You are not far off the mark, Lady Lanreath," Vasily said, his blue eyes touching her face briefly, intimately. It felt intimate, at least to her. Had he meant to be intimate?

She was a fool with men. She understood nothing.

"The Reading Room?" Mama said. Well done, Mama! She had not known Mama had it in her to play, at anything. She found even cards dull.

"No, though I do know how to read," Vasily said with a smile.

"In four languages," Lanreath said.

"Is that how you spend your time? Reading together?" Sophia said. "I am shocked, I must confess."

"I had not thought it possible for Lady Dalby to be shocked," Lanreath said, his dark eyes considering Sophia with far too much interest.

"You must not believe every rumor of me, Lord Lanreath," Sophia said. "Only the salacious ones."

Lanreath laughed, a burst of pure, involuntary joy. Vasily grinned at Sophia as if he would carry her off in the next instant.

"Which languages, Prince Vasily?" Toni asked, anything to break the web Sophia was casting over the two men. Mama made a noise of approval.

"The usual ones," Vasily said. "Russian, French, English, of course, and Greek."

"Greek? Is that usual now?" Mama said.

"It is for a Russian," Vasily said easily. Mama's tone had been a bit abrupt. Was Toni's tone abrupt? Was she how Mama had been twenty-five years ago?

Very possibly.

"Greek, yes," Sophia said. "You look very much like a Greek scholar."

Of course Prince Vasily looked absolutely nothing like a scholar, Greek or otherwise. He looked a lean and lethal hunter, a feral wolf in the blue white of a Siberian winter, or what she imagined a wolf in Siberia would look like. She had never been farther east than the Rhine.

"Thank you, Lady Dalby," Vasily said. "A most unusual compliment. I shall cherish it."

"All compliments should be cherished, Prince Vasily," Sophia said. "There can never be enough compliments in one's life."

"Surely a diet of compliments would turn the strongest of stomachs," Mama said.

"If an experiment is required, I shall gladly volunteer," Toni said, quite proud of herself for being so bold. It was quite unlike her, and that could only be to the good.

"What are we volunteering for? If it concerns Prince Vasily and Lord Lanreath, I certainly wish to be included," Bernadette said.

Toni sighed inwardly and turned to welcome her sister to their number. Toni might have sighed inwardly. Mama sighed quite audibly.

Bernadette, the dowager Countess of Paignton, was becoming something of a scandal. Well, actually, she was already a scandal. She had become a scandal through no fault of her own but that of her husband's wild behavior. To be thought wild in London was a feat indeed. Paignton had gambled lavishly and been wildly indiscriminate in his affairs. Indiscriminate and public. He had died a very public death in a duel with a very angry husband. Bernie, who had never been what anyone would call a sweet child, had exploded within the bounds of her marriage, copying Paignton's behavior to the best of her ability.

Bernie, most unfortunately, proved quite an able student in the art of debauchery.

"Lady Paignton," Lanreath said, nodding his head.

As far as Toni knew, Lanreath had been in Bernie's company less than a single handful of times. Of course, Toni rarely left the house. "Have you been introduced to Prince Vasily? He is an old friend of mine."

"Under what circumstances they became friends, there is still much mystery," Sophia said.

"Are not all friendships mysterious?" Mama said. "Who can explain why we prefer one person over another?"

"I can," Bernie said, staring boldly at Vasily. Bernie, for all that could be said against her, did have the one trait that Toni was coming to admire more and more fervently: Bernie was not at all intimidated by Mama.

"And probably have," Lady Staverton said, joining them. Anne Staverton looked quite unusually beautiful, and she always looked beautiful. She had left the room a beautiful woman and reentered the room a short while later looking completely ravishing. Toni would never had thought a trip to the necessary could inspire such a transformation.

"Anne," Vasily said, his light eyes burning like blue fire as he looked at Lady Staverton.

Really, first Bernie, who always looked as if she had just crawled out of some man's bed, and therefore snared every man's attention for a mile circumference, and now Anne Staverton, who had always seemed such a pleasant, mild sort of woman. Until now. What had happened to turn Anne from sedate to seductive? She surely looked the epitome of seduction.

Toni knew she had never, not even in the midst of losing her virginity, looked even remotely seductive.

What was *wrong* with her?

"Vasily," Lady Staverton said, smiling up at him with far more intimacy than the occasion warranted. "I still can't believe you're here. Are you staying long?"

"Longer now. My plans were loose. They are becoming more firm."

"Longer and firmer. The finest and most time-tested of compliments," Sophia said, again, quite bawdily. "Well done, Lady Staverton. You put the rest of us to shame."

"Shame, most assuredly," Lady Helston said. "Antoinette, Bernadette, I do believe that Camille and Delphine need us."

"I'm certain my sisters are fine," Toni said, digging in her heels, metaphorically and physically. "You go, if you care to. I would like to catch up with Lord Lanreath. We are family, after all."

"Yes, Mama, you go on," Bernie said, coming dangerously close to making a shooing motion with her fingers. She didn't, because no one, not even Bernie, was that foolish.

Mama, her pale blue eyes dangerously bland, Mama was at her most explosive when she appeared most bland, nodded and moved away across the room directly to the side of Camille, who stood in conversation with the Indian girl, Miss Grey. That was almost certainly a conversation that should be chaperoned. Where Delphine was, Toni could not tell. At least she wasn't with the Iroquois. Everyone knew the Iroquois were the most savage, the most fierce, the most ruthless of people.

How Sophia Dalby fit into that description Toni had never been quite certain. Sophia always seemed quite perfectly sophisticated and well-bred, at least once she had become Lady Dalby, and as that had been for two decades now, Toni didn't see any reason to look further back than that. It was well rumored that Sophia made a spectacular enemy, but Toni, who had no enemies, did not think it a bad thing to be a fearsome enemy. Certainly, if she had any, she'd want to be feared by them. Having enemies otherwise would be a most dangerous situation.

Toni did everything in her power to avoid dangerous situations.

It was very likely supremely cowardly of her. Perhaps she would become more seductive, more alluring, if she possessed the smallest pinch of danger in her aspect?

She feared that was quite beyond her.

"I fear she has moved beyond you," George Grey said to Dutton.

Dutton, having been knocked cold by Grey two years ago, did not enjoy his company in the slightest.

"Mind your own affairs," Dutton said.

"Don't have any to mind," Grey said, leaning his shoulders against the cream walls, staining them with bear grease, or whatever else the savages bedecked themselves with. "Yours are entertaining enough."

"Bugger off," Dutton said.

Grey smiled slightly, not enough to show his incongruous dimple.

"He is something to her. Maybe only a prod," Grey said, looking across the wide room to Anne and that Russian. They were staring into each other's eyes like long lost cousins.

No. Not cousins.

Lovers.

Hell and damn.

"I'm no ox to need prodding."

"Asses need prodding," Grey said. "Stop being an ass."

Dutton stiffened. "I take insult from no man."

"You're taking insult from a woman. From her. Right now," Grey said. "I'm trying to help you, you know."

"You're Sophia's pawn."

"No," Grey said, his black eyes deep and dangerous. "Her ally. At times. If the work suits me. In this, I am for you. This is a man's game. I want a man to win it."

"I've won it."

"Doesn't look like you've won anything."

"Anne is mine. She has always been mine."

"Does she know that?"

It didn't appear so.

Damn women for being so difficult. Though, in truth, he had always found women to be the most easily managed of creatures, certainly not nearly as challenging as a fine bit of horseflesh. Anne, damned Anne, had never fallen in line with either his expectations or his experience.

What the devil was wrong with the woman that she couldn't behave as any normal woman would?

He'd taken her, more than once, and she didn't give

any appearance of having been taken. In truth, he felt he'd been taken. And that was flatly unacceptable. Unnatural, too.

"She will," Dutton said, walking away from Grey without any further word on the subject. As if he would confide in an Indian.

"I suppose you'll rush over to Lady Staverton and encourage her to confide in you," Lady Helston said.

"Lady Staverton does not need any help from me," Sophia said, watching Anne bewitch Prince Vasily and bedevil Lord Dutton in one graceful move.

"I'm shocked," Lady Helston said, sipping her champagne. "I had thought you to be most anxious to involve yourself in everyone's---"

"Affairs?"

"Concerns," Yvonne said.

Sophia looked askance at Yvonne Helston, at her flawless profile, gone a bit soft about the jaw now, at her brilliantly white hair piled in abundant abandon upon her head. She was a woman who never came at something directly when an indirect route would serve. It was the French way and Sophia understood the French way very well indeed.

"It is true that I do enjoy being at the center of things. I have always believed that it is a woman's natural place in the ordering of the world, and I always act in accordance with my beliefs."

Yvonne grimaced in a most polite fashion and took

another sip of champagne, her gaze on her daughter, Antoinette. "That is your belief? You truly are no Englishwoman."

"Neither are you, darling."

Yvonne made a noise in her throat that was nearly a snort. Sophia suspected she was amused, and horrified at being amused. The orchestra Lady Lanreath had hired began a concerto by Corelli. Sophia had always enjoyed the sprightly sentimentality of Corelli. Such musical optimism was unfailing amusing.

"My daughters are most assuredly Englishwomen. To the bone, it would appear," Yvonne said. It was not said pleasantly. Sophia hardly faulted her.

"It is the price one pays when marrying into the English nobility," Sophia said. "Like all bargains, it is not a perfect solution."

"Your daughter did well enough."

"Darling, surely you are not ignorant of the details of Caro's relationship with the Earl. It was a most spectacularly lurid courtship. I am most proud of her for succeeding so well at it."

"I had heard something," Yvonne said. "I dare not credit gossip, Lady Dalby."

"But one simply must credit gossip, else what is the purpose of it if not to drive certain points home, illuminating certain facts and obscuring others? Gossip, as you well know, is a most effective weapon."

"A slippery weapon, easily fumbled."

"Not by an experienced woman of the world. Not by one such as you."

"Or you," Yvonne said, looking at Sophia with a clear and calculating gaze.

"What a lovely compliment. Thank you."

"It is not lightly given."

"As I am aware," Sophia said.

The single women in the room, Englishwomen all, watched the men in the room. Watched avidly, watched timidly, watched hopelessly. It was most amusing, pathetically so. The young widows in the room, also Englishwomen, did not watch. They engaged. They flirted, they speculated, they planned, and they took action. True, some took action more overtly and more boldly than others, Antoinette and Bernadette being two such contrasts, but they took action.

There was one exception to this, of course. One not so slight exception. Elizabeth Grey. She was not English. It made all the difference. Which was not to say that her differences were necessarily of a positive nature, but at least she was not timid and she was certainly not hopeless. The furthest thing from it.

But it was Anne Staverton, widow, English, who held the eye. She was holding the men in the room by the, well, not the beard. Or not *that* beard.

"She used to be more timid, did she not?" Yvonne said, watching Anne smile at Vasily and ignore Lord Dutton extremely pointedly.

"Before she was a titled widow, yes, of course," Sophia said. "As you and I both know well, her marriage has changed everything for her."

"She is wise enough to know it," Yvonne said.

"Naturally. Anne is nothing if not sharp."

"A matter of necessity, wasn't it?"

"And when is it not a matter of necessity?" Sophia said, casting Yvonne an amused look.

"I concede the point," Yvonne said with a stiff smile. Yvonne was a very stiff sort of woman. Sophia expected that Lord Helston had had very little to do with it.

Sophia merely nodded and took a sip from her glass. She did not look at Lord Ruan where he stood looking very solemn and mysterious, his rugged face half hidden in shadow. He stood talking to Lord Quinton, who was doing most of the talking, which was not at all like him. Whatever could they be talking about?

As if she didn't know.

⁂

"She won't heed me," Quinton said, looking a bit frantic and not at all like himself.

"If not you, then certainly not me," Ruan said, indicating by a suggestion of movement that he would like another drink. It was delivered by a well-shod footman in less than a moment. "You might be making too much of it."

"I am not the sort of man to make too much of anything."

"I'll concede the point."

"I don't require you to concede the point. I ask that you do something," Quinton said. "You clearly do not understand what Aysgarth is capable of."

"He can't be worse than Weslin."

The Earl of Westlin had first been Sophia's protector and then her most avid enemy for more than two decades. That he had died while Sophia was in

North America was the best reason for the absence of a rumor that she done him in; not that he had deserved a natural death, but death was rarely just and equitable. Pity.

"He's of a different type entirely," Quinton said, waving away the drink tray. "He's history with her is different, and his goals entirely different."

"I'll take your word for it," Ruan said casually.

He did not feel casual. He felt alive, bees crawling on his skin alive, and the urge to hold still and do nothing warred with the need to take violent, irrevocable action. He held himself very still; it was in his training to do so. Where training took root and flowered, nature receded and submitted. If he had ever been the violent sort, and he had, that man was forever chained to control learned in a harsh school. He did not mourn the man he had been.

"If you love her, protect her," Quinton said.

Ruan took a careful sip of his drink. It was Madeira. He did not care for Madeira. He lifted his glass and the footman took it upon his silver tray and hurried it out of his sight. Just so.

"If," Ruan said. "A mighty word, bearing much weight."

"I use it lightly."

"You should not. No matter what words are used, Lady Dalby does not need my protection, nor any man's. She has made that clear. More than once."

"A matter of pride," Quinton said.

"A matter of record. And she has earned her pride. I will not strip it from her."

"Ruan, if we could speak privately---"

"Excuse me, Lord Quinton. I believe Mr. Grey is beckoning me." Ruan moved across the room with unhurried steps and a steady heartbeat. Training had trumped the moment, as it ever did.

Mr. Grey was not beckoning. Mr. Grey was grinning. It was a signal, of sorts, and Ruan was just the sort of man to recognize it as such.

"Laying bets on how long Dutton can go before he hits someone," Grey said.

"Not how long before he gets a beating?" Ruan said.

Grey shrugged, a lifting of one shoulder that emphasized the coiled strength across his shoulders and back. "He's no longer a man to take a beating."

Ruan smiled in agreement. Things had changed. Dutton had changed. All to the good, as far as he could see.

"What do you know about the Russian?" Grey asked.

George Prestwick and Josiah Blakesley joined them in that moment. "Figuring odds? What's the wager?" Blakesley said, youngest of the five sons of the Duke of Hyde.

"About Lord Dutton, of course," Prestwick said. Prestwick's only sister had married Hyde's heir just two years previous, no future heir forthcoming as yet. They were, by all reports, quite diligently going about their duty to the title. Working at it night and day, it was said. Such industry was always commendable.

"Prince Vasily Borisovich Yusupov," Ruan said. "He's quite well-traveled, well-educated, well-fixed."

"Sounds a proper toad," Blakesley said, as only the young can say it.

"Nothing remotely like it," Ruan said.

Prestwick, a most observant, wry sort of fellow, looked at Vasily, at Anne Staverton flirting quite openly with him, at the other women in the room sighing quite loudly over him, the mamas making plans over him, and said, "He looks like trouble."

And that he did.

For a young buck on the Town, one did not relish the competition a man such as Vasily brought to the field.

"He'll take Lady Staverton and that's done with him," Blakesley said.

"Not bloody likely," Prestwick said.

Grey merely smiled and crossed his arms. His arms were quite stupendously long, his hands quite impressively scarred. Ruan was not impressed and not even remotely intimidated. He suspected Grey did not expect him to be.

"Dutton won't hand her over," Prestwick said.

"She's not his to hand over or not," Blakesley said.

"Does he know that?" Grey asked.

"Does she know that?" Ruan asked, smiling at Grey. He almost liked the Indian, if one could like without trust.

"A woman must be told," Grey said.

Ruan chuckled. "Does your sister know that?"

Grey uncrossed his arms and lost his amused expression.

"He acts like he has her, or has had her," Blakesley said. He was very young, perhaps not yet twenty-five. He could be excused.

"It's how she acts; that's the point," Ruan said.

They all looked at Anne in that instant. Dutton, by the most abundant good luck, was just coming to stand at Anne's side, taking her arm in a movement that was not, perhaps, as gentle as it should have been.

Anne, most beguilingly, did not seem to mind.

Anne was of a mind to snap at Dutton, either that or ignore him; she could not quite decide which response would infuriate him more, and in that momentary indecision, Dutton made up her mind for her.

It was completely adorable of him. How perfectly her plans were playing out. She should have done this years and years ago.

Dutton, looking quite completely enraged, took her most firmly by the arm, and said to the group in general and Vasily in particular, "You must excuse me. It has become extremely obvious to me, who knows Lady Staverton so very well, that she is not feeling quite the thing. Allow me to escort you to a more secluded spot."

He jerked her arm in a way that was nothing like a proper escort.

"How thoughtful you are," she said, trying to wrench her arm free. He did not release her. She could not do more without making a spectacle. "I feel fine,

Lord Dutton. More than fine, in fact. Have you met Lord Lanreath? This is his friend, and mine, Prince Vasily Yusupov--"

"How do you do?" Dutton said, cutting her off. "Come, Lady Staverton. I simply cannot allow you to exhaust yourself."

"She appears in the pink of health to me," Camille Thorn said, in what should have been an innocent tone and was not, quite.

Of course, virginal, young, unmarried Camille would want Vasily all to herself, and perhaps Lanreath as well. A sister-in-law marrying a brother-in-law was not unheard of.

"Thank you, Lady Camille," Anne said. "I *feel* in the pink of health."

"I should say so," Dutton murmured, running his thumb over the delicate inside of her arm.

"I'm certain Lady Lanreath must have a place set aside for the ladies, should they feel the necessity of seclusion," Lanreath said. It did not sound quite as innocent as it should have done.

Anne was beginning to think that nothing sounded quite innocent because Dutton was touching her. She could feel him against her, smell the citrusy scent of him, feel the beating of his heart . . . well, perhaps not that. But nearly so. She would swear to it.

"I'm quite certain Lady Staverton feels exactly that," Dutton said. "The need for seclusion. Isn't that so?"

He took hold of her pearled reticule, hanging innocently, well perhaps not, from her wrist, and yanked. The string broke, the purse fell, and buttons rolled across the floor in guilty abandon.

Dutton's buttons.

"Buttons? Are those buttons?" Camille asked. Really, for a young, virginal, unmarried girl she should not talk so much.

"Trouser buttons," Vasily said, smiling at Anne conspiratorially.

Dutton bristled at that smile. Anne could feel it. Yes, she could.

"My trouser buttons, if you must know," Dutton said.

There. That shut Camille up very nicely.

Anne didn't have any opportunity to enjoy Camille's shock because Dutton, as she should have expected and which she did enjoy, dragged her out of the room by the hand. She suppose she should be grateful he did not drag her by the hair.

Perhaps he could be induced to do that later.

Yes, she was nearly certain he could be.

How delicious.

Chapter 21

Naturally, and this was to be entirely expected, when Dutton announced that Anne Staverton had her reticule filled to bursting with his trouser buttons, all eyes went to his trousers to see, well, to check the condition of his buttons, what else? It was to be expected. Certainly Dutton should have expected it.

Dutton, his mind and hands full of Anne, did not expect it.

Dutton, his trousers filled to bursting with something very much unlike cold, unfeeling buttons, did not relish having every eye pinned upon that spot. *The* spot.

Nevertheless, he was not overly concerned where eyes were pinned as long as his body was pinned to hers. Immediately.

"That was most ungentlemanly of you, sir," Anne said, a bit breathlessly as she was stumbling to keep up with him.

He solved that problem by hoisting her into his arms and carrying her like a child. Or a bride. No, like a child. Definitely like a child.

Brides had no place in his thinking.

"Lord Dutton, have you lost your senses?" Anne snapped, green eyes blazing into his.

"Clearly," he said, kicking open a door, or attempting to. The door remained closed. "I don't suppose you'd turn the knob on that door?"

"You are mad," she said, crossing her arms over her lovely breasts. They pushed up nicely and improved an already stellar bosom.

He walked down the long second floor hall and kicked at another door. This time, it was opened by a brown-haired maid. Her mouth dropped open to reveal two crossed teeth and a red tongue.

"Lady Staverton is in want of a couch," he said, striding into the room. It was a drawing room, apparently for the ladies as it was done up in pinks and golds and the candles were newly lit. He did not lay Anne upon the couch. No, she could have got away from him then, or put on a pretense of escape. She had no more desire to escape what was coming than he did. "Go to Lady Lanreath and tell her that Lady Staverton is resting and is not to be disturbed."

"Shall I fetch a cordial, my lord?" the maid asked.

"By no means," Dutton said. "Leave us."

The maid obeyed. He had expected nothing less than prompt and certain obedience.

As to that . . .

Anne kicked and squirmed violently and so he did what any sane man would do: he dropped her onto the nearest sofa. She bounced off of it onto the carpeted floor. That wouldn't do her any harm.

"Are you mad?" she shouted, running hands over her hair.

"You asked me that before."

"I suppose an answer is beyond you." She rose to her feet with grace. He was hardly surprised. She moved with grace at all times and in all circumstances.

"My sanity is not at issue." Though he was beginning to wonder about that. "The issue, Lady Staverton, is the host of buttons which have been let loose. Given the metaphor of the button, the implied contract of the button exchange, you owe me quite a lot, don't you? Let's get to it."

Her hands froze, her eyes blazed, and her voice raised even further. Anne on fire, that's what he was witnessing.

He rather liked Anne on fire.

Her hair gleamed, her skin glowed, her eyes sparkled; she was a woman afire. Anger, lust, raw passion burned in her blood and bone. The careful Anne Warren was gone. Anne Staverton stood proudly in her place.

He had been interested in Anne Warren.

He was consumed by Anne Staverton.

Yes, consumed. He could admit it. He knew she felt the same for him. Consummation, conflagration, fascination. What would be left of them both after the fire turned cold he did not waste time in contemplating. Fires spread and died as they would. He would ride the blaze for as long as it lasted.

"I beg your pardon?" she said, straightening the seams of her gloves, looking at him through her lashes. Her lashes were gold. Hot, shining gold. "Excuse me. I misspoke. I beg for nothing, and never from you."

He barked a laugh. "I can but assume you mean that as a challenge."

"Oh, I think I am challenge enough for you, Ned, without any additional baggage," she said, staring at him without shame or modesty.

Ned? The last, and only, person to call him Ned had been his nurse. When his father had caught her at it he had threatened to sack her immediately. But then his dissolute father had fallen further into his cups and that had been the end of that. Nurse had stayed on, but she had never again called him Ned.

Anne, bold and bright, used the derivation as a

hammer. Nay, as an battle axe.

Was there ever a woman more perfect? No, not the woman, the moment. Merely that.

"The button challenge is yours, Anne," he said. "Stand and deliver."

"Oh, I shall. Never fear, Ned. I shall not leave you wanting."

As the words left her mouth, hanging like golden embers in the air, he was certain she would. Leave him. Leave him wanting.

Then he shook free of the oddity of the moment, watching as Anne lifted her skirts up to her waist, her white stockings held in place by white garters with seed pearls, her shoes white silk satin with pale gold ribbon bows, and nothing else. Nothing but the bold naked beauty of Anne.

He was not aware of crossing to her. He was not aware of heartbeat or breath or thought. He was captive of only one thought, one impulse, and that was Anne. Anne. Anne.

He was inside her. He had her, possessed her, controlled her.

He pounded that truth into her. Ground into her. Breathed into her mouth, his pulse in time with her heart. He was one with her.

"Ned, you are too fast," she whispered, one leg wrapped around his hip.

"Catch up," he snarled, walking a few steps, carrying her, and then falling down with her upon that delicate gold settee where she had landed earlier. Stupid of her to have moved. This was the place. This is where he wanted her. Needed her.

His hands did what was required, his mouth bit at her lips, devouring her like the tart she had never been. Whatever her mother had been, Anne had not been touched by it. He knew that now. Perhaps he'd always known it.

"Ned, you are too slow," she said, clawing at his back, pulling at his hair, wrapping her legs around his back and urging him on.

"Harpy," he grunted against her throat. "Can you not be pleased?"

"It's up to you to find that out, isn't it?"

He grunted a laugh, a bark that turned into a bite on her throat, the swells of her breasts, and he pounded and ground against her, merging them into one, making them one, fusing them with a raw hunger he had not known he could feel.

She screamed and shook in his arms, her head arched back and the cords in her neck taut.

"So, she can be pleasured," he said, kissing her face, butterfly kisses, the kind Nurse used to give him, back when she called him Ned. He was smiling. He could not remember the last time he had smiled, or felt like smiling.

"So, he can find ways to pleasure me," she said. He could hear the grin in her voice. "I am much relieved, I can tell you."

"I believe I still have all my buttons. An improvement."

"Oh, I don't know . . . " she said, a laugh bubbling up.

And, in the most startling development of all, he found himself laughing with her.

❦

"What do you suppose they're doing in there?" the Lanreath maid asked.

"Telling jokes," the Lanreath butler said in a most disapproving and sarcastic voice.

"I suppose she must feel better then," the maid, Agnes, said. Agnes was not attuned to sarcasm, particularly from so lofty a personage as the Lanreath House butler.

"If I were given to placing bets, which I am not, I'd wager ten pounds on that," he said.

"Isn't he the one who beat that butler to mash?"

"He is."

"He looked a rough sort when he burst into the room. I hadn't thought an earl could be rough as a cob."

"Inaccurate assumptions are the cause of many bad wagers in the world, as I am certain Winthrop now realizes."

❦

"Ten pounds that the buttons are part of a wager between them," Josiah Blakesley said.

His remark was met with blank, if not outright pitying stares.

"You won't get a wager on that, Jos," George Prestwick said.

"They have known each other long?" Prince Vasily asked.

The younger men in the room had wandered together with as much subtlety as iron filings when faced with a large magnet. Lady Staverton being so escorted, Lord Dutton's demeanor being so precisely as it had been . . . well, they were all men of the world, to one degree or another. They had known what was to come. Where, why, and how it was to come was more of a mystery.

George Prestwick, Josiah Blakesley, and Lord Raithby had been joined by Prince Vasily and Lord Lanreath with such alacrity that a time could not be put upon it. George Grey, easily of their age, had kept his distance, firmly planted at his sister's elbow. His sister did not look pleased. Neither did Raithby, but that was not the issue at the moment. No, 'twas all of Anne and Dutton.

What connection Vasily had to Anne Staverton was also a question that begged an answer, but George Prestwick knew better than to ask it.

"A year or two, and only casually," George said. It was not precisely true. It was also not precisely untrue. He did not know Vasily. He did know Anne, and liked her. He planned to proceed cautiously.

"Something quite more than casually, to hear Lady Louisa tell it," Jos said.

George did his best not to sigh audibly. Louisa was married to Josiah's older brother; Louisa had never cared overmuch for Anne Staverton.

"Lady Louisa?" Vasily said.

"Lady Louisa Blakesley," Lanreath said. "Formerly

Kirkland. Melverley's oldest girl."

George supposed he should not be surprised that Lanreath knew the players in the top tier of London Society, but he was, just a bit. Yes, Lanreath was of their number. But Lanreath, famously, did not concern himself with anything beyond his horses, his hounds, and his hunting fields. Perhaps he had experienced a change of heart, or perhaps one of circumstance?

"Ah," Vasily said. "Congratulations to your family. A most beautiful woman."

"You know Louisa?" Jos asked.

"We were never formally introduced, no, but I am aware of her," Vasily said.

One had the distinct impression that Prince Vasily did not miss much, particularly when it concerned women. Beautiful women.

Just what this London Season needed, another titled, eligible man.

George was not in any hurry to marry. Not at all. However, his father was in a hurry that he marry. It was nothing so significant as a problem, but it wasn't particularly enjoyable, being at odds with one's father. He happened to like his father. He did not want to be at odds with him. He also did not want to marry. He was, however, not adverse to the idea of appearing to look as if he were interested, even mildly. He would make his father happy and it would not burden him to any appreciable degree to do so.

But if the field was crowded with the likes of Vasily and Lanreath, for why else had he come to Town if not to acquire a wife?, and there was Raithby looking quite interested in women of a sudden, what was a simple man like himself to do? He was heir to a tidy fortune and would inherit the lowest title of them all, and only when his father died, which he would not sully himself by dreaming of, and his looks weren't bad, but they also were not spell-binding in the way of Vasily and Penrith, who, thank God for mercies great and small, was not in London at present.

Still, being possessed of a genial and even temper, George knew there was nothing to be done about any of it except to enjoy the company and the inevitable entertainment that always came with the company. He would marry next year. Or the next. Certainly he had time. His father, a solid man of business who had got his title the old-fashioned way, by buying it, would understand that he could not adequately compete with a prince.

"Lady Louisa has not, in the past, been overly fond of Lady Staverton," George said. It was quite diplomatically put, if he did say so. "I think it is equally well known that Lady Staverton was quite contentedly married to Lord Staverton and that she mourned him honestly and long."

It was not lost on George that the men were looking at him with something approaching raw amusement. Let them be amused. He was in need of a wife, or would be soon; he was not going to alienate Sophia Dalby, the most famous procurer of wives the Town had yet seen, and it was no secret to anyone that Sophia had taken Anne quite completely under her wing sometime in the far distant past and was not likely to over look any insult to Anne's character or behavior. Quite the opposite, in fact.

George was too fully his father's son to ignore a profitable alliance.

"Quite a warm defense, George. I wasn't aware that anyone was attacking Lady Staverton's character," Raithby said.

Louisa Blakesley had, but he was not so deeply in his cups that he would give voice to that bit of fact.

"I should think not," Vasily said, his eyes glittering with suppressed amusement. "She is a most interesting woman, quite memorable."

"You've met before?" George said.

Lanreath shifted his weight and mildly cleared his throat. Vasily ignored him.

"Yes. Years ago. Still, it was memorable," Vasily said, his amusement less suppressed.

"She appeared quite glad to see you again," Jos said.

"Certainly," Vasily said.

An awkward silence followed that single word, and the look of male satisfaction which accompanied it.

Again, they were all men of the world, to one degree or another, and certain looks could only mean certain things.

George took another deep swallow of his drink, determined to be well-fortified when he spoke to Sophia. Which he simply must do. Instantly.

※

"I simply must speak to Lord Ruan," Toni said. "He hasn't spoken to more than three people since he arrived."

"Leave him alone, Toni. He's doing what he wants," Bernie said.

"Standing alone in a corner?"

"Staring with all the subtlety of a wolf at Sophia Dalby. Yes. Precisely what he wants. Leave him to it. Now, if you want to talk to a man, there's that ripe Russian just waiting like a plum for some woman to grab him and run off with him. Why not you?" Bernie said, her green eyes looking quite seductively bewitching.

Of course she had noticed Prince Vasily the moment he had arrived. What woman wouldn't? But she was more distracted by the arrival of Lord Lanreath than anything else.

Why was he here? Why come to Town during the Season?

For a wife, of course.

And if he found a wife . . . and why wouldn't he? He was wealthy and handsome, titled and well-connected. He had to merely nod his head at a likely woman and she'd fall into his lap. Isn't that how she'd become Lady Lanreath? Her husband had nodded at her father, not even at her, and she'd fallen.

The older she became and the more she considered it, the angrier it made her. Which is precisely why she never thought of it. Best not to dwell on things that could not be changed.

"Why not you?" she countered. Surely she could not possibly be of any interest to a handsome prince. Bernie, however, would interest even a dead handsome prince.

"Toni." Bernie sighed dramatically. Two men turned

to look at her, at her lifted bosom, to be precise. "You simply must learn to fight for yourself."

"I have no idea what you mean."

"How well I know it," Bernie said. "When will you learn to take action? To see what you want and catch him up before he knows what's happened to him?"

"I do not want Prince Vasily."

"Then you are a fool."

"We are all not as you, Bernie," Toni said in a cold whisper. Toni was not the sort to burn hot. No, she burned cold. Cold in anger, cold in shame, cold in bed. Or so her husband had accused. She knew it to be true. "I don't want every man I see."

"Toni," Bernie said, her voice a warmly husky murmur of apology. "Not every man. But some man? You must break free of the chains that bastard Lanreath used to bind you. You have not been the same since your marriage."

"What woman is?" Toni said with a smile. "Are you?"

"No." Bernie did not smile in return. Small wonder. "I have no wish to be."

"Clearly."

"Toni, there is no shame in taking a man to your bed. You have done your duty to your father and your husband. You can now please yourself. Look at Anne Staverton. She is hardly shy in making her wants known. Lord Dutton jumps at the twitch of a single finger."

"Yes, that is quite new, isn't it?"

"She has found her power, and she is exercising it."

"She does seem quite changed."

"Beautifully changed."

"Bernie, I have no Dutton, sniffing at my heels for years."

"You could have. If you tried."

Toni thought of the single time she had tried, and then pushed the thought from her. A single effort, a single failure. Why did she put so much upon that?

Because she was a cold, suppressed woman.

Unless that woman was in the past, as Anne Staverton was no longer Anne Warren, poor widow with no connections and no place in Society?

Yes, things could change, and a woman could be the author of the change.

"Very well," she said. "I think I will try. But not tonight."

"Just don't think about it too long or you'll think yourself out of all my persuasion," Bernie said, smiling with a beautifully calculated air.

"I've agreed. Best to leave it at that."

"I suppose we must leave it precisely as we found it," Anne said.

"I don't suppose that's possible. We've torn one pillow and scratched the surface of a table," Dutton said.

He sounded quite pleased with himself. She felt quite pleased with herself, truth be told. How well, how very well things were progressing. She had him quite precisely where she wanted him.

He was obedient to her wishes, came when summoned, and behaved as required. Dutton the wolf had been sweetly trained to become Dutton the well-mannered lap dog. If only she had done this years ago, but of course, she couldn't have done. It was only her equal footing in Society that had made the difference; becoming Lady Staverton had changed everything.

Thank you, dear Stavey.

They lay upon the sofa, Dutton's feet on the floor, Anne wrapped around him like a vine, her head on his chest. His coat lay on the floor, and if she were not mistaken, was covered in pet hair, how poetically accurate. His cravat was twisted and loose, his chest bare. She had dreamed of his chest, pale and covered in a light coating of glistening hair. It was better than her dream of it. As was he. She had dreamed of what it would be like, this baring of bodies, joining, panting, heaving.

It was not as she had dreamed. It was more. More powerful. More elemental. More soul-baring.

She did not want him to know that, obviously. Dutton was just barely managed as a lap dog. She had no wish to feed the wolf that lurked within.

She sighed, kissed his chest, that glorious skin, and lifted her head to begin the process of putting herself back into order.

Dutton pulled her back down and kissed her roughly, his hands in her hair, on her neck, her back, her bosom, which was bared. In her catalogue of his dishabille she had ignored her own state. She was dressed, but barely. Her dress was more in the manner of a belt at this point. She would look a ruin when she reentered the salon. She smiled just thinking of it.

"Stop smiling, you witch," he growled. She could hear the smile in his voice.

She bit his lip, trailing bites down his throat, that glorious throat, nipping at the muscle that joined neck to shoulder. He was so muscular. How had dissolute Lord Dutton not turned to bone and whiskey?

"I'm happy."

"Is that a compliment?"

"Take it however you like."

"What an offer," he said, lifting her up so that her breasts dangled above his face.

She chuckled and rolled out of his arms, after a few minutes of searing pleasure, of course. "We must return to the others."

"Must we?"

"I must."

"I say you must not."

And here, here and now, she must begin the game again. Without the game, he was lost to her. Boredom, his every wish fulfilled, Dutton would lose interest. She held him by a thread of a leash, the tiniest and most fragile of ties. It would always be so. She could never hold him hard and fast, his link to her forged in iron. No. Not Dutton. He was flame, moving, ever moving. He could not be leashed, not for long.

She played a game she had learned in childhood. She knew this game. She knew it well and she could play it if required. With Dutton, there was no other way. She wanted this, this hot play, this seductive laughter, the game of rejection and control and passion and need. Need first denied and then permitted and then denied again.

"I do not answer to you, Neddy. Have you not yet learned that?"

She got to her feet, her skirts falling in a wrinkled mass. Her bodice was quickly adjusted. Her hair was not too horribly awry. There would be no possibility for speculation as to what had happened between them in this half hour; she saw no reason to pretend otherwise.

Of course, there was Vasily to consider. Vasily was . . . but no. He would not be a problem. Of course he would not.

"And I answer to you, I suppose," he said, lying upon the sofa, the torn pillow smashed against his hip, goose feathers spilling across his lap, one white feather sticking to his belly; his chest gleaming, his eyes gleaming, his smile the gleaming smile of a wolf. It was not a monumental leap to imagine him as the wolf who had just devoured a fat, white goose.

She would not be Dutton's goose, not even an imaginary goose.

"Do you? How lovely. I require help with my bodice. Do help, won't you?"

She wanted him to lunge up in anger, expected it, in fact. But Dutton, clever, dangerous Dutton smiled at her, his blue eyes sparkling with comprehension.

Damn.

"Fix it yourself. If I come near you, I'll rip that dress off your lovely white skin," he said. He said it easily and with a smile hovering at the corners of his mouth.

"That would hardly serve the purpose."

"It would serve my purpose most well."

Unfortunately, most unfortunately, looking at him

lying there, looking far more seductive than usual, which was saying quite a lot, she wanted nothing more than to throw herself upon him and devour every inch of him.

"We are at cross purposes then," she said, looking for her gloves. One was on the scratched table. The other was . . . hanging from the unlit candelabra in the center of the room.

"I doubt that very much," he said. Arrogant sot. He'd always been such an arrogant sot. She wished that put her off somehow, but no, it didn't. "Come here, Anne. You know you want it."

"It?"

"To bask in passion's glow. To bathe in love's fountain. To swim in the rivers of Eros."

"It sounds quite vile. No thank you." It was very difficult not to laugh. She managed it, just.

"Put it however you like, dress it up in poetry and metaphor, if it pleases you."

"Hardly that. I can't think when I've felt more revolted."

"Agreed. Let's call it what it is. Lust. Passion. Desire. We want each other. Why dissemble?"

"Dissemble? I've not dissembled in the least particular. I enjoy sex with you, dear Ned. I enjoy it when I want it, where I want it, how I want it. Has that not been made clear to you? I did think I was being so forthright in my wishes and desires. I do not want you now. I don't want *it* now, if that is language which suits you better. When I do want you, I will make it known to you, you can rest assured. When I no longer want you, I will make that equally clear."

"You shall always want me," he said, rising to his feet, his eyes looking quite lethally wolfish. She left her glove dangling from the candelabra; she couldn't reach it and she wasn't going to linger. What had happened to her lovely lap dog?

"You are more certain of that than I. Somehow, I doubt it."

And on those words, she hurried out the door. She had the advantage of being fully, or nearly, clothed. She used that advantage. With Dutton, one had to be ruthless.

Chapter 22

When Anne Staverton walked into the lovely, massive salon of Lanreath House every eye in the room turned to her. This was not remotely an exaggeration. Her gown was a complete ruin. Her hair was mussed in the most charming way imaginable. She was missing a glove, the right.

That bare right arm was as erotic a sight as if she had appeared stark naked. More so. There was something about partial nudity that was so much more seductive and suggestive than total nudity. In the right circumstances, at any rate.

This was just such a circumstance.

Sophia could not, could not possibly, have been more delighted.

Darling Anne truly was a genius at this sort of thing. High time she realized it, too. And beyond time that Lord Dutton, sad, silly Lord Dutton, come to terms with the stark reality of Anne Staverton in the full force of her feminine power.

What a spectacular evening. The arrival of Prince Vasily and Lord Lanreath was the cream on top. What delicious trouble would they, between them, spark?

The possibilities were nearly limitless.

A shiver of anticipation tickled along her spine.

"The fact that you find such obvious delight in the dramatic, and one could almost say traumatic, moments of others is one of the most mesmerizing aspects of your allure."

Ruan. Darling Ruan.

She did feel something for him. She would be a fool to deny that, and she was hardly a fool.

A fool for love? Never.

"Darling, I thought you had washed your hands of me. And here you are, not a week later, waxing poetic about my allure."

"Don't say you're disappointed in me."

"Hardly that," she said, looking up into his sharp green eyes.

He was a splendid looking man, a man not in the way of the sheltered London beaus who wore padded coats and brightly polished boots, their hair arranged meticulously to look ruggedly outdoorsy. The Marquis of Ruan was none of that. His face was weathered and splattered with small scars gone pale with time; his body was hard and lean; his gaze was direct and fearless. He was a man as she had been taught men ought to be. He was a warrior, to the bone and through the heart, a warrior. He did not need a battle to prove it. The proof was in his eyes.

"What do you want for Lady Staverton, Sophia? This? And at Dutton's hands?"

"I want for her only what she wants for herself. Since she wants Lord Dutton, for the moment, I can only be delighted for her that she has him. She does have him, darling, in precisely the way she wants him. What better circumstance for a woman of means and position?"

Ruan studied her, his eyes poking and prodding, seeking the depths of her thoughts. He had not the talent to reach the depth of her thoughts. No man did. No man would.

"She toys with him."

"He had it in his mind to toy with her," she countered. "You do not find the current situation comically just? I had thought you a man of more sophistication, Lord Ruan."

"I am gratified that you think of me at all, Lady Dalby."

His voice was a low, thrumming murmur that set her spine to tingling again. They had a history, the two of them. A strange, coiled history that did not follow any of the paths she had previously followed where men and women were concerned. It was intriguing. He was intriguing. A mystery. A man she could not read in a moment. She was, she dared to admit, mesmerized by him, if slightly. In the life she had lived, he was far beyond her expectations.

"You must know that I think of you, my lord," she said, forgetting Anne, forgetting Dutton, forgetting everything but Ruan.

"I had hoped so. Do you think well of me?"

"I do. A rare compliment from me."

"How well I know it."

They smiled in the same instant, a soft smile between adults caught in a world of infants.

"Why do you care so much about Lord Dutton?" she asked.

"I care only because you care. If you are intrigued by him, then so must I be."

"That is a compliment of the most high degree, Lord Ruan, to admit to having your thoughts and efforts concentrated where I casually point. I have much power over you, it seems."

"You know you do," he said, his smile miles gone, his eyes blazing like blue-green fire.

"You do not regret it, or more, fear it?" she asked,

all inclination to tease him gone from her like smoke in a gale.

"I am too far gone to regret or fear anything if it concerns you," he said, taking her hand in his, tracing the joint of her thumb through her glove. She shivered and almost could not hide the fact. "Are you not the same? Are we not, the two of us, too far gone for regret or fear or deception?"

She let her hand continue to rest in his, but the shiver died a cold, hard, instantaneous death.

"I have rarely felt regret or fear, my lord. Deception? I deceive no one, about anything. I am Lady Dalby, a woman who follows her inclinations and seeks her pleasures where she will, a woman who answers to no one. Was there any confusion about that?"

He lifted her hand and kissed it, a soft kiss that she could not feel through her glove. But she did feel . . . something.

"Lady Dalby," he said, dropping her hand in the proper fashion, "about you there is only mystery. Astonishing, mesmerizing mystery. I am helpless to turn from it. Or from you."

"Men, I have found, are much attached to mystery and elusiveness in women. It is our most enduring weapon," she said, speaking the truth fully. Would he know it?

"You insult me," he said mildly.

She smiled in response, truly amused.

"I have no wish to insult you," she said. "It is the farthest thing from my intentions."

"And your closest, most intimate intention?"

"Lord Ruan, you ask me to bare my mysteries to

you? How unchivalrous."

"Another insult," he said with a smile. "How can I endure it?"

"A man endures what he must to attain what his heart demands," she said, another truth.

"My heart? I am puzzled that you did not name another part of my anatomy."

She laughed, a lighthearted laugh that she had not felt in years. "My attempt at recompense for the previous, unintended, insults."

"Ah, a lady to the core. I expected no less of you."

"Lord Ruan, I suspect you are attempting to seduce me with mild and chivalrous flattery."

"Lady Dalby, I suspect you know that I will attempt to seduce you with any means at my disposal, flattery the least of them."

"And the most of them?"

"I may," he said, running a finger down her arm from elbow to wrist, the span of her glove, "resort to Lord Dutton's method of simply yanking you from the room."

Her heart, strangely, so strangely, began to race. Only Ruan could make her heart do anything so unusual as racing. Even in the deep woods of upstate New York she had not forgotten that.

"And now we come full circle. You would do to me what so concerned you regarding Lady Staverton?"

"You have convinced me. Lady Staverton is doing exactly as she pleases. Why shouldn't you enjoy the same?"

"You are so certain I want from you what she wants from Lord Dutton?"

He smiled, a slow, careful slide of a grin that did not quite reach his eyes. His eyes were quite serious and intent, a fact she found quite gratifying.

"I know I am willing to put whatever effort it takes into making you want it. Is that not a fine starting point? You are Lady Dalby, a woman who famously knows what she wants and does not hesitate to take it."

His eyes blazed, warm and welcoming, encouraging her to leap, to trust, to abandon all caution and all care. She felt the call of it and of him. She *felt* it, she, who felt almost nothing.

"Want me, Sophia. Take me," he said.

She almost did. Then and there, she almost did.

***

Anne almost turned and walked out of the room. She almost did. The only thing that kept her in place, staring blankly at her accusers, and certainly they were accusing her, albeit silently, of behaving horrendously and scandalously, and she had of course, not that she truly cared, but the only thing that kept her standing stock still was that Vasily, that cursed Vasily came hurrying over, took her arm and led her to a quiet corner and pushed her, truly pushed her, down upon a chair upholstered in ivory silk. It was all meant to be solicitous, she supposed, but it was very inconvenient and indeed, completely off purpose since it made her even more of a spectacle. Why not allow her to enter the room and melt into the crowd?

Vasily, and she had quite forgotten this about him,

was not a man to melt into a crowd. Quite the reverse.

"Anne, sweetling, are you quite well?" he said. Vasily did not have a Russian accent; no, his accent was quite appropriately English aristocrat, but he did have something different about his intonation that, absurdly, made his voice even more appealing than the norm.

"I am perfectly well," she said, trying to stand. "Thank you."

He pushed her back down, drawing a seat next to her so that they sat face to face and knee to knee. How positively inconvenient. Every face in the room was aimed straight at them. It was rather like facing a firing squad. And she, missing a glove. She sighed in frustration.

"I know that look, Anne. I know what he has done to you," Vasily said, looking far less alarmed than his words suggested.

"Nothing was done to me, Vasily. I was a full participant," she said.

Really, she never spoke this bluntly to anyone else, not even Sophia, but there was something about one's first. Certain barriers were quite unable to be resurrected with one's first amour, even if she had been bought and paid for. A first was a first, no matter the circumstances.

Perhaps she might make some use of that with Dutton?

Anne felt her annoyance with Vasily lessen, just a bit.

"But of course, sweetling," he murmured, stroking her wrist. Her naked right wrist. "I should know that better than anyone, shouldn't I?"

"Vasily, do not try to play the rogue with me," she

said, grinning as she yanked her hand out from under his. "I knew you as the callow and naive youth you were."

"Never callow. Only inexperienced," he said. "We taught each other, did we not? Lessons learned together. Sweet lessons they were." He had clasped her wrist again, both of them, and held them in one of his hands, the other hand dangerously on the loose.

"As I remember it, darling Vasily, you exploded in less than ten seconds." She said it on a laugh. It had been quite completely laughable, after all.

"Anne! I was a youth!"

"A callow youth."

He grinned. "A callow youth," he agreed. "I have aged admirably. As have you."

"Thank you, Vasily."

They smiled at each other in a warm glow of mild affection that she found surprising. Vasily? She had not thought of him for years. He had been a moment in her life, a frightening, unavoidable moment, and she had never been deluded about that. That he had remembered her at all was something of a shock. How many women had tumbled into his bed since she had?

"I would not have thought you'd remember me, Vasily," she said.

The eyes in the room were still on them, all except Sophia's and Ruan's, who were engaged in a most intimate, most pleasant conversation by the look of it. It was a bold vote of confidence that Sophia clearly didn't feel the need to monitor her or advise her about either Dutton or Vasily, and that gave Anne even more confidence.

She could, and would, manage this. And she'd do it beautifully as well.

"Not remember you? I could never forget you, sweetling. You live in memory like the first fire of winter."

She chuckled. "Prettily put. I don't suppose you've written a long, slightly morbid Russian poem trumpeting my virtues? No? If you care to compose one now, I'll wait."

Vasily laughed outright, a most charming sound that quite took the watchers by surprise.

It was then, in that precise moment, that Dutton walked into the room, her white glove twirling in his hand like a child's toy.

She stiffened. She flushed. She fluttered. And Vasily felt all of it. He was still holding both of her hands, after all. She was capable of only so much sophistication, unfortunately.

"A poem would not serve me well enough," Vasily said, leaning back in his chair and looking at Dutton over his beautifully tailored shoulder. "I shall leave you to him, Lady Staverton."

"No. Don't," she said. She did not have anything so formal as a plan, but Vasily was Vasily and Dutton was most definitely Dutton and, certainly, inevitably, some things must surely fall into place? "Stay. Will you? Will you stay, Vasily? Will you tempt me? You tempt so beautifully."

Vasily looked into her eyes intently, the pale blue of his eyes still as shockingly beautiful as when he had been a callow and naive youth, his face still sharply chiseled and his nose still as aristocratic. He looked a prince of the north, and yet, to her, he was still Vasily the youth, the boy who exploded in ten seconds. He would never, could never, make her feel as Dutton did. Dutton made *her* explode in ten seconds. And he did not even have to touch her to do it. All he need do was enter the room and her heart exploded. When he touched her, she trembled. When he spoke, she shivered.

Vasily, Vasily the first, understood all this, and he understood what she wanted of him. And Vasily, darling Vasily, was . . . not kind enough, no, for no one could say that a Russian prince had any use for kindness, but he was sophisticated enough and pleasant enough to play the game for as long as it amused him.

"To be a temptation to any woman, particularly a woman as lovely as Lady Staverton, is a challenge I cannot resist and an honor I cannot refuse," he said, lifting her hands in his, kissing one and then the other, his lips lingering on the bare skin of her right hand, his eyes devouring her. Only she would see the playfulness in their depths. And she did see it. But she dared not play this game with Vasily for long; Prince Vasily Borisovich Yusupov was not a man to toy with, especially as a pawn against another man.

No, this must happen quickly or she would lose all control of the situation and the men.

Which presupposed that she had any control now.

"Darling Vasily," she said, leaning toward him, determinedly avoiding looking at Dutton. "What a man you've become."

"I would show you even more fully the man I've become," he said, raising her to her feet. "To be rejected without even the courtesy of an audition. And between two such old friends as we."

"We are hardly old friends."

Vasily tucked her naked hand into the crook of his arm and began a circuit of the room. All the women looked at her with astonished envy, which was quite completely gratifying even if slightly uncomplimentary. The men looked on speculatively. Dutton did she knew not what. She was *not* going to look at Dutton.

"Old lovers, then. Even better, wouldn't you say?"

"I would not say. I offer no opinion on the subject," she said primly. In an undertone, leaning against his shoulder, she said, "Thank you, Vasily. Thank you for this."

"This? The most beautiful woman in the room is on my arm, and in my thoughts. For what should you thank me?"

"Vasily," she whispered, cocking her head until she could see his eyes. "Thank you."

"Thanking him? For what, dear Anne?" Dutton said. "Please answer most carefully and most completely, my dear, won't you?"

Dutton stood directly in front of them, his blue eyes cold, his mouth hard, his hands clenched. Her glove hung like a limp white flag of surrender, twisted around his fingers, pointing toward the floor.

"Have we been introduced?" Vasily asked in his most regal tones. Vasily could be quite regal when he had a mind to be.

"I am Lady Staverton's escort for this evening. And you are not," Dutton said.

"I believe, and it has ever been so, that the lady

decides whom her escort shall be," Vasily said, patting Anne's hand where it rested on his arm. "Lady Staverton has made her choice. Obviously."

"Lord Dutton, may I say---"

"No, you may not," Dutton interrupted. "I have your glove, Anne. What more is there to say?"

"Yes, thank you for retrieving it," she said, holding out her hand for it.

Dutton smiled wolfishly, the sod, his dark blue eyes scoring her heart. He held out the glove, dirty now, small wonder, like a beau presenting her with a flower. 'Twas no flower and he was no beau. No, he was Dutton and he was doing what Dutton always did: confusing her, confounding her, tempting her to fall into his arms, disappearing into oblivion and ruin.

Ruin. But that was not true. She had been ruined from the start. She had risen from being ruined, risen far above her ruinous beginnings. What could Dutton, or anyone, do to her now?

"The glove is mine, Anne. The buttons are yours," Dutton said.

"A tailor is needed, I should think," Vasily said with a superior smirk.

"This is between us," Dutton said, snarling slightly. Dutton snarling did not bode well for future peace.

"If by *us* you mean we three, then I heartily agree," Vasily said. "If we are to catalogue what bits of clothing are where, I have a green garter of Anne's in my wardrobe, a most cherished memento, I can assure you. Do you remember, sweetling, how I slipped that garter off your leg? You giggled like ---"

Dutton, who, if one wanted to catalogue it, was the

most consistent of men in certain lights. Dutton dispensed with punches the way a woman discarded ribbons. It was, she might be forced to admit, one of his most predictable of behaviors. Also, one of his most endearing.

Vasily, who had clearly been provoking Dutton to just this end, quite adorably of him, took the first punch, which happened to be to the mouth, in good form. That was all he gave Dutton. After that, it became a rain of blows given and taken, Anne quite ruthlessly pushed out of the middle of it to land with admirable grace, all things considered, on a small chair occupied by George Prestwick. Mr. Prestwick, who should have released her immediately, did not. In fact, he murmured something about the unpredictable nature of fisticuffs and wrapped an arm about her shoulders, tucking her against his body in such a way that she was shielded. Mostly.

She could see Sophia and Lord Ruan standing in a far corner watching with mild amusement and not one bit of surprise. Sophia caught her eye and gave her a small and silent ovation. Anne grinned.

It was all rather marvelous, wasn't it? And she had managed things well, hadn't she?

Dutton was fighting over her. It was all completely wonderful.

Vasily, who had provoked Dutton as a favor to her, did rather more than she expected of him, truly engaging in the fight and not walking away or giving in when he could have done. Men were like that when they fought, keeping on when the whole point of the thing had been accomplished.

Anne looked across the room. The men were watching with hot interest, the women with astonishment. That, too, was typical. Men did seem so very interested in fighting, at any hour and in any situation. It was rather perplexing when one considered it; she rarely considered it for that very reason.

The orchestra, understandably, lost their timing and their place in the piece, Mozart, she surmised, as they stared in shock at the fight. Dutton happened to be delivering a solid blow to Vasily's mid-section, right in the center of his rather stunning blue waistcoat with red embroidery at the pocket seams, and so the musicians' preoccupation was well explained. Lady Lanreath snapped her fingers sharply, nodded stiffly, and the music resumed.

In the most strange of coincidences, or perhaps not, to give the musicians their due credit, the music, most definitely Mozart, happened to find itself in the same rhythm as the fight.

It was quite remarkable.

It was equally amusing.

They were fighting over her. She had never had anyone fight over her, and here was a prince and an earl, bashing into each other quite joyfully, Vasily's right eye very red and swollen, Dutton's lip bleeding, looking better than either one of them had ever looked, if she could judge. And why should she not judge? She had every right to have an opinion on the matter.

Could she help it if she were grinning?

Lady Lanreath smiled at her from across the room and raised a glass in toast to her. Anne blushed and dipped her head, then turned the dip into a nod of recognition and acceptance.

Lady Paignton, who surely had caused more than a fight or two, watched the fighting men and, quite like her, licked her lips. She then threw a smirk of approval at Anne that caught her completely unprepared. Lady Paignton was only on friendly terms, one might say *intimate* terms, with men. Never women, unless the women were her three sisters, and that was a supposition based on very little.

Elizabeth Grey was suddenly at her elbow, a most unwelcome revelation, and said, "Well done."

Anne turned her head slightly, only slightly as she did not intend to miss a single second of this glorious fight, which at that moment consisted of Dutton staggering back against a table, knocking over three or four Italian goblets to the floor, Vasily lunging after him so that they landed in a pile of legs upon the carpet. Anne responded, "You approve? You astonish me."

"Men should fight. It is their way, and they are good at it. Or they should be. A man who does not fight for a woman, for food, for life, is not much of a man."

In the most completely remarkable moment of the entire evening, Anne found herself in complete agreement with the disagreeable Miss Grey. She would not have thought it possible. Life, if lived carefully, was truly capable of the most remarkable surprises.

"You don't think it disgraceful?" Anne asked.

"Admirable," Elizabeth said. "How did you do it?"

"To be honest, I'm not quite certain. A matter of ownership, I should think."

Elizabeth nodded with sharp economy. "Something to consider."

"I beg your pardon?"

"Nothing," Elizabeth said.

It was very difficult to keep pace with Miss Grey in a conversation as she did nothing to help one along. One felt a half step behind, or perhaps ahead, the entire time.

"Nothing?" Anne repeated, sounding quite stupid, she was sure.

"I think they are at the end of their strength," Elizabeth said, changing the subject yet again. Or perhaps not. Anne simply could not be sure of anything regarding Miss Grey. "A good showing. They did well."

Dutton and Vasily had, in truth, reached the limits of their endurance. They were both short of wind, bruised, and unsteady on their feet. As to whom was the victor, why, Dutton, most assuredly.

The orchestra slowed their playing, drawing the notes out on their strings, waiting to see if a reprise might be necessary, a fresh burst of sound to accompany a fresh burst of fists.

Alas, it did not seem so.

Yes, alas. She had waited for this, without quite realizing that *this* is precisely what she had been waiting for, for years upon years. She was due her day as the damsel and Dutton, even more certainly, was due his day as the jousting knight, bloodied and not too badly broken.

It would do him nothing but good.

"You are satisfied, sweetling?" Vasily asked, blatantly unconcerned with his injuries.

"Honor has been satisfied," Dutton said, answering

for her, the swine. Dutton was simply horrendous at chivalry. "You will not speak to Lady Staverton in such vulgar tones again. Understood?"

"I believe that is for the lady to decide," Vasily said, lifting his chin.

The orchestra, in truly hopeful manner, began a lively Vivaldi piece.

"As the lady is to be my wife, I shall decide," Dutton said with a martial air.

Vasily, that coward, bowed curtly to Dutton and, with a polite smile to her, walked across the silent room to Lord Lanreath. In moments, they left the room together. To get a proper wash and new linen, one could only surmise.

The lively Vivaldi piece trailed off with a disconsolate tone; the players decided upon a Corelli piece of languid tempo, their disappointed faces matching their mood.

Anne watched Vasily and Lanreath leave, then watched the room, the stares, the open speculation; she watched it all in a haze. It was a dream, a blinding dream. It was a nightmare. She had expected none of it, not one piece of it. Not the fight and not the proposal.

She did not want it.

"No."

She did not know where the word had come from, from her own lips, she supposed. Yes, she must have said that. Because she meant that. She truly did.

"But he fought for you," Elizabeth Grey said, so typically falling into the wrong conclusion and then ridiculously announcing it to one and all. The girl had no subtlety whatsoever. When she had a moment to think of anyone but herself, she would feel some deep sympathy for her. Or something very like sympathy. Pity. Yes, pity and horror. "He has won the right to you."

Gad, was she still speaking? Of course she was. She was always doing the wrong thing at the wrong time. But were not all wrong things, but the very definition, done at the wrong time? Could there be the wrong thing at the right time? The right thing at the wrong time?

"He has won the right, perhaps," Sophia said from across the very large room. It need not be explained that *everyone* heard every word of this peculiar conversation. Anne heard it all from a very great, fuzzy distance. "He has not, however, won the right to make Anne's decision for her. Only Lady Staverton has the power to decide whom to marry and whom to . . . discard."

Dutton's head lifted sharply at the word, his jaw clenched in pulsating fury.

"Discard?" he said.

"Disregard?" Sophia said, by way of appeasement, one might suppose. If one were very stupid. "I leave the choice of words to you, Lord Dutton. The choice of action, however, remains with Lady Staverton, does it not?"

The wrong thing at the wrong time. The right thing at the wrong time. The wrong thing at the right time. And then there was the right thing at the right time. This was that, precisely that.

The fog lifted. She found her bearings, and she found her words.

"Indeed it does," she said. "I am sorry you were bloodied on my behalf, Lord Dutton," she said, not sorry in the slightest, "but I have no intention of ever marrying again."

She turned to make a lovely, stately exit, the orchestra playing the Corelli somberly, their hopes for more blood-letting cast down, when Dutton grabbed her arm, her waist, and then her arse and hoisted her over his shoulder and strode from the room.

"No, Lady Dalby," Dutton said, "the choice is mine. Come, Lady Staverton, it is time you were home and in bed," he said, as is he were not carting her like a sack of potatoes! "I'll just see you safely there, shall I?"

She could not take breath to answer before he had pushed open the door and was halfway out of the room. She did have time to see Josiah Blakesley bend down to scoop up a handful of Dutton's trouser buttons. Mr. Prestwick, she saw, was in possession of her glove. Neither man gave any appearance of remorse.

And wasn't that so typical of men?

Chapter 23

"Did Dutton just propose to Anne Staverton?" Delphine asked.

"He most certainly did," Yvonne answered. "It might be the most violent proposal ever proffered."

"Violence does not seem to lessen the quality of it, does it?" Camille said.

"I should say it enhances the quality," Bernadette said.

"Kindly do not lead your young sisters astray, Bernadette," Yvonne said stiffly.

"Is it being led astray to learn how to acquire a proposal of marriage from an earl?" Antoinette asked. It was slightly subversive of her. She knew Mama would notice. For once, she could not summon the strength to care. "I should not have thought so."

Mama cast her a disapproving glance. Toni returned the glance with one of her own. Mama blinked and looked away.

How very interesting.

Toni took a deep breath, perhaps her first since leaving the nursery, and looked about the room, considering . . . well, considering every man she saw, and a few she did not see. What she wanted to do with said man she had not decided. She didn't suppose she had to decide anything immediately. One step at a time was adventurous enough, for a start.

"Well. That was daring of him," Jos Blakesley said.

"Lord Dutton as always been an adventurous sort,"

George Prestwick said.

"A drunken sort, I would have said," Raithby said.

"Some men require drink to dare," George Grey said.

As usual, his comments ran along the edge of insult. George Prestwick, far from finding it offensive, found it amusing. Life was so much more pleasant if one searched for the amusement in everything. It was always there, if one looked closely enough.

"Do you think he means to marry her?" Jos said.

"I don't think he meant to marry her this morning, but he means it now," George said.

"Sounds about right," Grey said with a cheerful smirk. He looked his absolute most deadly when he smiled. Must be some odd Iroquois thing.

"Well, it shan't happen to me that way," Jos said, looking nearly grim.

"Going to be logical about it, are you?" Raithby said.

"Of course," Jos said.

"The most sane course, highly logical, is to pick a wife based on her fortune," Raithby said. "In fact, might as well let your father do your picking for you. He'd be truly logical about it all."

At that remark, they all, quite understandably, took a mental and physical step back. There was logical and then there was mad. Logic, yes, stupid not to be, but there had to be some . . . that is to say . . . some measure of gut level attraction. Something beyond a list of assets on a ledger.

"Are you going to let your father make your choice for you?" George asked.

"Hell, no," Raithby said, looking across the room.

One would suppose he was looking at his father, Lord Quinton. One would be wrong.

⁂

"I suppose you think that by carting me out of the room, arse first, that I shall succumb to your less than obvious charm and accept you," Anne said, kicking her legs. Dutton slapped an arm around them and kept walking. "You would be quite completely wrong."

A Lanreath footman standing at the bottom of the stairs stared open-mouthed as they passed him on the way to the front door. The front door, fortunately, stood quite a distance from the stairway and across an exceptionally wide marble-floored hall. She had quite a good view of the marble floor.

Her hair fell out of every single pin in a single whoosh.

Her view was instantly much worse.

"I can't think why you proposed marriage," she said, pulling at his coat hem violently.

He slapped her, hard, across the buttocks.

"I can't think why either," he said. "It came to me quite suddenly."

"The notion might leave you just as suddenly."

"I don't think that likely," he said, sounded not one bit winded. "The door. Lady Staverton and I are leaving. She feels unwell," Dutton said, speaking to the porter.

"I do not feel unwell!" she snapped.

"Lady Staverton has recovered," Dutton said. "I am

relieved. We need a private place so that she can rearrange her person."

"We do not need a private place!" she said sharply.

"Lady Staverton does not require a private place. If she does not, then neither do I," he said to the two, no, three footmen standing in the hall. "I am determined to accommodate Lady Staverton in all things."

"Put me down!"

"In most things," he amended.

Dutton kicked at a door with his foot, it was opened with astonishing speed by a maid, and then they were in a corridor that led to the working core of the house, to judge by the noise.

The light was dim, the maid was waved away, and she was dropped onto her feet before she could catch a breath. Her hair fell in long ropes down her back, over her breasts, and in her eyes. Dutton grabbed her hair, pulled her to him with it, and kissed her with the hot need of a green boy.

She was not going to succumb to passion, not even raw, bleeding passion. Of course it was flattering. Of course she felt herself heat in response to it. Of course Dutton had her, once more, pressed against a wall and was treating her with all the care one would show a ten penny whore.

The real problem was that she didn't mind as much as a real lady would.

In fact, she didn't mind at all.

"Is this how you treat the woman you asked to marry you?" she said, yanking his hair and pulling his mouth off of her for a second.

"Apparently so," he said, lifting her in his arms and

twirling her so that his back was against the painted wall and she was trapped only by his arms. Such strong arms they were. He still wasn't even winded.

"It's disgraceful," she said, wrapping her arms around his neck and her legs around his hips. She was disgraceful. Had she learned nothing by being Lady Staverton?

"It is me we're talking about," he said, kissing her throat, her shoulders, grinding into her.

"Aren't you ashamed?"

"Of course not," he said. "I never feel shame. It's the best part of my charm."

She laughed. She shouldn't, she knew she shouldn't, but she couldn't help herself. He really was the worst influence.

He kissed her mouth again, tenderly, softly. Quite unlike him, actually.

"I don't want to marry again," she said.

She had to say something, anything to stop this softness that was creeping into her bones. One could not be soft with Lord Dutton. He would destroy her in a moment if she were soft and vulnerable. She meant it, too. She had no wish to marry. She liked her freedom and she'd worked hard to attain it; freedom from want, from poverty, from shame, from the whims of men. Dutton would be the absolute worst person she could marry, if she did marry, and she wouldn't. He would devour her for breakfast.

"I don't want to marry at all," he said, grinding his hips into her, trailing kisses along her shoulder.

She felt soft and weak. Impossible. Unacceptable. She must stop this immediately.

"Well, then," she said, lifting her chin so that he could kiss her throat.

"But I want to marry you, Anne," he said, lifting his head to look into her eyes.

"That makes no sense."

"I know it," he said, dropping a kiss upon her cheek, turning so that her back was against the wall. "You turn everything inside out. You make me want things, make me do things, that I shouldn't want and shouldn't do. I do them and want them in spite of it."

"That hardly puts me in a good light. Are you saying I'm a bad influence on you?" she said, both insulted and delighted.

"A horrible influence. I'm not the man I was. I am sober and diligent, responsible and sober. I said it twice; it's that horrific. I hardly recognize myself. Someone should lock you up. I volunteer."

She laughed, the sound buried in the curve of his neck. Such a lovely, long neck, so beautifully shaved, so delicately scented.

"What is that scent you're wearing?" she asked, burying her face against his skin.

"Lust."

"You don't sound very reformed to me."

"It's a slow process. It will take you the rest of your life to complete my reformation."

He kissed her and she melted into him. The scent of him, the words of love, for these were words of love from Dutton. Of that she had no doubt whatsoever. He was not a man to gush or wax poetic. He was not a man to make ardent vows. No. He was Lord Dutton, after all. She knew with whom she dealt.

This, this repeated insistence that she marry him, couched in humor, terse in delivery, was as emotionally vulnerable as Lord Dutton was going to get.

She understood him perfectly, and she did not expect anything of him which he was not capable of delivering. In fact, this was far more than she would have dreamed of expecting.

She had him precisely where she wanted him, except that she did not want to marry him because she did not want to marry at all. She was nearly certain of that.

But if she did marry, it would be to someone who made her feel what he made her feel. She had married once for survival and once for advancement; surely if she ever did marry again, she could marry for love.

Love. Passion. They were close enough to be often confused.

She never confused them; she had too much life experience for that.

Oh, dear. What had she done?

She had felt passion for Dutton for an age. Somehow, inexplicably, she had made the perfectly horrible decision to fall in love with him.

"Say yes," he said, his mouth against hers.

"I think you are a brute."

"I am a brute. Say yes."

"I was not aware that you were so desperately in love with me."

"Liar. You know exactly how desperate I am. I will marry you anyway, liar that you are."

"I have not said yes."

"You will."

"You are arrogant."

"I am. Say yes."

He let her slide down his body until her feet touched the floor. Her arms stayed wrapped around his neck. He leaned down to her, his face inches from hers, his hands on her hips.

She longed to grind her hips against his. She refrained. Some decorum, however meager, must remain.

"I have conditions."

"Of course you do," he said.

"Say you love me," she said.

"I love you," he said in clipped tones.

"What do you love about me?" she said, running her hands along the long stretch of his shoulders.

"Everything. Nothing." He blinked, his gaze going soft and confused, and so completely adorable. "There is no explanation for it."

"What a proposal."

"It's heartfelt."

Anne laughed, joy suffusing her. She had confounded Dutton; he had fewer defenses than a day old pup. And she had done it all by herself.

"No doubt as to that," she said, her words garbled by laughter. "You are quite undone, aren't you, Lord Dutton?"

"Completely. Satisfied?"

"Completely," she said, leaning her head against his chest, her cheek against the beating of his heart.

"Does your ladyship require aid?" the Lanreath butler interrupted, coming from who knew where. Her eyes were filled with Dutton, and her hands. And her heart.

"Her ladyship does not," Dutton answered.

The butler, and she could not, at this moment, remember his name though she had known it for years, cleared his throat in a most ponderous manner and said, "Lady Staverton, shall I escort you back to the drawing room?"

Dutton stopped looking at her long enough to stare at the butler. The butler, to his immense credit, did not blink, twitch, or flinch.

"Your name?" Dutton asked.

"Johnson, my lord."

"Johnson, Lady Staverton, of whom you have such interest, is in need of a butler."

"Are you offering me a position, my lord?"

"I am," Dutton said, facing Johnson, holding her hand tightly in his.

"Lord Dutton, I do not think--" she said.

"Lady Staverton," Dutton interrupted, "has recently discharged her butler, a poor excuse for a man and hardly worthy of the role of butler in such a stellar dwelling as Staverton House."

When Johnson held his tongue and continued to stare at Dutton with a hard brown gaze, Dutton said, "You know the man to whom I refer?"

"I do."

Dutton grunted and Johnson cleared his throat. Apparently they were in complete agreement about Winthrop and needed no further conversation to clarify it.

"I will pay you five percent more than you are currently getting," Dutton said.

"*You* will pay--" she sputtered.

"Lady Staverton and I are soon to be wed," Dutton continued, ignoring her completely, "and she will, naturally, be living at my home, but as Staverton House is without a butler and as Lady Staverton is in need of a butler until she is the Countess of Dutton, the position is yours. Naturally, we cannot guarantee that Staverton's heir will keep you on, but I must assume you will give him no reason why he should not."

Johnson stared at Dutton for a few moments, his gaze shifting to hers for a moment before returning to Dutton. Well, but she'd rather look at Dutton, too.

"Eight percent," Johnson said.

Dutton grunted and nodded his assent.

"It shall be a pleasure to serve you, Lady Staverton," Johnson said, bowing to her. She did so wish her hair were in better form. "Now, shall I show you to the dining room? Dinner has been served."

Johnson preceded them out of the corridor into the brighter light and space of the hall. Anne was hurriedly trying to braid her hair into something resembling a style.

"You've hired me a butler," she whispered.

"I have. You were in dire need of one," Dutton said, walking sedately at her side. *His* hair was not a complete ruin.

"You knocked my last butler to the ground."

"He got off lightly."

"You hired me a butler," she repeated, a smile working its way across her mouth.

Dutton looked askance at her, his blue eyes twinkling. "It was the least I could do. A lady of the realm cannot be expected to function properly in

Society without a competent butler."

It was the most romantic thing he could have said to her. She, a lady of the realm, at least in his eyes. And did she care what anyone else thought? She did not.

"Yes," she said.

"Yes. Of course. Perfectly obvious," he said as they followed Johnson up the stairs.

"No. Yes," she said. "Yes. I'll marry you."

Dutton did not so much as pause, the arrogant sot. He said, "Of course you will, Anne. There was never any doubt about it."

"Of course there was doubt about it! I refused you, you know."

He waved that away. Actually waved!

"Don't you want to know why I said yes?" she prompted.

He smiled at her, a devilish smile.

"No, not because of *that*," she said.

"I'm devastated."

She laughed. He *looked* devastated.

"I'm going to marry you, Lord Dutton, because any man who can manage household staff the way you can is a man worth marrying," she said. "I shall have the most well-run, well-staffed household in all of London. A woman would be a fool not to marry a man who can do that."

Dutton, darling Dutton, smiled at her, his heart in his wickedly blue eyes. "Yes. She would."

Chapter 24

Sophia was waiting for Anne when she arrived at one the following afternoon. Elizabeth and George had been sent to ride in the park and told not to return until tea time. Anne, she knew, would want privacy. So would Lord Dutton.

"Freddy, have you heard?" Anne said as she was welcomed into Dalby House.

"I did. Got him good, didn't you?"

"It was quite startling."

"Long time coming, the way I see it. He needed taking down."

"Well, I don't know that I'd put it that way," Anne said, walking at his side to the white salon.

"I never would have put money on Lord Dutton taking him down, though. Heard he did a good job of it."

"I beg your pardon?" she said, halting, stunned.

"Dutton. Knocking that bastard Winthrop to the dirt. Wish I could have seen that."

"Fredericks, I was speaking of Lord Dutton's proposal of marriage!"

"Oh," he said, grinning lopsidedly, "there was no surprise as to that. Saw that coming years ago."

"You did? But how could you?" she stammered.

"In you get," he said, a hand to her back and propelling her into the white salon, closing the door firmly behind her.

Sophia stood to greet her, her dress falling in graceful ripples to the floor. She was wearing rose pink with sprigs of white embroidery in a leaf pattern scattered upon the bodice. Her hair was up and twisted into a simple coil, her jewels were emeralds and rubies, and she looked as fresh and innocent as a maiden of fifteen years. Anne did not know how she managed it. She had stopped looking innocent when Vasily had jumped into her bed.

"Darling, you've done it. I knew you would," Sophia said, arms outstretched.

Anne, a bit bewildered, walked into her embrace.

"I appear to be the only one astonished by the tide of events," she said once they were seated upon the matching settees before the hearth.

"Darling, you can't think he could resist you?" Sophia said, smiling. "He was a challenge, to be sure. A more stubborn man would be hard to find, but you managed him brilliantly, as I knew you would."

"You knew I would? I had no such confidence."

"Anne, darling," Sophia said, her gaze serious and her smile gone, "that is precisely it. You lacked confidence."

"I needed you, Sophia," Anne said, the familiar wave of panic lapping at her. "I needed you, and you were not there. You were with your niece instead, and Miss Grey, if you'll pardon me, does not respect you as I do!"

"Elizabeth is my concern, and I am not at all concerned about her," Sophia said smoothly. "You, Anne, have been my concern since your mother sold you to Prince Vasily. I have tried to guide you onto a more prosperous path ever since."

"Not the path of righteousness?" Anne said.

"One and the same, darling," Sophia said, smiling with a wicked glint. "But, Anne, surely you can understand now what I did and why."

Did she? She was not sure she understood anything at all. She had relied upon Sophia for counsel and support. Sophia, gone to America for two years, had not been there to lean upon. And Anne had faltered. That is what she understood. She had needed her counselor and her counselor had been absent.

"I needed you," she said.

"You most certainly did not. In fact, you needed the opposite," Sophia said. "Darling, surely you must see that what began so well between us had become poisonous for you? You are a woman of immense intelligence and resilience. All you lacked was confidence in your own abilities. Just look at Lord Dutton. You managed him brilliantly, once you relied on your own knowledge and experience, and you did it with far more speed than even I credited you with. Why, he was pudding in your hands in just days! Did ever a man fall so swiftly into marriage? Darling, you are to be congratulated."

"I did not intend to marry him," Anne said, her thoughts whirling. "I did not plan for him to propose marriage."

"Didn't you?" Sophia said, a smile playing around her mouth. "Lord Dutton, with an insulting lack of subtlety, wanted to toss you upon his bed and be done with it and with you in a matter of hours, if not minutes. You refused him, rejected his plans for you, and forced him to dance to your plans for yourself. He danced, darling girl, and he danced at your pace and to your tune."

"I must confess that he did not give me the trouble I was expecting from him."

"Because he is a child, poor dear, in such games, and you, darling Anne, are a master. He wanted you, you rejected him, you married darling Stavey, and could meet him as an equal when the time came to do so. You would not be his toy."

"No, that is true."

"In order to have you, he must give you his name and his title."

"No, that is not true. He had me, as you must know."

"Darling, you underestimate yourself and overestimate Lord Dutton. You also forget the volatile power of an old lover."

"Vasily?"

"Of course, Vasily. Was there another?"

"No," Anne said, gazing deeply into Sophia's amused eyes. "You sent for Vasily?"

"Well, not precisely *sent*, but I did suggest to Lord Lanreath that his friend might enjoy a London Season. *This* London Season."

Anne burst out laughing. "But that was horrible! To see him, to have Dutton in the same room, to have Vasily behaving as if I had just stumbled out of his bed, and that we would resume things without pause."

"Oh, yes. Horrible," Sophia said. "I can't think how Lord Dutton endured it."

"You were helping me."

"As little as possible. A nothing, really. You do not need me, Anne. You are very well able to take care of yourself, Lady Staverton."

Yes, she was, wasn't she? She had known how to take care of herself and how to manage Dutton. She had done it all, using instinct and experience, and she had . . . Lord Dutton to show for it.

Not to mention a butler.

⁂

Lord Dutton arrived an hour before tea time, a most inconvenient time for callers, but Sophia did not expect the Marquis of Dutton to change his ways simply because he was in love.

"Lord Dutton, what a pleasure," she said, curtseying before him. He bowed his response, a scowl upon his brow. Poor, confused Lord Dutton. "Won't you be seated?"

She sank down upon a small chair covered in ivory silk damask, forcing him to face her on an equally small chair. A tiny revenge, yet still so pleasant.

"Lady Dalby, as you are undoubtedly aware, I am to marry Lady Staverton."

"A most delightful pairing. I'm quite certain you shall both be deliciously happy."

"You are not going to throw a rock into the works," he declared. "I shall not allow it."

"Why should I want to do any such thing? I am delighted, honestly so. In all things, Lord Dutton, I am scrupulously honest."

He snorted and refused her silent offer of tea. She filled her own cup and let the silence between them stand as she did so.

"You have been against me from the start, Lady Dalby. Respond honestly to that, if you dare."

"Oh, a dare. I do so love a dare," she said, taking a sip from the black Wedgwood cup. "Why do you believe I've been against you?"

"It's been obvious."

"It is only obvious, Lord Dutton, that I have been very much for Anne," she said, studying his face. He did not have much of the look of his father; they had the same shade of blue eyes, but not the shape. The mouths were different completely and the brow only slightly similar. His hands, how well she remembered his father's hands, weren't remotely the same. How reassuring. "If that has meant I have been against you, then logic dictates that it is only because you have been against Anne."

His brow furrowed further, angry and quite possibly confused.

He had not known his father well; everyone knew that. His father had been a drunken sot from before his birth, well known for it, actually. In that, he had been on the road to becoming much like his father.

"It goes beyond Anne," he said. "I know it does."

"How do you know it does?"

"Damn me for a fool," he grunted, "but I can feel it. You wish me ill, Sophia."

"Lord Dutton, I do not," she said.

"And honesty was to be your calling card?" he said sourly.

"Oh, I think something more interesting than honesty for my calling card," she said lightly, "but I am speaking the truth. I have never wished you ill. Quite fully the opposite, in fact."

No, truth was never to be her calling card, but she

did not lie, especially not in this, to this man.

Lord Dutton's hair was shining, his eyes were clear, his manner brisk and efficient. Hardly the Lord Dutton of two or three years ago. He had been following his father's most dissolute and debauched habits. She would not have it so, not if she could help it. It had taken years of manipulation and maneuvering, but look at him now. He was the picture of health and about to be happily married to a woman who could manage him with a smile on her face and in her heart.

It was the perfect happy ending for the son of the man who had orchestrated her rape.

"I know what he did," Dutton said, looking her squarely in the eyes. What a fine man he had become. It was a joy to see him so. "I understand why you'd want revenge."

"Darling," she said, leaning forward, setting her cup down, "no one knows what your father did better than I. I do not hold you responsible for another man's acts. I am not as uncivilized as all that."

"Aren't you?"

"Well, perhaps," she said, winking at him. "If the occasion requires it. In your case, it did not. You were a child at the time, at no fault whatsoever. Your father bore the full brunt of his actions, as it should be."

"Then what have you been about these years? I know you have been manipulating things, trying to force me to things."

And succeeding, too, but no reason to push his lovely nose into it.

"To help you, darling. Can you not see it?" she said. "And of course, to help Anne. It was clear from the first that you two were meant for each other, and I simply could not allow her to associate with a man as, well, I leave the words to you."

He, clearly, had no wish to put words to it. It would have been distinctly unflattering.

"I am not like him," he said, his brow lifting.

"Not at all," she assured him. *Not anymore.*

"I sometimes wondered," he said, a most vulnerable remark, and one the Dutton of two years ago could never have spoken.

"Wonder no longer," she said softly. "Can I not tempt you with a cup?" she said.

"No," he said, smiling, rising to his feet. A most spectacular looking man. Lucky Anne. "I must be going. There are details to be seen to. The wedding is to be in six weeks. I'll have no rumors of Anne *needing* to marry."

"How thoughtful of you," she said, offering her hand.

"No, purely selfish," he said, kissing her hand with more gallantry than she had ever seen in him. So, so unlike his father. "I won't have my wife fodder for the rumor mill."

"Yes, I can how selfish an act that is," she said. "Well done, Lord Dutton. Well done."

He bowed, tears glistening at the corners of his remarkable blue eyes. "Thank you, Sophia. For everything."

And before she could reply, he was gone. Just as well. She had nothing more to say on the subject, her own eyes irritatingly moist.

Chapter 25

Sophia was dressing for a musicale at the Duke of Hyde's, having great difficulty in deciding between the ivory silk shot with gold thread and the cream muslin with the lace overlay on the bodice, both dresses slightly out of date as she had not been to a modiste in months and simply must see to her wardrobe before the Season truly began, when George knocked once and entered without waiting for her reply.

It was quite unlike him. She had no trouble at all in guessing the cause.

"She must go home," George said, stalking into the room like a wolf about to pounce on a mouse. A mouse? How completely absurd.

Sophia was wearing a silk banyan with brilliant red poppies on a field of dark blue. It was her favorite dressing gown as it had been her husband's. He had died wearing it.

She sat on the chaise, tucked her feet up underneath the banyan, and waited.

"She is unhappy. She must go," George said.

"Is she? I thought she was making the adjustment quite well."

"No. She must go," George said.

George, quite obviously, was capable of being quite charming, even occasionally effusive, by Iroquois standards, but that was only under certain circumstances. His sister in London, attracting male attention, was not one of those circumstances. In this instance he was sounding more and more like her brother, John.

"John wants her to stay," she said, looping her arms over her drawn-up knees. Poor George. He was quite undone. "What can I do?"

"Send her home," George said, staring her down, or attempting to.

"Darling, what is wrong? She can't be that unhappy. I thought she was getting on quite well."

"Too well. She must go."

"George, surely you trust your own sister."

He stared at her, his dark eyes as hard as flint. "Don't work your games on her, Sophia. She is your blood. Don't you want her well out of this pit?"

"London is the pit, I presume?" she asked, stretching out her legs. "Sit, darling. You're wearing me out."

He sat, but not happily.

"She shouldn't be here, Sophia."

"You've had a change of heart, surely."

"It is her change of heart that scares me."

Sophia raised her brows. "You are afraid? Of what, darling? Elizabeth is perfectly safe."

"Not perfectly."

"Well," she laughed, "I don't suppose anyone is ever perfectly safe. But what harm can befall her in London?"

George looked at her, his brows lowered and his mouth grim. "Men."

"There are men everywhere, George," Sophia said. "I assumed you were aware of that."

"Don't play that game with me, Sophia," George said. "I know you too well."

"What game do you assign to me? The fact that there are men on every continent on Earth? I am hardly responsible for that."

Before George could answer, Elizabeth burst into the room, without benefit of even a cursory knock.

"I want to go home," Elizabeth said. "Oh, there are you are George. What are you doing here?"

"Meddling in your affairs, darling," Sophia said before George could do more than open his mouth. They were a pair, the two of them, both so darkly beautiful, so elegantly savage. She quite adored them both, not that she made a spectacle of herself over them. That would have been quite awkward, particularly with Elizabeth.

Elizabeth, garbed in a riding habit that looked quite the worse for wear, and she'd only had the thing a day, turned to her brother and snapped, "I can take care of myself, Brother. You do not need to speak for me. Or act for me."

"Why not? We are in agreement. I told Sophia it's time for you to go home."

Sophia said sweetly, "If your brother thinks you must go home, I suppose he should decide it. He knows London better than you, darling, and must, therefore, know what is best for you."

Elizabeth bristled visibly. George sighed and shot Sophia a look of such annoyance that it was all she could do not to laugh. She merely shrugged her shoulders and looked as innocent as possible.

"I know what is best for me, Brother, not you."

"You want to go home. That is enough for me," he said.

"Well, if George is satisfied, I suppose that's all that matters," Sophia said.

"My satisfaction is equally important," Elizabeth

said.

"Naturally, darling," Sophia said smoothly. "Now, I really must dress for our evening at Hyde House. Or, given that George wants you away from all the delicious London men, would it be wiser for you two to remain here, safe?"

Elizabeth rounded on George like a striking snake. "Away from the men? I am not a child, George, to be shielded behind walls and moats from something as simple as men."

"You know how protective brothers can be," Sophia said. "It's the main part of their charm, isn't it? So adorable of them, really."

"I don't notice my father being overly protective of you," Elizabeth said.

"True," Sophia said, stretching her arms behind her head in a languid movement. "I suppose he trusts my judgment."

"Sophia, you know that is not the issue," George said. "Elizabeth, we are in agreement. Let's go home. Immediately."

"Yes, before you get hurt," Sophia said. "These London men really are formidable. Just ask . . . well, anyone, if you doubt me."

"I can take care of myself," Elizabeth said. "The men are nothing. Pale and weak, nothing of which to fear."

"What a comfort to hear that! Aren't you comforted, George? Your darling sister is in no danger from the men on this island kingdom. Why rush off, if that's so?"

"I think we should go home," George said, crossing

his arms in that way men had when they had run out of words and had decided to make their will law by simply wishing it so. Adorable.

"I want to stay," Elizabeth said. "I'm going to stay. You will not think I am a coward, George. I will not let you think that."

"I understand completely, Elizabeth," Sophia said. "I should feel the very same if my brother ever tried to tell me what to do. Which, naturally, he would never dream of doing. He knows I can take care of myself quite beautifully. As can you, most definitely."

"I can," Elizabeth said, her black eyes lit from within by a combative glow. "And I will."

Sophia smiled and rose to her feet. "It's settled then. You're both staying. How perfectly delicious. I'm so delighted that we've reached an accord. We're all going to have a simply marvelous time tonight. I'm quite certain of it, aren't you?"

George and Elizabeth, in answer, stormed out of her room. If Dalby House had been shoddily constructed, her door would have slammed shut. But, of course, it did not.

Made in the USA
San Bernardino, CA
09 August 2015